THE PRECIOUS WENTLETRAP

Deborah Elaine Lindsay

COPYRIGHT © 2020 DEBORAH ELAINE LINDSAY

All rights reserved. No part of this book may be reproduced or transmitted in any form or by any means, electronic or mechanical, including photocopying, recording, or by any information storage and retrieval system, without the written permission of the Publisher, except when permitted by law.

Copyright © 2020 Deborah Elaine Lindsay

All rights reserved.

ISBN: 9798664276855

DEDICATION

The nurses who served in Vietnam bandaged the hearts and souls of our fallen military heroes when our nation could not and would not. This book is dedicated, with the deepest gratitude and admiration, to these nurses, especially those who never came home: Lieutenant Sharon Lane, Lieutenant Elizabeth Jones, Captain Mary Klinker, Captain Eleanor Alexander, Lieutenant Hedwig Orlowski, Lieutenant Jerome Olmsted, Lieutenant Kenneth Shoemaker, Lieutenant Pamela Donovan, Lieutenant Carol Drazba, and Lieutenant Colonel Annie Graham.

Humpty Dumpty sat on the wall;
Humpty Dumpty had a great fall;
All the king's horses and all the king's men
Couldn't put Humpty together again.

                        Mother Goose

PROLOGUE

It wasn't a soothing summer rain. It was a hard rain that beat angrily against the ground creating ugly indentations in Lydia's dirt driveway. Maggie felt as tormented and confused as the raindrops that were being pelted unmercifully against the windowpanes by that howling wind. And she knew that wind; she knew it well. She could feel its chill gnawing at her soul even safely seated inside this warm room. Suddenly, lightning streaked across the black skies followed within seconds by thunder so loud that it seemed to share the very room with them. Maggie didn't flinch. For nothing out there was as terrifying as the storm that raged within her. Slowly she turned away from the window and looked across the room towards Lydia.

"Lydia," she said, barely audible, "I've heard it asked 'if a tree fell in a deserted forest, did it make a sound?'" She paused for a moment to allow Lydia to fully comprehend her question; it was important that she understood. "But I think the real question is, 'if a soldier died thousands of miles from home, did his country see him?'"

Lydia looked into Maggie's eyes. As usual, Maggie couldn't read her expression. After a few moments, Lydia responded, "Maggie, I think the only question that matters is 'Did you see him?'"

Maggie looked back out into the raging thunderstorm and thought, "Oh yes, I saw him. I still do every day."

CHAPTER ONE
Fire

Maggie Prescott sank down into the sofa in the waiting room, kissed the tiny blonde curls on top of her daughter Katie's head, and then pulled her against her chest. While Katie slept peacefully in her arms, Maggie gazed around the room. Despite the passing of twenty years, surprisingly little had changed. Large pastel illustrations of Peter Rabbit and other equally beloved Beatrix Potter characters still brightened the walls. Children still played boisterously with the toys in the far corner while their mothers impatiently flipped through the magazines that had been scattered around the waiting room for them. Maggie closed her eyes. Even the sounds of the waiting room- children's noisy, excited voices, mothers' tired reprimands, and a baby's cry- remained unscathed by the passage of time.

Maggie opened her eyes and turned her head to the left expecting to be comforted by more nostalgia. But this wall's solitary decoration, an immense oil portrait, caused her entire body to stiffen. She could feel her blood pulsating against her temples. Sweat began to dampen her silk blouse so that it began to cling uncomfortably to her skin. She thought she had been totally prepared to talk about her today. Why then did just looking at her portrait unnerve her so? And yet she was unable to look away. She stared into those unforgettable green eyes. Their passion penetrated her soul, kindling feelings that had lain dormant for so long.

The subject of this portrait wasn't smiling fully. Just a hint of laughter played at the corners of her mouth as if she had just done something that amused her. Her flaming red hair fell loosely around her shoulders. "Fire" had been her nickname in

Vietnam. Looking at this image of her on canvas, Maggie remembered how well that name suited her. Maggie could feel the warmth radiating from her delicate, ladylike facade. Maggie so wanted to reach out and touch her. Even more intense was Maggie's need for Fire to wrap her arms around her, just one more time. Maggie's throat began to tighten.

"I see you enjoy looking at the portrait of Dr. O'Brien's daughter, too. She was incredibly pretty don't you think?"

"Excuse me," Maggie said, turning her head slightly to face the woman sitting next to them.

"Dr. O'Brien's daughter, Kate. That's her in the portrait. Don't you think she was gorgeous?"

Maggie only gave her a polite nod but it was all the encouragement needed.

"I think she was an only child. They say she died very young. In Vietnam. Can you imagine that?" She shook her head slowly back and forth. "Poor Dr. O'Brien." She looked expectantly at Maggie, waiting for her response.

"Yes, she was quite beautiful," Maggie softly replied then looked quickly away before the woman could ask her anything else. She leaned her head back against the sofa and closed her eyes to bring Kate into focus. Memory after memory rushed at her yet all she had been able to say to this stranger was that "she was quite beautiful." Such empty words. But then again, maybe there were no words capable of capturing Kate's mystique. Just when Maggie had thought she knew everything about her, Kate had left her to stand alone with thousands of questions reverberating in her mind. The English language was devoid of words to express the tremendous joy their friendship had brought into her life and the intense sadness her death had imparted upon it. Thoughts of Kate had perpetually caused this duality of emotions to churn inside her, eating away at her soul until she knew her survival depended upon her avoiding thoughts of Kate all together. But today was different. Kate's image on canvas had somehow unleashed an outpouring of emotions inside of her. For once, she didn't try to stop herself from reliving precious moments with Kate.

She smiled recalling what a tomboy Kate had been. She was always the last one caught in "Kick the Can." Even Jeremy Withers, the fastest boy in their class, had trouble catching her. Maggie could still hear her laughter and see her red hair blowing in the wind as she ran. Kate was always happiest when faced with a true challenge. Maggie's thoughts wandered to that tall pine tree in Kate's backyard. They had spent hours in its graceful branches. Kate had never been satisfied staying on the lower branches. How she loved to climb so high, almost to the top.

"Please, come down now," Maggie would plead. "You're scaring me."

"Oh, don't be such a worry wart," Kate would laugh back. "Climb up with me. It's just like being in a big swing. The wind blows you back and forth. It's so peaceful."

Kate was always the stronger one. Never brave enough to climb to the top with her, Maggie never experienced the peace Kate was talking about. It had always eluded her.

Maggie's thoughts strayed to the red pocket jackknife that Kate had cherished, keeping it safely tucked away in her pocket at all times. No matter how much the boys cajoled and pleaded with her, she wouldn't consider any of their trades for it, not even for the latest Beatles album. Maggie remembered the late summer night when they were about ten years old, camping out in a pup tent beneath their beloved pine tree. Deliberately, Kate cut a deep gash in her left middle finger with the knife without showing any signs of distress or pain at all. Then she handed the knife to Maggie solemnly saying, "Cut your finger now so we can become blood sisters for life."

Maggie hesitated. Sickened by the sight of that red stream oozing from Kate's finger, she was afraid of what the sight of her own blood would do to her.

Kate had sensed her fear. "Come on, Maggie. I promise it won't hurt."

But it did and Maggie cried.

"You big baby," Kate teased for just a minute until she realized how upset Maggie really was. "I'm sorry. I shouldn't have forced you into it," she said, throwing her arms around Maggie's shoulders and squeezing until Maggie was able to relax and laugh at herself, too. How Maggie treasured and missed dearly that aspect of Kate's personality. Kate never forgot how to make her laugh at herself, no matter how deeply the pain cut.

Maggie tried to remember just one of the countless secrets Kate had whispered to her in the dark that night, under the strictest confidence of course. She couldn't remember a single one. Why? She supposed that the reason didn't really matter. All that mattered now was what she could remember. Memories of Kate and their friendship flooded her until all she could see were fragmented threads of their moments together, delicately woven across the tapestry of time to create an exquisite, impressionistic masterpiece. Kate's flaming red hair and Maggie's dirty blond curls had been virtually inseparable for years. They had been together in Nam, too, until Kate had left Maggie standing alone to face the storm.

"Katelyn Prescott. Katelyn Prescott." The nurse called out her daughter's name from the doorway of the waiting room.

Maggie quickly opened her eyes, stood up with Katie in her arms, and grabbed her diaper bag. Her mind raced chaotically as she followed the nurse down the hallway. After reviewing for weeks what she would say to Doc, those well-rehearsed words suddenly sounded hollow to her. *Should I have come after all?* she thought.

They entered the exam room. "You can put your things there," the nurse said, pointing to two pale-blue exam room chairs. "Then please place her on the examination table and remove all her clothing down to her diaper." While Maggie undressed her, the nurse asked her questions about Katie's feeding, sleep and wake patterns, and development. As Maggie concentrated on each question, answering as completely as she could, she felt her body finally begin to relax again. She smiled down at Katie waving her arms and kicking wildly as the nurse wrapped a paper measuring tape around her forehead to measure her head circumference followed by obtaining her body length. She documented Katie's measurements in her medical record, and then placed her on a cold scale, causing her to fuss for a few moments. "Sh, sh now little doll baby," she said, before smiling and handing her back to Maggie. "Katelyn is getting big. She weighs twelve pounds today and she is twenty-three inches long. Dr. O'Brien will be in soon to examine her. Do you have any questions for me before he comes in?"

Maggie shook her head. "I can't think of anything right now. Thank you for everything."

The nurse smiled back then brusquely left the room, pulling the door shut behind her. A few minutes later the door opened again and Doc walked back into Maggie's life. His head was bent intently over Katie's chart. Maggie noticed his hair had turned a beautiful snow-white, but otherwise little had changed. He was still so tall and slender. Perhaps his face had a few more wrinkles. Maybe he walked a little more stiffly. Suddenly, he looked up. She painfully watched his practiced doctor's smile disappear the moment their eyes met and her identity registered with him. He stood there, a powerful six-foot man, looking as helpless as little Katie. Maggie began to sweat again. She felt so cruel for coming back unannounced after all these years. She fought the urge to run out of the room.

He spoke first. The years hadn't changed the fatherly intonations of his voice. "Maggie, is it really you?"

She nodded her head as she walked towards his outstretched arms still cradling Katie. He hugged Maggie tightly as if he were afraid she would vanish again if he relaxed his hold on her.

"I just can't believe it's you," he said hoarsely.

Finally, she felt his arms slowly loosen around her. He gently pushed her an arm's length away. She saw tears trickling down his face now. He had trouble speaking. "Let me get a good look at you. How long has it been? Could it really be that the last time I saw you was the day you and Kate flew off..." His voice trailed off. He didn't have to say Vietnam. They both knew.

She felt the warmth of her own tears against her cheeks. Her voice cracked when she began to speak, hesitantly at first, but with ever-increasing strength as his warm, blue eyes encouraged her. "Just look at the two of us. We're a mess. We always were so emotional. Remember how mad it made her?"

"Yes, yes," Doc said, "I remember. I can still hear her little foot tapping so impatiently and hear her saying 'Stop it you two! It's only for a year. It's only for a year.' Do you ever wonder who she was really trying to convince?"

His question took her by surprise. She avoided his eyes and thought for a moment, not knowing quite how to respond. "It was only supposed to be a year," she said quietly, looking into Doc's moist eyes. "She didn't know she was saying goodbye to you forever or she never would have gone."

"Oh, I'm not so sure about that, Maggie. She was so stubborn. Irish through and through."

Katie began to fuss. Maggie rocked her gently in her arms.

"It's OK, Sweet Pea," Doc said, smiling down at her, allowing Katie to wrap her tiny fingers around his index finger. Neither of them spoke for a few moments.

Doc broke the silence. "Where have you been all these years? You don't know how hard it was losing you both."

"I'm so sorry. I never meant to hurt you. I always intended to come back to you. 'Tomorrow I'll go,' I said time and time again. Until tomorrow turned into years. I've been all around this country looking for something. Just don't ask me what it is because I've never found it. Not in Manhattan or Baltimore. Waco or Phoenix. Not even back home here in California. I tried so hard. I must have started and quit a hundred jobs. I don't really even remember most of them. My life is a blur of places and faces. All except Nam. It reaches out and touches me when I least expect it. With such clarity, everything comes rushing back as if it happened just yesterday. I don't understand why. All I do know is that much of my life has been spent thinking about Kate and others I knew in Nam. I know you're her father. But she was my best friend. Perhaps my only friend..."

Doc gently squeezed her arm. "I know, Maggie. I remember

too. My mind is full of images of the two of you together." He smiled at her. "What a pair! So much laughter and noise. God, I miss that beautiful noise."

"Me too... I miss her, Doc." She turned away from him and placed Katie down on the examination table for him. She kicked her legs and waved her arms again excitedly with wild random movements.

Doc walked around to the other side of the table. "She is beautiful, Maggie." He looked across the table directly into her eyes. "Tell me. What really brought you back today?"

Not ready to share the real reason yet, she said instead, "I guess she did. I just needed you to meet her. I married a man, Adam Prescott, five years ago. Katie here is our first child." She gently stroked Katie's cheek. "I guess you'll have to thank little Katie for my coming back."

Doc smiled down at Katie then looked up questionably at Maggie.

"Yes, she's Kate's namesake. Katie doesn't have her red hair. But look at that dimple. Does that remind you of anyone?"

They laughed together while smiling down at Katie. She continued, "you don't know how many times I almost came back. I even got as far as your parking lot a few times. I wanted so much to talk with you about Kate and Vietnam."

"Tell me. What stopped you? Didn't you know how much Mama and I loved you?"

"I know." She reached out and held on to his sinewy hand for a moment before letting go. "I think at first I didn't come because I felt so guilty. She told me how much you and Mama O'Brien hated her going to Nam. I felt like it was all my fault that she died. I was the one who initially suggested that we should sign up under the buddy system and serve together, you know."

Doc nodded. "I remember."

"I was so afraid I had talked her into it, against her will. Part of me still feels that she would be here with us today if it weren't for me."

"You're right about one thing, Maggie, we didn't want her over there. Not our only child. But you're completely wrong blaming yourself. We never blamed you. Don't doubt for a moment that she would have gone, no matter what. Even without you by her side. She was so determined to help those boys. 'It's in their eyes, Daddy,' she told me. 'I can't stand seeing all the pain in their eyes.'"

"You're right. I remember now watching her eyes tear up each night in our nursing school dorm as we watched the evening news. Perhaps she really would have gone without my encouragement. I wanted to go to protect my brother, Jason, from being drafted, but Kate's motives were completely altruistic. She just wanted to help as many of those soldiers on TV as she could."

Doc looked right into her eyes. "Did she? Did she help them like she wanted to?"

"Yes. You would have been so proud of her. She was a damned good nurse."

"That doesn't surprise me. She always tried so hard. She threw herself fully into everything she did."

Maggie nodded in agreement. "She was incredible. There we were fresh out of nursing school one day, then at the 71st Evacuation Hospital in Pleiku, Vietnam the next. Not quite. But it sure felt that way to me. I had a difficult time adjusting to the pace. But not Kate. I think even the nurses, who were short, I mean the ones who were scheduled to come home within the next few months, learned something new from Kate before they left. Did she ever tell you the nickname they gave her?"

Doc shook his head. "No, I can't say I remember her mentioning a nickname."

"They started calling her 'Fire' within the first month of our arrival at the 71st."

Doc smiled. "I loved her red hair, too. I think they chose well for our Kate."

"It wasn't just her hair. Sure, her appearance was a part of it. Her hair blended in so completely with the red dirt which surrounded us and literally covered us most of the time, but it was so much more. She just was Fire. She burned with such passion for the welfare of the boys. Such intense energy and warmth radiated from her. They claimed her spirit belonged to Pleiku. She had a way of warming everything that she touched. I saw a tired, weary staff become revitalized because of her."

Maggie paused a moment wondering if she should continue. She didn't want to hurt him any more than she had already, but she wanted him to know a portion of the truth now, to prepare him for what she would share later. She looked across into his questioning eyes then gently continued, "I'm sorry to share this with you, but Pleiku was a God-forsaken hospital. Broken, mutilated bodies arrived nonstop on so many days. I remember thinking that there weren't any whole eighteen and nineteen-year-old boys left in the world. I often felt so completely inadequate to really help them. I mean what do you say to a young kid who will never run again? 'Sorry. You're lucky to be alive. Your family still loves you.' They were such empty words when I was staring into their sad, frightened eyes. And then I would look across the Emergency Room (ER) at Kate. Time after time, she made napalm-burnt boys and double leg amputees smile. I just don't know how she did it, day after day. Not once did I see pain register on her face when she was with the boys. I never knew how much it upset her. I guess I thought she was stronger than she really was. I thought she could take anything."

"Now, now Maggie. I think you're wrong about her ever being upset. Kate did possess tremendous amounts of inner strength. Even as a small child. Nothing of what you just mentioned was in her letters. I really don't know what to think. We saved every one. Perhaps I should read them again and see if we missed anything. What I do remember is anecdotes about you and the children and how grateful she felt to be able to care for our wounded soldiers. And I remember how her letters had initially confused Mama and me. She sounded like she was on vacation instead of in a war zone. After a while, after we received so many with the same message, we believed her. We consoled ourselves by remembering why she had gone in the first place. Mama and

I couldn't choose her life for her. No matter how much we wanted to. In the end, all that mattered to us was that she was living out her dream. We tried to be happy for her."

After hearing Doc's words, Maggie felt that familiar heaviness in her chest as she thought, *I guess no one knew about her pain then, until it was too late.* Her throat tightened as she thought about the loneliness Kate had borne alone. *Why hadn't she reached out to any of us?* She took a deep breath, fighting tears. As her throat muscles began to relax, she said, "After she died, Doc, I hated myself for being alive. My name should be on that wall in Washington, D.C., not hers. Never hers. I was a nurse doing my share in Pleiku, but she was our soul. How could she have died when so many of us needed her?" She turned away so he couldn't see her tears beginning to form. But he knew.

"Now, Maggie. It was so long ago. You don't know what it means to have you here today. I've missed you so much. And look at little Katie. She needs you, too. She wouldn't be here without you."

Listening to the soothing quality of his voice, she began to believe some of his words. She turned back and looked down at Katie.

Doc smiled at her. "There, that's much better now. Mama would have loved to have seen you today. She would have been as bad as us, crying and laughing at the same time."

"I promise to come back another time, for a real visit with the two of you. I thought it would be so difficult to see you again. I realize now how much I missed you and Mama O'Brien. How is she? I can't wait to see her again, too."

"I'm sorry, Maggie. Mama passed away a little over two years ago. I buried her beside our Kate at St. John's Cemetery. They're beneath a large pine tree overlooking the Pacific. Nothing but the best for my girls..." Abruptly, he stopped talking and turned towards Katie. "That's enough talk for one day, Maggie. Let me examine Katie for you now."

"I'm so sorry. So very sorry." Her words were just the tip of the cold despair that was engulfing her. He didn't answer. His attention was focused solely on Katie now. Watching his gentleness with her daughter, Maggie's thoughts began to drift, carrying her back to happier times. During her childhood she had often daydreamed that Kate was her sister and gentle Doc was her father. She had relentlessly fabricated this dream from the California sunshine.

"Maggie. Did you hear me? I would like Katie to have her first immunizations today."

Doc's words terrified her. She saw Kate's mutilated, bloodied body; the image wouldn't leave her. She put her hands behind her back. Doc mustn't see them shaking. "No," she said, trying to speak calmly so he wouldn't guess the truth. "This isn't a good day for immunizations. Adam and I have plans tonight that we can't break. I promise to bring her back for them soon."

"OK, Maggie. You're the boss. Don't forget to set up an appointment with the nurse for her shots next week on your way out." He hugged Maggie one last time then gently kissed Katie on the top of her head. "Thank you again for coming back today. You don't know what this means to me." With a tremulous hand, he wrote his home address and phone number on the back of one of his appointment cards and handed it to her. "Call me soon. I look forward to meeting your Adam."

Realizing she couldn't put off any longer the real reason for her visit, she picked up the diaper bag and looked into Doc's warm, blue eyes. At this moment she had intended to give him Kate's journal from Vietnam which was tucked safely in the diaper bag. But standing there now, looking at this gentle man, she couldn't. Perhaps because she was a parent herself now, she understood what the truth would do to him. She refused to hurt Doc by opening the door and allowing him to see what horror his only child had really experienced during her last year of life. She knew, too, that this was only part of the reason. She wasn't ready yet to cut this last thread connecting herself to Kate. She still needed Kate's thoughts beside her. So, she walked out of Doc's office uncertain if she would ever be strong enough to return.

CHAPTER TWO
Awakenings

Katie slept peacefully in her car seat as Maggie drove out of the city and headed for their home in Carmel Valley. She turned on the radio to stifle the harsh sounds of San Jose's 5:00 pm congestion and to try to push Kate and Doc to the back of her mind, for a few minutes anyhow. Her afternoon encounter with Doc had wreaked havoc with her emotions. She felt as if she were teetering on the edge of a cliff, a frequently recurring and disturbing feeling that she had learned to live with over the years. As she neared Salinas, "Will you Still Love Me Tomorrow" filtered from the radio. Linda Ronstadt's plaintive voice involuntarily brought her back to her first full day at the 71st Evacuation Hospital located in Pleiku, Vietnam, on the Cambodian border deep within enemy territory. Arriving by chopper the previous day, she remembered that she had been startled to see concertina wire surrounding the hospital complex and four guard towers strategically positioned around it, providing additional protection. She wondered why seeing these fortifications had instilled fear in her instead of bringing her comfort. Perhaps it was because, for the first time, she realized that now she would be living in a war zone. There was no turning back.

"...And remember, he needs to go back to the operating room (OR) in less than fifteen minutes." Captain Pollard looked intently at Maggie. "Is everything clear?"

Maggie nodded but remained silent.

Captain Pollard hesitated as if she might say something else to her, then abruptly turned and walked away, leaving Maggie alone with her patient. Fearfully, she looked down at the wounded soldier lying on the stretcher. He was sleeping, but every few seconds his arms and upper body shook spasmodically and he cried out softly, "Mama, Mama." Without disturbing him, she carefully wiped the blood off his dog tags with part of his torn uniform shirt. "Campbell, Martin E." was engraved into the steel along with his social security number, his blood type and his religious preference. For a split-second she wondered, *Marty, where are you from? Who will mourn you if you die?* She tried to formulate a plan of care for him to prepare him quickly for the OR. If only she knew where to start.

His face was such a pasty white and he writhed in pain. She desperately tried to recall what they had taught her at Fort Sam Houston in Texas during basic training and what she had put into practice for six months at Walter Reed Hospital prior to coming to Vietnam. She had learned how to give injections, start intravenous (IV) lines, draw blood, apply splints, dress and pack wounds, and so many other important nursing skills for the recovering Vietnam soldiers in that stateside military hospital. Perhaps most importantly, she had learned to treat the whole patient. Those soldiers still "lived" in Vietnam. Meeting their emotional needs was often the top priority. For example, because they had lived with so much daily horror, she was taught to never startle them, to never wake a sleeping soldier by touching him; rather from a safe distance, she was to call his name softly.

She carefully lifted the sheet up and peeked beneath it so as not to wake him. The extent of his injuries frightened her. Despite the intact splint, she could still see bone emerging grotesquely from his right leg, like a jagged white dagger. Blood oozed from multiple tiny craters in both of his legs, a few of them bearing steel fragments. He had a large abdominal dressing and blood was already beginning to seep through it from his gunshot wound. Despite her desperation to help Marty, she couldn't remember what to do first. *What had Captain Pollard just given her for orders?* She picked up his documentation but was unable to concentrate on it. She knew she could easily care for recovering soldiers, but this was different. This was an unstable, freshly wounded soldier in critical condition who was depending on her for his survival.

She looked around the ER. Dozens of stretchers, all bearing wounded soldiers, filled the ER and she could hear more Dustoff helicopters approaching in the distance. The other nurses and corpsmen were scattered around the ER in a flurry of activity—bending over stretchers, calming the soldiers, starting IV lines, taking vital signs, drawing blood work, reinforcing dressings, inserting airways, and applying splints. They were functioning as a well-trained, efficient team. She got the sick feeling that she didn't belong here. She turned, fully prepared to bolt out the door.

She looked up and saw Major Bradshaw, chief nurse at the 71st, walking rapidly towards her. Her face was so tense. She was shouting, but Maggie couldn't comprehend her words until she got a little closer. "Lieutenant Taylor. Are you deaf? Don't just stand there with your mouth hanging open. Reinforce that abdominal dressing. Start two IV lines. Get some vitals. He can't go to the OR until you stabilize him and it looks like he needs to go there now!"

Maggie looked down at Private Campbell, still moaning softly on his stretcher. She felt as if she were shaking uncontrollably on the edge of a huge ravine, the water swirling angrily hundreds of feet below her. She was beginning to lose her balance, but paralyzed in place; she couldn't step back to safety. If only she could find something to grab on to. But there was nothing here for her.

With her face contorted like a gargoyle, Major Bradshaw continued to shout at Maggie. "That's an order, Lieutenant Taylor! Now! Move!"

Suddenly, a large black hand was wrapped around Private Campbell's wrist taking his pulse. Maggie looked into the big brown eyes of one of their skilled medics. "L. Powers" was lettered across his front shirt pocket and his shoulder insignia was that of a sergeant. Looking into his eyes, she knew instantly that he had been in Nam for a long time. His presence reassured her.

He looked directly at Major Bradshaw and spoke quietly but firmly. "Everything is under control here, Major. I will assist Lieutenant Taylor for a few minutes."

"Lieutenant Taylor shouldn't need your help, Sergeant," she said coldly. "But I suppose you can stay with her for a few minutes." She turned towards Maggie. "You have five minutes to get your ass in gear. Understood?"

Maggie nodded. "Yes, Ma'am."

"Thank you, Sergeant Powers," she whispered as the major walked away.

"Don't worry about it. It's my job. Now, let's get to work. What do we have here, Lieutenant?"

"Private Campbell has a compound fracture of his right leg, multiple shrapnel wounds to both legs, and a gunshot wound to his abdomen. He needs to go to the OR in less than fifteen minutes."

"Well, we have our work cut out for us then. What have you done so far?" He looked at her intently. When she didn't respond, he softly spoke, "Private Campbell. Private Campbell. Can you open your eyes and look at us for a moment?"

Private Campbell slowly opened his eyes and looked up at Sergeant Powers. He seemed confused and tried to sit up.

Sergeant Powers gently pushed him back down on the stretcher. "Hold on there now, Private. You have to let us help you. Do you remember what happened to you and where you are?"

"I know they carried us to the chopper after we got hit." Intense fear suddenly filled his eyes and he tried to sit up again.

"What about my buddies! I just need to know if my buddies made it. Have you seen them? Can you find out if they're OK?"

Sergeant Powers gently pushed him back down on the stretcher again. "We can check into that for you, but first Lieutenant Taylor and I have to get you ready for the OR. You need surgery. You'll be going to the OR in just a few minutes. Do you understand what's wrong with you?"

He nodded. "Yeah. I've been shot up pretty bad. My stomach kills and my right leg hurts even worse."

Sergeant Powers nodded. "That's right. You've got a lot of shrapnel wounds on both legs, a gunshot wound in your abdomen, and a very broken right leg. The good news is that we can fix everything. You'll be in pain for a little while longer. I'm sorry, but we can't give you anything right now because you're going to surgery soon. Do you understand?"

He nodded again. "I'm tired. Mind if I just close my eyes and rest for a while?"

"I understand. We just have to ask you a few important questions first and we want to let you know what's going to be happening to you. Lieutenant Taylor and I will be starting two IV lines and drawing some blood work. We need to insert a Foley catheter to drain your urine during surgery and we'll be taking your vital signs often. Can you handle all that before you go to sleep?"

"Yes, believe it or not, it sounds a hell of a lot better than what I've been doing for the past week. Maybe the last month."

"I hear you Private. We can tell it's been really heating up out there. We haven't seen this many come through here for a long time. But don't worry about a thing now. You've done a lot for us. Now, it's our turn to help you." Sergeant Powers looked at Maggie. "Why don't you get a set of vitals and go through the pre-op questions with him while I go gather all the supplies we'll need to get him ready."

"OK. I can do that," she said in a surprisingly calm voice now. As Sergeant Powers walked quickly away, she placed a blood pressure cuff on his left arm. His pressure was down to 90/60. She then placed her stethoscope on his chest to auscultate his breath sounds. His lungs were still bilateral, equal and clear. She moved her stethoscope over his heart to count his heartbeat. His apical pulse was strong and steady but mildly elevated at 115 beats per minute. These findings were consistent with his injuries. He was in pain and had lost a lot of fluid which needed to be replaced as soon as possible.

"Private Campbell, I have to ask you a few questions now," she said softly. She smiled down at him after he opened his eyes. "I promise it will only take a few minutes. Are you allergic to anything?"

He shook his head. "Nothing that I know of. I haven't been sick much in my life so I don't really know."

"It's all right. Don't worry. When is the last time you ate or drank anything?"

"It's been a while now. Haven't eaten since we engaged Charlie yesterday morning and my water ran out last night around 2100 hours."

"I know it may not feel like it to you, but that's good news. You'll do fine in surgery. I promise we'll get you something to eat and drink as soon as we can after surgery. But I'm afraid it will just be IV fluids for now." She checked his dog tags again. "It says your blood type is A positive. Is that correct?"

He nodded. "That's right."

She patted his arm. "OK then. You can rest for a moment. That's all we need until Sergeant Powers returns with the supplies for your IV lines and your Foley catheter."

She documented all the pertinent information in his pre-op chart, then looked up, relieved to see that Sergeant Powers had returned with his arms full of their supplies. He placed them all at the foot of the stretcher.

"How are his vitals?"

"His pulse is elevated slightly and his pressure is down to 90/60 but he's holding his own for now."

"OK. Let's put his gown on first then. I want to check him over completely for any additional wounds. It's important we identify them all. I'll need your help in positioning him and you'll need to document each and every wound in his pre-op record on the outline of his body using both the anterior and posterior views."

"Private Campbell." There was no response, so Sergeant Powers called out a little louder this time. "Private Campbell, I'm sorry. It's time. We need your help to get you ready as soon as possible."

They worked as a team to remove his clothing and put on his gown. They moved him as a roll and inspected his entire body for any additional wounds. Maggie documented everything.

"He'll need to go to X-ray before surgery, Lieutenant Taylor. Shrapnel can be tricky. The pieces of metal aren't always visible to the naked eye. If we miss any scraps, they can lead to sepsis and death." They repositioned him as comfortably as possible. "Are you comfortable drawing a complete blood count, blood type and electrolytes?"

"Yes, we did that hundreds of times at Walter Reed."

"Great. You do that while I insert his Foley."

They worked quickly and quietly, both aware that they only had a few minutes left to get him ready. He slept fitfully through all their poking and prodding, but cooperated as much as he was able. They continued to inform him of what they were doing so that he was fully prepared every step of the way.

"I'll get another set of vitals while you drop his blood work over there," Sergeant Powers said, pointing to the blood collection station. "They'll come by soon to pick it up."

"His pressure's down to 80/50," Sergeant Powers said when she returned. "We need to get his IV lines in now. I don't usually subject them to this but we need to get them in together." He tossed her a liter bottle of fluid, tubing, tape, a tourniquet, alcohol solution and an 18-gauge catheter, while keeping a complete set for himself. "Connect your tubing and flush your line first. Good."

As they looked for suitable veins, he spoke to her in a deep, soothing voice, thick with a New York City accent. "I grew up in the Bronx, Lieutenant. I remember way back when my dad gave my little brother, Leon, a brand new, cherry-red two-wheeler for his birthday. Leon loved it, but he didn't know how to ride a two-wheeler. He was afraid to try because he knew he would fall. He told me he wasn't afraid of getting hurt but he didn't want to scratch the paint on his new bike. Dad didn't understand. He thought Leon was a sissy. He screamed at Leon in front of our neighborhood. 'You git your ass on that bike and ride it or I'll give it away. Do you hear me, Son?' When Dad went back in the house to get another beer, I helped Leon get on the bike. I told him that I would run beside him and protect him and his bike if he fell. That's all Leon needed. Someone to walk beside him."

He paused and looked across at her. "I think that's all anyone ever needs. People don't learn shit when they're screamed at, but if you can just stand beside them, they catch on real quick. Ain't that right, Lieutenant?"

"That's right Sergeant Powers. Thank you." She looked around the room and sighed. "There's so many of them. How are we going to make it through the day?"

He looked her directly in the eyes. "Exactly like we just did. One soldier at a time. I know you can do it, but keep me in mind if you ever need help again."

They finished working on Private Campbell together and then she stabilized another and another for over seventeen hours. Somehow, with Sergeant Powers' support, she had managed to survive her first full day at the 71st. She and Kate had arrived in Nam at the tail end of the Tet Offensive, so this day, the horror of a mass casualty or a "push" as they called it, would be repeated often over the next few months. And each time, just as in her first experience with a push, her jungle fatigues would be covered with so much dried blood that it would stick to her skin. She would have to soak her shirt with water to remove it.

Later, back in her hooch, one of six Quonset huts, each housing ten nurses of the 71st, she washed her hands over and over again. She just couldn't seem to get the blood off of them.

Kate gently pulled her away from the bathroom sink. "Look at your hands, Honey. They're clean. It's all over. You can rest now." They walked together down the narrow center hallway of their hooch which was lined on each side by a row of five private rooms for the nurses. Kate and Maggie's rooms were directly across from each other. Kate looked at Maggie with concern. "Why don't you come in my room for a minute and we'll talk."

They sat down in her room. "I know we've only been here a few weeks now, but I don't think I can survive a whole year over here, Kate. I think maybe we made a mistake in coming."

"Try not to think about the whole year. Just think about tomorrow. Do you think you can help them some more tomorrow?"

Maggie nodded. "But there's so many that are so badly wounded. I can barely stand to look at them. I feel ashamed to admit this, but sometimes the extent of their injuries makes me feel sick to my stomach."

Kate wrapped her arms around Maggie's shoulders and squeezed. "I know. Try not to be so hard on yourself though. I'm sure we all feel that way sometimes. I think the secret is to look directly into their eyes. Focus on them because they are mirrors to their souls. If their eyes scream out fear, it's our job to calm that fear. If they overflow with sadness, we have to find a way to bring them just a moment of hope. I'm not saying you should disregard all your nursing assessments and tasks. We can't miss anything critical. And we both know that time is always the enemy, but don't ever forget their eyes. Make sure you truly see them and help them. Most often, they just need reassurance that they'll be OK."

"But what about the ones that won't be OK? What about the ones you know aren't going to make it? How can looking into their eyes help anything at all?"

Kate squeezed Maggie's shoulder one more time then let go of her. "Oh Maggie, don't you see? Those are the ones that need our help the most. I spend extra time with them and almost never look away from them. Their souls are petrified and I try my best to allow them to leave this earth as peacefully as possible."

They sat in silence for a few moments. Maggie reached over and gently touched Kate's hand. "Thank you for trying to help me. I'll try some of your suggestions tomorrow. I honestly don't think I could survive here without you."

Kate laughed. "Oh hush. You're a lot stronger than you think.

You're doing a great job." She turned away from Maggie. Silence filled the room. Maggie was just about to ask her another question when Kate smiled at her and said, "Tomorrow will be here a lot sooner than we would like. I'd like some time to write in my journal. Would you mind if we called it quits for tonight?"

"Of course not," Maggie answered giving her a quick hug. "I know how you enjoy doing that. Have a good night."

It wasn't until much later, lying in her bed in her own room, that Maggie finally relaxed. She fell asleep with the soldiers' faces imprinted on her dreams.

CHAPTER THREE
Locked in the Past

Arriving home, Maggie pulled open their massive oak front door and walked inside with Katie in her arms. Katie whimpered ever so slightly and nuzzled Maggie's blouse with her delicate mouth. Camille, their Spanish nanny, must have heard their car drive up for she stood in the foyer, smiling with her arms outstretched. "Let me take Little Miss Katie for you."

For once, pangs of guilt didn't tug at Maggie's heart for employing a nanny to do the things she thought any good mother should be doing herself. Gratefully, she handed Katie to Camille. "Thank you, Camille. The trip to San Jose has exhausted me. And I believe Katie is hungry. Would you be able to give her a bottle now? There's still some of my expressed milk in the fridge for her. If you need me, I'll be upstairs soaking in the Jacuzzi."

Ten minutes later, eyes closed, body totally immersed in the warm, vibrating water, she finally felt her heartbeat slowing and her breathing was becoming so much more relaxed. *There must be a God after all,* she blissfully concluded. Suddenly, from the distance she heard it, that unmistakable sound of a chopper. *No! No! Not now!* Her mind screamed. *I'm not ready for them.* She opened her eyes and jumped up, dripping wet, fully prepared to put on her jungle fatigues, flak jacket, and helmet, pull on her army boots then run the short distance from her hooch to the 71st ER to assist with the wounded from the Dustoff chopper. And then she saw the hanging geraniums on her balcony and realized she was home now. The war was over. She sank back down into the water, but it was too late. She couldn't return to her previous state of relaxation. Regretfully, she climbed out of the Jacuzzi and dried herself off with a large, green bath towel.

After throwing on a comfortable but sexy, mauve jumpsuit that accentuated her figure, she went into the kitchen and began to rummage around to find something to prepare for dinner. It was a beautiful late-summer evening. She decided that a barbecue on their deck might soothe her nerves. She pulled out a few T-bone steaks and marinated them with Adam's favorite steak sauce. She set them aside, then partially husked two ears of corn so that they could be easily grilled. She prepared some asparagus for grilling as well, and then began throwing together a salad. She was tossing the final ingredients, delicious, fresh cherry tomatoes, into the salad, when Adam walked into the kitchen.

Watching him walking towards her, she was reminded that they had definitely left their youth behind. At forty-three, he was quite bald and the little remaining hair on both sides of his head was graying rapidly. His athletic build had eased into love handles and an ever-expanding "beer belly." She smiled warmly at him and handed him a glass of California red wine. "Welcome home, Sweetheart."

He placed his leather briefcase on the black granite kitchen counter and pulled her into his arms while simultaneously reaching for the glass of wine. He kissed her softly on the lips before releasing her. He looked questionably at her. "What's all this about? Are you trying to spoil me?"

She laughed. "I'd love to say 'yes' but it would be a lie. I guess I just had an unsettling day and I thought a little wining and dining tonight would be good for both of us."

"That's right. You took Katie to the pediatrician's today. I still don't understand why you insisted upon taking her all the way to San Jose when there's perfectly good doctors around here in Monterey or Salinas."

"But Adam, remember what I told you? Dr. O'Brien is the best. I thought we both wanted only the best for her."

Adam laughed and threw his arms up in the air. "I give up then. When you put it like that, I'll have to agree with you every time.

How did she do? Is she fussing from her shots?"

She was taken aback. She hadn't expected Adam to know anything about Katie's immunization schedule. "She didn't get her shots today," she said while staring down at the salad to avoid his eyes.

"That's unusual, isn't it? Craig told me today that his kids got their first shots at their two-month appointments. He told me not to expect much sleep tonight." Adam laughed. "He even offered the couch in his office for me to sleep on tonight."

"I guess Dr. O'Brien just does things a little differently."

"Well, if he's really the best and she'll get them soon, I guess it's OK." He grabbed his briefcase off the counter. "Wait for me to light the grill. I just want to get out of this suit and check on Katie first."

She felt tremendous relief as he walked out of the kitchen. She poured herself a very small glass of wine and took a large sip. *What should she do about Katie's immunizations? She knew Katie needed them but she also knew she couldn't be there when their daughter got them. How would she explain this to Adam? She couldn't tell him about Nam. Or could she? Should she? She knew he loved her. It's been twenty years. Maybe it was time.* She took another large gulp of wine then set the empty glass down on the counter. She pictured his face as she told him. *He would be furious. What would he do? He's was her husband. Didn't he have the right to know? Isn't it time she trusted him with this piece of her life? They had taken that vow together- 'til death do us part.* She poured herself one more glass of wine and sipped it slowly this time. She sat down on the island stool, placing both of her hands on the counter to steady herself as she teetered so close to the edge of that cliff.

Ten minutes later, Adam came back downstairs, much more comfortably attired in beige Bermuda shorts and a short-sleeved polo shirt. "Katie's fine. Sleeping like a charm," he said, stepping through French doors to the deck.

She followed him outside, carrying the T-bone steaks, corn, and asparagus on a large, colorful Pyrex platter, a roll of aluminum foil, the bottle of steak sauce and a brush. "Can you first cover one third of the grill surface with foil for grilling the asparagus?" she said, handing him the roll.

He carefully placed the foil on the grill then lit it before bowing gallantly to her. "It's all yours, Madam."

Laughing at his antics, she placed the asparagus on the foil. She then laid the ears of corn on the uncovered section of the grill and dropped the steaks next to them. She brushed more barbecue sauce on the steaks before sitting down next to Adam on the cushioned porch swing while their dinner cooked. Adam wrapped his arms around her and pulled her close. She leaned back comfortably against his chest, closing her eyes for just a moment to fully saturate her senses with that summer evening. She breathed in his gentle touch, the warm westerly breeze caressing her face, and the symphony of crickets warming up in the distance. The aroma of the steak cooking suddenly sickened her. Somehow the night's melody had become distorted. She was overwhelmed with the smell of napalm-burnt soldiers. She fought the sensation, focusing first on the song of the crickets then the warmth of his skin against hers, but her attempts were futile. In desperation now, she tried to fill her mind with images of California sunsets over that majestic Pacific Ocean. She imagined enormous waves crashing on the beach and slamming against the large, gold and burnt-orange cliffs. But horrid snapshots of those infected burns kept pushing those pleasing images aside. The stench suddenly gagged her. She pushed herself free from his arms and ran inside to their downstairs bathroom and vomited.

It can't be starting all over again. Not after all these years. She hadn't had an episode like this for five years. Why is this happening again? Why now? She held a cool washcloth to her face for a few moments, before dropping it into the sink. She looked down at her hands. They were covered with blood! She washed them vigorously, harder and harder. But the blood wouldn't come off. She felt the warmth of her tears against her cheeks and her throat tightened uncomfortably.

There was a soft knock on the bathroom door. "Are you all right Sweetheart?" When she didn't answer him, Adam opened the door slowly and looked in. He saw her tears. "What's the matter? Why are you crying?"

She held up both hands for him to see. "Look at them. It won't come off."

"What won't come off? I don't see anything on them but water."

She looked down at her hands again, surprised and so grateful to see that Adam was right. Her hands were just wet. She dried them while Adam waited.

He put his arms around her while they walked back outside. "I think you've been hitting the wine bottle a little too hard, Darling," he laughed. "Why don't you just sit down and relax. I'll finish the grilling for us."

When his back was to her, she looked down at her hands, relieved each time to see that the blood had not come back.

"I believe our steaks are done now. Sample a bite for me," Adam said, gently lifting her chin and placing a small piece of steak on her tongue.

She closed her eyes, allowing the steak to intoxicate her taste buds. She opened her eyes and smiled at Adam. "Once again, oh great god of the grill, you have achieved perfection." They laughed then sat down together to eat dinner on their deck table. Both very hungry, they dined in quiet, comfortable silence for a few minutes.

She broke the silence first, "How was work today? Any interesting new cases?"

"As a matter of fact, Craig tried to give me what most people would call an interesting case. One that I'm sure will make national headlines. But I refused it."

"Why? That's not like you, especially when you're pushing hard to make partner this year. You've never been camera shy before."

"It's not the publicity, Maggie. I just can't take this one." He looked at her with intense anger in his eyes. "They're damn

Vietnam Vets. He was a medic and she a nurse. They have two children. They want to sue the government for Agent Orange damages."

"I thought there were already funds set aside for those affected by Agent Orange?"

He nodded. "There are. But they want money for their kids. They claim that their children have birth defects directly caused from their dual exposure to the chemical."

"It sounds interesting to me. You don't think you could reconsider taking this one?"

She jumped as he banged his fist on the table. "Damn it! Not you, too. I thought you understood me? You know how I feel about that war and anyone involved with it."

"I do," she said softly. "But the war ended twenty years ago. How long will you condemn Vietnam Vets for?"

"Forever. Does that answer your question?"

"But those children didn't participate. Aren't they entitled to help if Agent Orange was responsible for their defects?"

Adam clenched his fists so tightly on the table that she could see his knuckles becoming white. "I argued with Craig for almost two hours today about this. Frankly, I'm surprised. I thought you would understand and support me on this. I thought you felt the same way I did about those bastards that went over there to kill and maim and destroy that tiny, helpless nation."

"But Adam, you said that they were a medic and a nurse. They weren't killing. They were saving lives."

"No! They were patching up soldiers as fast as they could so that they could return to their killing fields."

She continued to plead with Adam. She was determined to make him understand for she knew that their future might depend on his understanding and acceptance. "I don't know Adam. Did you ever think that maybe they didn't even want to be there? That they would have given anything to have been home. Perhaps, they were even drafted?"

"No. You're dead wrong about that. I think I might have felt differently myself if that were the case. Perhaps, I might have been able to consider accepting this one if they had been forced to participate in that war. But they both volunteered. They went under their own steam. In fact, that's half their case. They want us to prove that they volunteered to help our country in its time of need, and now, in their time of need, the country is abandoning them."

"I don't know, Adam. I can see their point. It was so long ago. Maybe it will help you to take the case. Do it for the children."

Adam looked directly into her eyes. His voice was low, controlled, and filled with such hatred. "Listen to me, Maggie. I won't repeat myself. I won't take this case or any other like it. Ever. I refuse to have anything to do with anyone who participated in Vietnam. Maybe you can forget and forgive what happened over there. But I can't. I won't. I watched on TV every night as they destroyed that poor nation's land and its people with such superior weaponry. They were killing flies with cannons. Can you imagine raising Katelyn Marie below the ground? Can you imagine her growing up without ever seeing sunlight or trees or grass? Only cold, raw dirt for her to play with?"

She shook her head, unable to answer him.

"That's what our military made them do. Whole generations of children were forced to grow up in tunnel cities underground because of our constant bombing. Still, we wouldn't stop. We destroyed so much of that tiny nation. And for what? Can you think of anything good for either side that came out of that atrocity?... You don't have to answer. It's a rhetorical question. We both know what the answer would be anyhow." He paused for just a moment before looking directly at her.

The anger she saw in his eyes chilled her and told her there was nothing she could say to change his mind.

"I will never defend anyone who was over there. And I won't discuss it with you again. Do you understand?"

Unable to verbalize any of the emotions battling within her, she simply nodded her head in response. Abruptly, Adam stood up and walked into the house. She waited until his footsteps

CHAPTER FOUR
Duty's Price Tag

After completing her first two weeks at Pleiku's 71st Evacuation Hospital, Maggie's body was adapting to the grueling twelve to sixteen-hour days. She didn't think she would ever become accustomed to the stark, primal pain etched upon the soldiers' faces though. *How long will this go on? How many more broken boys will come through our doors before we say, "that's enough?"* She had no answers, could think of no solutions, so she kept quiet and tried to help them as best she could.

"Haskins, Christopher P." arrived on Friday at 1643 hours or 4:43 pm. When Captain Pollard, who was running triage that day, assigned him to her, time stood still. She knew she would never be able to forget him or this moment. Up until then, she had cared for soldiers in only two triage classifications, either they had simple wounds requiring very little care or they had serious wounds that needed immediate attention and stabilization before they could be brought back to the OR. Christopher was different. He was alive, but Maggie knew instantly that he was in extremely critical condition. Yet, Captain Pollard had simply asked her to offer him more morphine for the pain in ten minutes, hold his hand, and stay with him. *Had she misunderstood her orders?*

She looked around the ER and was grateful to see Kate leaning over a soldier on the next stretcher. "Kate! Kate! Can you come here for a minute?"

Kate hurried over. Her eyes saddened for just a moment when she looked down at Chris. She smiled at him. His body, from the neck down, was bloodied and mutilated. She squeezed his hand and spoke softly to him, "How are you doing, Chris?" We're going to help you now."

Chris smiled weakly at Kate. He tried to speak but it seemed to take enormous effort for him to do so.

"It's all right," Kate said. "You don't have to say anything. Just lie back and rest."

But Chris wouldn't give up. "Photo… Pocket," he finally got out.

"You have a photo in your pocket you want to look at?"

Chris smiled weakly at her. Kate reached into the torn, blood-spattered pocket of his fatigues and pulled out a wallet-sized photo of him and a beautiful, blond-haired girl. She wore a lavender gown with baby's-breath in her hair. Chris was decked out in a gray suit. They were holding hands, looking adoringly into each other's eyes. On the back of the photo, in feminine scroll, was written "All my love forever, Shannon." Kate held the photo close to Chris so he could see it clearly. He stared at it for a few minutes. They could see tears beginning to well in the corners of his brown eyes and trickle down his cheeks. A few minutes passed. Unable to hold them open any longer, his eyes closed and his breathing became irregular and spasmodic.

"Oh my God, Kate. I think he's dying! Should we call for a doctor? What do we do?"

"Stop it, Maggie," Kate said in a quiet, firm voice. She grabbed Maggie by the arm and pulled her a short distance from the stretcher. Her words softened. "There's nothing we can do for him."

"You're wrong. I'm sure we can help him. Shouldn't we at least try?"

Kate looked firmly into her eyes. "You're right. We might be able to help him, but it would take hours in the OR to do it. Even then, his chances are so slim."

"But we owe it to him and Shannon to try. It's our duty. It's why we're here."

"Maggie, stop. Look around the ER. If we tie up the OR for that long to try to save Chris, how many others are we going to lose?"

"But it's not right. We can't play God, picking and choosing who lives and who dies. I won't do it."

"I understand. I know this is difficult for you. I'm not asking you to play God. Just listen. Can you hear more Dustoffs in the distance? We have so little control over here. We can't tell them to stop bringing us their wounded so we can concentrate on Chris and others wounded just as badly as him. The choppers have no place else to go. We're their only hope. We have to be ready for them."

"But what are we supposed to tell Shannon? We can't just let him die. There has to be another way. Please, Kate. We can't let him die."

"Please stop. You can't fall apart like this every time we lose one of them. Look around. These boys need us. We have to try to save as many as we possibly can. We can only do that by following the orders from triage." She sighed. "We have to get back to work now. I'll stay with Chris for you. I was working on Private Winslow. Why don't you go insert and IV line on him?"

Maggie understood some of what Kate was trying to tell her. There were so many stretchers, so many wounded surrounding them. And she could hear the Dustoffs landing now. Soon more stretchers would be coming through the ER doors. Maybe Kate was right. Maybe this was the only way. She forced herself to stop crying. "No. Thank you anyhow, but I want to stay with Chris. I'll do my best to help him, if that's all right with you?"

"Yes, I know you can do this. I'll be right over there if you need me again."

Maggie returned to Chris's side where he slipped in and out of consciousness for the next twenty minutes. Each time he awoke, she held his hand, looked into his frightened eyes and tried to calm his fears. It seemed to comfort him the most when she held up Shannon's photo for him to see and whispered that Shannon would always love him. Finally, his eyes closed and his chest stopped rising. She placed her stethoscope on Chris's chest and listened for his apical pulse for one full minute. Hearing none, she asked one of the ER doctors to pronounce him. She stared at the photo of Shannon and him one last time, before placing it back into his pocket. With Sergeant Lance Powers' help, she placed Chris in a body bag. They wheeled him to their makeshift morgue, where he would wait, alongside the others, for his final flight home. She looked around the morgue. "There are so many of them, Sergeant. Why are we here? It can't be right."

Lance looked around the room for a moment, then back at Maggie. "How many have we lost today?"

"I don't know," she said sarcastically, stunned by his question.

"Well count them then," he said gruffly.

Angrily, she turned away from him and began to walk away.

He grabbed her arm and held her in place. "Count them. Damn it!"

Something in his voice frightened her. She did what he asked. She counted the body bags. "I think there's twelve. Are you satisfied now? Do you mind if I go back to work?"

"Actually, I do mind. I want you to listen to me for a moment... Please." He began to speak much more softly. "I used to wonder what we were doing here, too, Lieutenant. But not anymore. I signed up in '66. At boot camp, there was a soldier in my platoon, half Chinese and half Vietnamese. He was tiny. And quiet. But so tough. A lot of the guys in my platoon hated him. Not for anything he had done. They just hated him, plain and simple, because they were ignorant. They didn't understand him and they didn't bother to try. They just concluded because he was Asian, that he was the enemy. He was the reason that they were going to war. And so, they hazed him constantly, without mercy. Just before inspection, someone made sure that his cot looked like shit, or his locker looked like a cyclone had blown through it, or his brass was tarnished. Our platoon sergeant must have known what was going on. He had to have. But he was just as ignorant. So Sarge just kept on dishing out demeaning punishments. The poor bastard scrubbed our latrine floors on his hands and knees, marched in the heat for hours with an M-16 on his shoulders and a forty-pound backpack strapped to his back, and shingled the roof of our barracks in the full afternoon heat. But he never broke."

"I'm sorry, Sergeant. I do feel badly for him, but I 'm afraid I just don't see your point."

"If you hold on for just a few more minutes, I think you'll see it. You asked me why we're here and I'm trying to tell you."

She nodded. "OK. I'll listen for a little longer."

"You remember that I grew up in the Bronx. I was as tough as nails. But I know I couldn't have taken it as long as he did. It got to the point where I just couldn't stand it any longer. I was so ashamed to be part of that platoon. Look at me, Lieutenant. Every part of me is big and mean. It only took a few brutal punches to a few choice faces to stop Hoang's nightmare. He and I became very tight after that. Hoang's with the Infantry now, stationed north of here. Right outside of Hue. Ever heard of it, Lieutenant?"

She shook her head impatiently.

"It's their imperial city, modeled after Peking, the Forbidden City of China. Most people imagine Vietnam as huts with thatched roofs, but Hue was a beautiful city built along both sides of the Perfume River. The river broke the city into two distinctly different settings. On one bank was a modern city with lovely European style architecture. The other bank housed an almost impenetrable fortress, complete with a huge, stone Citadel.

"You're right. I haven't seen anything like that around here. I hate to say it again, but where are you going with this?"

"Just give me a chance. I'm almost there. The key word is 'was.' It was a gorgeous world with its Citadel and all, but the Tet offensive in January took care of all that. Nothing much left to it now. It's a city of rubble with seventy-five percent of the population homeless. It took hundreds of years to build and less than a month to demolish."

"I'm still not sure I see your point. After all, I'm sure our weapons had something to do with its destruction."

For the first time, Lance seemed visibly agitated. "That's right. Our firepower wiped out that city. Unfortunately, the

Vietnamese use gasoline or kerosene to heat their homes. So, when rockets hit them, in a matter of seconds flames consumed their entire houses. We weren't trying to rip apart their city. It just happened. And we had to do it. We had no choice. The Viet Cong had taken over that city and were so entrenched. They were in the sewers and gutters. Everywhere. They perched their snipers on every high point in the city. From almost every 2nd floor window, they would fire upon our soldiers and marines who were trying to retake Hue. We lost so many. We had over a fifty percent casualty rate. Modern Hue was retaken before the Citadel. It took an additional two weeks to penetrate that fortress. Finally, on February fourteenth, Hue belonged to our side again."

"Now listen carefully. This is the part I wanted you to hear, Lieutenant. I received a letter from Hoang last week. His platoon was out patrolling the countryside surrounding Hue less than a week after our side regained control of the city. They came across a Vietnamese woman- a very pregnant Vietnamese woman- and an old man walking together. They looked so weary, so exhausted. The platoon waited while Hoang questioned her. She told him that her husband was an educated man, a translator and an accountant. He had served in the South Vietnamese Army for a short time, but they had transferred him to Hue to work for the government instead. Just two days after the Viet Cong took over Hue, she said that the Viet Cong had invaded their home in the middle of the night. At gunpoint, they took her husband. And he was just one among hundreds abducted from their homes throughout the city that night. The soldiers forced the men, young boys, and even some women that they had rounded up, to march out of the city. With many other women, this pregnant woman had followed behind the communist soldiers and their captives. She had walked for miles, until she just couldn't go on. She eventually returned home, but her husband never did. None of them ever came home."

"Did Hoang ever find out what happened to them?"

"Yes. Here in Nam only a few have televisions. They don't watch the daily news like we do in the States. The Vietnamese communicate by word of mouth. The woman told Hoang that it hadn't taken long for word to reach the families in Hue. Their loved ones had been killed and buried in a mass grave in the countryside. That's why Hoang's platoon found her walking so far from the city. She was searching for her husband's body to take him home to be buried properly."

"But how did she even know where to look?"

"Like I said. Word of mouth. Some had watched. They passed on what they could. Hoang convinced his platoon to help this woman. They eventually found the mass grave. Hoang said that there were hundreds of bodies. Most of them had their hands tied behind their backs and their skulls were smashed in. It appeared that the majority had died kneeling. Worse yet, some bodies showed absolutely no signs of violence. Almost as if they had been buried alive."

Maggie covered her ears with her hands for a moment. "Please stop. I don't want to hear anymore. Why would anyone kill all those innocent people? They did nothing wrong. It's inhumane." Maggie shuddered and looked away from him momentarily before turning back again. "I need to know, though. Did they ever find her husband's body?"

"Yes. He was one of them. They brought him back to Hue for her."

He stopped talking and looked directly into Maggie's eyes. "Do you see what I'm trying to say?" he said softly, gesturing towards the body bags. "You're right. We're losing some. Twelve today. Perhaps the same amount, or even more, tomorrow. And the next day. And the next. But I don't think that they're dying needlessly. Don't you agree? We have to help these people. We can't just let them be slaughtered. The next time you lose a soldier, remember what that woman lost. And how. Remember what that whole city lost. We have to stop the Viet Cong. We have a duty to help these people."

Maggie returned to the ER and tried to reassure herself as she worked over their stretchers that the boys were suffering and dying for a good cause. But Shannon and Chris kept creeping back into her thoughts. Chris's body might have been flown home, but his face had remained behind. Shannon and Chris would forever be a part of her dreams.

"Nurse. Nurse. Help him. Please, help Chris!" Shannon, still wearing her lavender gown, cried out to her while Maggie lay helplessly, unable to move, in the middle of the ER floor with blood covering her hands.

CHAPTER FIVE
Confessions

Maggie awoke shivering and feeling frightened, her nightgown saturated with sweat. She untangled herself from Adam's arms and got out of bed. After pulling on a fresh nightgown and checking on Katie, she returned to their bedroom. By the soft glow emitted from their night light, she could see Adam was still sleeping soundly. In direct contrast to his relaxed breathing, she felt as restless and edgy as a caged tiger. She was overwhelmed with a desire to hold her Vietnam memorabilia. She walked softly over to her dresser and removed a large manila envelope that she kept safely hidden in the back of her bottom dresser drawer. A few minutes later, safely curled up on the living room couch, she hugged the envelope to her chest. Doubt permeated every ounce of her being. Should she open it? Indecision paralyzed her.

Finally, her need to touch her past empowered her. With a renewed strength, she dumped the contents onto her lap. After rifling through a dozen or more photographs, mostly of her and Kate interacting with delicate Vietnamese children, she picked up a small joke book and softly kissed the cover. "I miss you, Jake," she whispered, before closing her eyes and leaning her head back against the soft sofa cushion, allowing her thoughts to run freely, thinking of him for a few precious minutes. Gently, she put the book down on the coffee table, before picking up Kate's dog tags. She squeezed them tightly in her left hand. Finally, she opened up Kate's journal. She felt relieved that she had chosen not to give it to Doc. Reading Kate's journal always wreaked havoc with her emotions. Feelings of intense sadness and anguish conflicted with an even stronger sense of love and comfort as she read Kate's prose, written in a flowery, feminine scroll with black ink on those notebook pages that had begun to yellow over the passage of twenty years. Maggie could see her so vividly, sitting on her cot at the end of another long day in the ER, head bent over her journal, writing away. As Maggie read her words, she felt so close to her that she could almost feel her presence in the room. All the pain that Kate had felt, but chosen not to share with her, was so blatantly obvious in her poetry.

"Oh Kate, you helped me so many times. Why didn't you ever let me help you? Why did you suffer alone? Didn't you know how much I loved you? We all loved you," she whispered as she slowly turned those precious yellowed pages. Her eyes were drawn to her poem entitled "The Children's War." She read Kate's words aloud softly as she remembered her best friend.

The Children's War

So, it's one, two, three
I just can't count them anymore.
Scores of broken boys are lying
On stretchers across the floor.

"Nurse, nurse forget me.
Just don't let my buddy die.
No. Wait. Hold my hand.
Mom, it hurts so much," they cry.

I know too many boys are dying
In this grisly Children's War.
One question gnaws at my soul,
"What are they fighting for?"

Their body bags are stacked
In the corner by the door.
Oh God, give me strength.
I just can't fill them anymore.

She closed Kate's journal, unable to read anymore. She brushed just a hint of tears off her face. Suddenly, she was aware of the slightest motion from the corner of her eye coming from the bottom of the stairs. Her hand dropped fearfully to her lap when she saw him, standing there silently with Katie in his arms, watching her. Frantically, she began to shove Kate's journal and the photographs back into the envelope as Adam walked towards her.

"How long have you been standing there?"

"Long enough to hear you read that poem. What would possess you to read such horror aloud in the middle of the night?"

She didn't answer him. She just continued to try to stuff all those photos back into the envelope, but her hands were shaking now, making it an impossible task.

Adam laid Katie down on the sofa and picked up a few photos. Maggie was in one of them, wearing her jungle fatigues. He held it up to her. "Can you, please, explain to me why you're wearing a damned army uniform in this photo?"

The hateful, insidious tone of his voice stirred her. "I'm wearing a uniform because I was in the army."

"You were what?!" His tense body language frightened her and he spoke with an intensity she had never before heard in his voice.

Suddenly afraid of the impact the truth would have on him, Maggie spoke quietly forcing Adam to strain to hear her. "I said I was in the army. I was stationed at the 71st Evacuation Hospital in Vietnam from February of '68 through March of '69."

"I don't believe this," he said, glaring at her with such contempt. "This can't be happening. Tell me. Were you drafted or did you volunteer?" That word was said with such hatred that it seemed to hang in the air for a few seconds.

She looked directly into his eyes before answering. "I volunteered."

"I guess I could ask why. But I don't even care to hear your answer."

Katie began to whimper a little louder on the couch and to wave her arms and legs frantically. Maggie picked her daughter up and rocked her in her arms. Adam walked over to their fireplace and placed the palms of his hands on the stone. He leaned against it with his back to them. His silence tore at her emotions with more intensity than his earlier explosion of angry words had.

After a few minutes of silence, he turned around to face her again. Somehow, he had managed to compose himself. His face remained tense, but his words were much more controlled now. "Are you telling me that while I was incarcerated for demonstrating against that monstrous war, you were playing 'Florence Nightingale,' helping all those baby killers? Do you have any idea how much I suffered, locked away like a caged animal, for over thirty-six hours on three separate occasions? But I endured it. It was a small price to pay to stop that war." He paused for a moment and stared intently at her. "How could you not have told me about something as crucial as serving in Vietnam? I know that you knew how I felt about that war. For all these years you've misled me. I believed our principles were one and the same." He glared at her. "You don't have to answer. To be honest, I'm not sure I even want to know. I don't know who you really are. I feel like I've been living with a stranger."

She hadn't seen those hate-filled eyes for over twenty years. Strangers, possessing those same hateful eyes, had cursed and spit at her when she had stepped off the "Freedom Bird," the plane that had flown her back home from Nam, and she had walked onto the California streets wearing her army fatigues. She had endured it then, but she refused to endure it now; not in her own home. Perhaps for the first time in her life, she was proud of her work in Vietnam. She knew that she had helped so many suffering boys. She knew, too, that they weren't "baby killers." She remembered so many of the soldiers had been wounded, sometimes fatally, because they had refused to fire upon Vietnamese children. The world had had its facts screwed up for too many years. She couldn't let the lies and half-truths continue. She looked directly into Adam's eyes and spoke in a strong, even, controlled voice. "So, you think you had it tough because you had to sit on your ass on a jail cot for over thirty-six hours. How would you have liked to work on maimed soldiers for those same thirty-six hours, without more than a few twenty-minute breaks? And, can you imagine with all our medical expertise, soldiers' bodies so mutilated that there wasn't a thing we could do for them but hold their hands and help them die?"

He tried to interrupt her but she put her hand up to silence him before continuing. "Our so-called 'soldiers' were mostly eighteen and nineteen-year-old boys. Do you honestly think they wanted to be there? Don't you know that they would have given anything to be home, kissing their girls, cruising in their cars, or playing baseball instead? Daily, I watched them cry for their mothers, ask about their buddies, give me messages for their girls, and die, so bravely, in the corner of our ER. And it was my job to give them a reason to live. Or help them die when they were too broken for us to fix. I called them the 'Humpty Dumpty soldiers.'"

She paused and he let her continue without any signs of interruption this time. "Don't you understand, Adam? Like those wounded soldiers, I was doing my part to help in a war that I didn't start or even believe in. I did it for the boys, for our country's boys. Finally, when my job was done and I could leave, I came back to the States, not expecting glory, but hoping for a 'Welcome home, Maggie' or perhaps a 'thank you.' Instead do you know what I received for working a minimum of twelve hours per day, six to seven days per week, for over a year? I'll tell you what. I was spit at by people like you who didn't even know me nor have the decency to ask me about my beliefs before they cursed them. I stood there unable to say a word and just took it back then. But I'll be damned if I'll take it now; not from my own husband who should love and respect me. Either you will apologize to me now, or you can walk out that door."

Her heart pounded against her chest and the palms of her

hands were wet and clammy, but she didn't back down. Not this time. She continued to look into Adam's cold eyes, hoping to see some spark of hope... Something... Anything to cling to. But they remained so bitterly cold.

After a tense silence, he responded, "Do you really expect me to apologize for the principles by which I've lived my entire life? I wasn't just some stoned teenager following blindly on the coattails of some cause that I didn't fully comprehend. I was the campus voice against the atrocity called 'Vietnam.' I hated everything Vietnam stood for. I find that I still do. I will never apologize for my beliefs. Given your ultimatum, I have no choice but to pack my things." He turned around abruptly and walked up the stairs.

Maggie picked up Katie and gently brought her to her breast. She was still nursing when Adam came back downstairs. He walked out the front door without saying goodbye to either one of them. Maggie didn't cry when the door slammed behind him. *Hadn't they called her "Ice" in Nam?* She had learned to feel nothing in that world of unbearable pain. She knew that she could do it again.

CHAPTER SIX
Humpty Dumpty

"*Darling, I'm so sorry for hurting you. I can't believe that I allowed a war that ended twenty years ago to come between us. Will you take me back?" He looked at her pleadingly, with those baby blues that ripped her heart apart. Remorse was drawn in painful lines across his face. She happily watched him sweat for ten long seconds before running into his outstretched arms.*

Such was the fanciful substance of her daily daydreams over the next few weeks. It seemed that the more she tried to live up to her Vietnam nickname, "Ice," the more her mind became saturated with thoughts of Adam until dreams of them played almost nonstop in her head, like a worn out forty-five. And they were composed of the same surreal trash that fills the cheap romance novels that line the corner newsstand's shelves.

I don't need that self-righteous bastard, she told herself while simultaneously finding it increasingly more difficult each morning to crawl out of bed. Finally, she just remained there wallowing in her misery. After one full day of this self-inflicted solitary confinement, Camille walked into her bedroom, carrying a breakfast tray which she placed beside Maggie on the bed.

"Go away, Camille," she said, pulling the covers tightly around herself creating the illusion of an impenetrable fortress. "Can't you see that I don't want to get up? And I certainly don't want to eat."

"I'm not going to leave you, Mrs. Prescott. I don't understand why Mr. Prescott left you. I guess it's none of my business. But little Miss Katie, that precious baby is my business. She needs you. Please eat for her." She walked over to the sliding door that led to their balcony and pulled open the drapes. "Look at this beautiful day. You should be outside enjoying it with Miss Katie. Haven't you cried long enough? It's time to move on."

"You don't understand what you're asking me to do, Camille. I can't move on. There's no place left for me to go." She rolled over in the bed, turning her back to Camille. A few minutes later, Camille walked out of the bedroom. Maggie heard the door close and Camille's footsteps fade away down the stairs. Hours later, she heard her footsteps again. They stopped in the hallway outside her bedroom door.

Go away, Camille, Maggie thought when she heard the knock on her door, but she said nothing. After a few moments, the door opened and a stranger walked into her bedroom. She was short and heavy-set, dressed in an extremely outdated, dark-blue suit. Her gray hair was pulled up into a bun, pinned haphazardly at the nape of her neck with many loose, dangling strands of hair. She peered at Maggie through thick, dark glasses and carried an attaché case in her right hand.

Maggie sat up in bed, pulled the covers up to her neck, and stared back at her. "Who are you? What are you doing in my room? Does Camille know that you're here?"

She completely ignored Maggie and her questions, choosing instead to walk slowly around the room studying everything intently. She even had the audacity to pick up their wedding portrait and study it for a few moments, before returning it safely to its home in the center of Maggie's dresser. Finally, she sat down in the rocking chair in front of the window and placed her attaché case beside her on the floor. She stared at Maggie through those dark glasses, and then spoke for the first time. "To be honest, your bedroom disappoints me. I was incredibly eager to see it. I guess you could say I was 'intrigued.' I found myself wondering what could be so fascinating about a bedroom that a person would choose to remain in it for days at a time. While I must admit that it's a lovely room. So tastefully decorated. I can find nothing compelling or exotic enough to captivate a person for days on end. So, I find myself stumped and I am forced to ask you, Mrs. Prescott. Why are you still in this room, in bed, at three o'clock in the afternoon?"

Maggie couldn't believe this was happening. This complete stranger sat in her bedroom, staring at her and acting as if she really thought that she would answer her ridiculous question. "Who the hell are you?"

The strange woman spoke softly, giving no indication that she was either surprised or offended by Maggie's hostile question. "My name is Lydia Rothschild. I'm a psychologist. Camille asked me to come see you today."

"Camille had no right to do such a thing. I'm fine. And I definitely don't need a shrink!"

"Then I must repeat my question, Mrs. Prescott. Why are you still in bed at three in the afternoon?"

Maggie glared defiantly at this "Lydia Rothschild" and refused to answer her. Lydia, in turn, sat calmly in the chair, rocking slowly, showing no signs of shock or anger or disappointment. She simply sat there, peering at Maggie through those thick, black glasses with an unchanging countenance. And somehow, Maggie just knew that this woman would sit there rocking and staring at her as long as it took for her to respond to her. She couldn't take it any longer. "I'm still in bed because I can't think of a single good reason to get up! Are you satisfied now?"

"Are others' satisfaction or dissatisfaction with you important to you?"

"What!" Maggie couldn't believe what she was hearing. "You're not like any other shrink I've known."

"Oh. Tell me more. What should a psychologist be like?"

"Well, for one thing, they don't make house calls. They have ritzy offices with large, uncomfortable couches. After you are lying blatantly exposed on their couches, like a defenseless laboratory animal, they bombard you with endless, probing questions about your past. After months, maybe years, of endless analytical questions, they successfully strip you of every meaningful moment in your life, and then the shrinks proclaim that you are healed and send you naked into the streets."

"It sounds like you envision us to be on a higher authority

level than yourself. You've described us as powerful adult figures while you, the patient, are more like a totally helpless child or victim. But have you ever imagined a psychologist who was on an equal playing field? More like a friend to share a cup of tea with or to lean on as needed?"

"Are you really from this planet?"

"Yes, I'm real. I'm sitting here in your bedroom, asking your permission to become your friend. I would like to see if, together, we can help you leave this room. You've told me that there's no good reason to leave, but is there a good reason to stay?"

"I can think of one very good reason- *Humpty Dumpty*. That's me. And I don't care if you have all the king's horses and all the king's men in your attaché case, I know that I can't be put back together again. Not ever."

Maggie expected her words to have an impact on Lydia. She didn't know exactly what kind of effect, but she thought she would see surprise or sadness or something. Instead, Lydia just sat in the rocking chair with her facial expression unchanged, watching her.

"Have you always given up on yourself this easily?" Lydia finally asked.

Lydia's words infuriated her. "This easily! How can you say that when you don't know a damned thing about me?"

"And what do you think I should know?"

"How about this? My father left when I was four. I can't even remember his face. My mother drank herself to death. My best friend was killed in Vietnam. And my 'loving husband' has now walked out on me, too. Does this satisfy you? Does that sound like a nice, easy life?"

"I think that, perhaps, you may have misunderstood my words, Mrs. Prescott," Lydia said with a gentleness that surprised her. "I never meant to imply that your life had been easy. I only meant to express my belief that you may be giving up on yourself too easily. I believe life is a precious gift."

"Do you really expect me to forget about everything, get out of bed, and go play in the sunshine, as Camille suggests, as if nothing is wrong? You may find that an easy thing to do. But I don't. God help me, but I can't think of one good reason to get out of bed and face more pain. And I know it's out there just waiting to find me again."

"You're absolutely right," Lydia said quietly at first, but with increasing strength and conviction as she continued. "If you get out of this bed, you'll certainly experience more pain in your life. In fact, I'll guarantee that people that you care dearly about, will either leave you or die." She stood up and walked across the room to the foot of Maggie's bed. "I want you to feel your pulse, Mrs. Prescott. That's right. Take your right hand and place it on your wrist. Feel the life pulsating within you. You're alive! But unless you get out of bed and start living again, you'll never feel joy or love again. And that's what living is truly about." She smiled and looked gently into Maggie's eyes. When she spoke again, her words were almost a whisper. "You told me that you need a good reason to get out of bed. If you strain hard enough, I'm certain that you'll hear it."

Lydia began speaking in a much more business-like manner. "I'm going to leave you now. I'll put my business card on your dresser. My cell phone number is on it. You may call me any time of the day or night. While I offer traditional office hours in my practice in Salinas, I'm available to you anytime that you need." She smiled. "I'm always willing to make house calls as well. It's important that you know that I work exclusively with Post-traumatic stress disorder and think we could work well together. The next step is totally up to you. Please remember, though, I want to be considered as your friend." Lydia turned around, placed her card on Maggie's dresser, and then walked out of the bedroom.

Maggie listened to her footsteps fading as she walked down the hallway and stairs. She heard the muffled sounds of conversation, then the opening of the front door. As the door closed, she also heard Katie's soft cries. Slowly, she pulled herself to the edge of the bed and sat with her feet dangling over the edge for

DEBORAH ELAINE LINDSAY

a few moments. She stood up and pulled on her robe, suddenly overwhelmed with the desire to see, feel, and hold her daughter.

CHAPTER SEVEN
A Breath of Hope

Dr. Lydia Rothschild's waiting room was unique; unlike any other that Maggie had previously been in. Just like the outdated clothing Lydia chose to wear, the room's colors, drab olive and gold, were in style over two decades ago. And yet, Maggie found these tones strangely comforting, for it was in those decades that she had lived most of her life. In Maggie's experience, the majority of psychologists decorated their waiting rooms with lovely, aesthetically pleasing artwork, perhaps to soothe their patients or decrease their anxiety. In direct contrast to this, Lydia's walls were covered with intense water-colored illustrations of Civil War soldiers, focusing upon their faces. She couldn't stop staring at these drawings. The soldiers' eyes spoke to her for they were filled with the same stark, primal pain that she had seen in the wounded boys in Nam. And somehow, after all these years, seeing that pain again calmed her. She felt like she was finally in a room where she belonged.

The door opened and Lydia stood there smiling at her. "I'm happy you came, Mrs. Prescott. Please, come in."

Lydia's office didn't surprise Maggie either. It, too, was from a bygone era. A massive, mahogany antique-desk stood in the far-left corner of the room. Its cluttered surface mirrored Lydia's appearance. There were no couches in the office; rather, four large easy chairs, badly in need of re-upholstering, were arranged around a well-worn braided rug. She knew instantly that these chairs would be incredibly comfortable.

Her eyes were drawn to the right where an extraordinary glass display case stood on large, intricately carved wooden legs. The case's dimensions were enormous. Perhaps ten feet long, five feet wide with an eighteen-inch depth. She felt compelled to walk towards it. "May I see your display case more closely, Dr. Rothschild?"

"Please do. This is your room. Your hour. You may do whatever you wish here. And please, call me 'Lydia.'"

"Only if you will call me 'Maggie,'" she said as she walked across the wide pine floor to stand next to the display case. She peered down through the glass, surprised, but not shocked, for nothing about this woman could ever shock her again, to see a battle scene from the Civil War. Literally thousands of tiny painted soldiers filled the display case. Whether the soldiers wore gray or blue, wore boots or had bare feet, carried a rifle or a sword, walked or rode upon a horse, the level of precision for each was breathtaking. The battlefield, itself, was created with the same attention to detail, so that grass, trees, hills, rocks, stone walls, and fences all appeared so real. "Where did you get this? It's beautiful."

"I made it. It took me over five years, but I painted every soldier and horse, every wagon and cannon by hand. Model train enthusiasts helped me design the landscape. I can't take credit for the display case, however; I hired a local carpenter to build it for me."

Despite the battle scene's unbelievable, detailed beauty, she wasn't at all surprised to hear Lydia admit that she had created it. Maggie could clearly envision her, dressed in an old housedress, sitting at her kitchen table, cluttered with tiny bottles of model paint, brushes, and other paraphernalia, peering intently through those thick glasses, painting her soldiers, for hours on end.

"What battle is this? I'm afraid I know almost nothing about the Civil War."

"This is Pickett's Charge which occurred in the afternoon of the third and final day of the Battle of Gettysburg. It was the climax of that battle." Lydia pointed to the endless sea of gray uniforms. "These are the Confederate soldiers marching in proud formation up the grassy, gentle sloping hill to these fortified

Yankee positions. I'm afraid it doesn't take a vivid imagination to guess the outcome of this charge."

Maggie was completely engrossed by the scene. "I know the Yankees won but I have no idea how. I would love to hear as much as you can tell me about this battle."

Lydia smiled warmly. "Entire books have been written on the Battle of Gettysburg. I'm afraid it would take hours to properly address it, but I'd be happy to share some basic facts with you. The Battle of Gettysburg escalated to become, at that time, the largest battle ever fought in the Western Hemisphere. All historians claim that it was a pivotal battle in the war; some think it was the single most important battle of the Civil War because it ultimately determined the outcome of the war. I agree with them. To fully understand the Battle of Gettysburg, you have to know how war was fought in that era. When they met here, on the outskirts of a tiny Pennsylvanian town called 'Gettysburg,' during the third summer of the war, July first through the third of 1863, both armies were composed strictly of volunteers. Most men didn't receive a salary, and each soldier supplied his own weapon and equipment. Few soldiers owned horses so they walked, often barefoot, from one battlefield to the next or were shipped by train. Both sides were hungry, forced to scrounge for food from local farms and plantations. The weather was hot and humid with temperatures in the nineties."

Lydia paused for a moment to measure the impact of her words. Maggie looked up from the glass and smiled at her. "You have a way of making the scene come to life."

Lydia continued without hesitation. "From the onset, the Rebels were handicapped because they were fighting without their eyes, their Cavalry. Traveling on horseback, separately from the bulk of the army, the Cavalry scouted for enemy forces. Once found, they reported the details back to headquarters. Without its Cavalry, the army was unaware of its enemy's strength, location or strategy. During the first two days of the Battle of Gettysburg, the Rebel forces were blind. Their Cavalry unit, led by Stuart, didn't arrive until this final day of the battle. On the other hand, the Union's Cavalry commanded by Major General John Buford was the first unit to be positioned on this battlefield. General Buford recognized the great advantage the Union would have if they were able to control the high ground. His unit fought bravely on the first day of the battle to maintain that strategic advantage. They were located here, Maggie, atop these hills, where they could see for miles. They saw the Rebel army amassing and reported this information. In response to this message, the Union force swarmed by the thousands to Gettysburg. The Rebel army, without its Cavalry, was unaware of the Union's approach, position or numbers."

Lydia paused again for just a moment. Maggie could sense her sadness, yet found she was hungry for more details about this battle. "Please go on. I still have no idea of why or how the Union forces achieved their victory. It sounds like positioning was extremely important. Do you think the Yankees just had stronger leaders or perhaps a better strategy?"

Lydia looked across the glass at her with just a whisper of a smile. "Actually, if leadership were the deciding factor in this battle, the Rebels would have won hands down. Robert E. Lee, the most beloved Civil War general, on either side, led the seventy-thousand-men-strong Confederate Army of Northern Virginia. Lee's men all but worshiped him. Many would have given their souls for him... All he had to do was ask. General Robert E. Lee gave orders for his Army of Northern Virginia to take the offensive and march into Yankee territory. Not all of the Rebel leadership agreed with this tactic, but they were unable to sway General Lee's opinion. Lee had lost his most cherished confidant, Stonewall Jackson, to friendly fire one month prior to the Battle of Gettysburg. Perhaps, if Stonewall Jackson had still been alive there would not have been a Battle of Gettysburg. This was actually last battle in the Civil War that the Rebel army was on the offense. For the remaining two years of the war, the South was always on the defense."

"On the other hand, the Yankees were just becoming acquainted with their new leader, Major General George Meade. President Lincoln gave him command of the Union's eighty-thousand-men-strong Army of the Potomac just three days before the start of the Battle of Gettysburg. They say Meade vacillated like a pendulum over his decisions and had yet to earn his men's respect. Some claim that he even suggested a Union retreat on the morning of the third day of battle. If not for the strong opposition voiced by his commanders, history might have unfolded very differently."

"What do you think was the key factor then?"

"You were on the right track a few minutes ago. Look at the terrain and the answer becomes obvious. Do you see how the Yankees literally controlled every piece of high ground? Major General John Buford knew how important this high ground was and sent word to Union forces to make haste into Gettysburg so that they could maintain control of it. Even though the Rebels eventually out-powered the Union forces on the first day of fighting, Buford still strategically retreated to these hills- Big Round Top, Little Round Top, Cemetery Ridge, Cemetery Hill, and Culp Hill. He refused to give up the high ground. Also, do you see how the hills formed a fish hook? This is an excellent high position to defend from because it allowed General Meade to move his troops around easily to support any areas that suffered substantial losses. Meade further bolstered his forces by having them dig breastworks at night to use for protection when they engaged the Rebels.

"During the first two and a half days," Lydia said, pointing at the terrain through the glass, "heavy fighting occurred here and here and here, on the union's flanks, as the Rebels tried to dislodge them from their strong, high-ground positions. Daily, the Rebels caused damage, but by night Meade reinforced his weakened flanks by providing them with fresh forces that had originally been positioned in the center of the battlefield, up here along Cemetery Hill and Ridge. Realizing that the Union's central position was now considerably weaker, on the afternoon of the third day, Lee ordered a frontal attack there. Lee sent three of his divisions, fifteen thousand men commanded by George Pickett, hoping that they might be able to break through, thereby severing Meade's forces in half-"

Maggie interrupted, trying to fully understand what Lydia was saying. "It seems like that would have been a good strategy and yet I know it didn't work. I know the North eventually won at Gettysburg."

"You're right. The plan failed miserably. Lee gave his second in command and close friend, Lieutenant General James Longstreet, command of this assault. Historians report that Longstreet had reservations about Lee's strategy. He even told his artillery chief, 'I believe it will fail.' They say that Longstreet was a crude, inarticulate man. He tried desperately but was unable to find the right words to convince Lee to change his mind. And so Longstreet had no choice but to follow orders that he felt were doomed to fail. After giving his men their attack orders, knowing full well that most would be marching to their deaths, Longstreet is said to have wept. And this, Maggie, the climax of the Battle of Gettysburg, is what I have recreated here."

Lydia pointed through the glass toward the miniature soldiers in gray. "Prior to launching his attack, General Lee ordered the largest artillery barrage that had ever occurred in North America. His cannons stretched over two miles and fired at the well-fortified Yankee positions for over an hour. It was so loud that the sound of cannon fire could be heard forty-five miles away in Harrisburg. In the beginning of this Rebel artillery barrage, General Meade's cannons fired back at them. After a time, however; General Meade ordered his cannons to cease firing, leading General Lee to mistakenly believe it was now safe to send in his infantry. Fifteen thousand Confederate soldiers then marched for almost a mile in the open while the Union's artillery, rifles, canisters and shrapnel rained upon them as heavily as hail. Can you picture it? The Confederate soldiers struggled so hard to make it up these grassy slopes. But they were falling like dominoes under all that fire, and all the regrouping in the world couldn't save them."

Maggie nodded. "I can see now why it would be so difficult. They were just out in the open for too long. You said almost a mile? I can't imagine anyone doing it alone, but they had fifteen thousand men. Lee must have felt it would be enough, that some would make it to the top. Do you know how far they got?"

"The Rebels never made it past this wall," she said quietly. "Their formation dissolved into the horrific chaos of retreat after losing six thousand of their original fifteen thousand attack force. Lee's retreating trail of wounded, heading back to Virginia stretched for miles. Over twenty thousand Confederate soldiers were wounded or killed in this three-day battle. Although the war dragged on for almost another two years after Gettysburg, the Rebels never recovered from their losses here; they never again would be able to mount an offense against the Union forces. It was the beginning of the end for them."

They both stood for a few moments in quiet reverie, gazing down through the glass at the doomed Confederate soldiers.

"What motivated you to make this replica, Lydia?"

"That's a very good question. Let me see if I can explain it to you." She looked directly into Maggie's eyes. "I feel the greatest pain a man could endure would be to be asked to fire upon his own brother. Therefore, the greatest horror our country has survived is the Civil War, a four-year long wrenching, brutal battle between brothers. You might remember that the Civil War came to its bloody conclusion at Appomattox, but I feel the Confederates actually lost the war here, at Gettysburg. In my mind, this battle signifies the real end of that war. I recreated this replica of the Battle of Gettysburg as a symbol of hope for my patients. Do you see, Maggie, that if our country has not only survived, but recovered, from a nightmare as terrifying and incapacitating as the Civil War, then there's no pain or horror you've experienced, no matter how unbearable you believe it to be, from which you cannot recover too?"

Maggie nodded her head in agreement but was unsure if she was totally convinced. "Perhaps... Honestly, I've never thought about it quite like this before." She looked down through the glass, one last time, before looking up into Lydia's eyes. "I couldn't help but notice the water-colored illustrations of these Civil War soldiers hanging in your waiting room before I came in. I've never seen artwork quite like that in a psychologist's office either. For some strange reason, they seemed to comfort me. I don't know why."

Lydia smiled. "Good. I'm glad they somehow helped you. We're such funny creatures. We think that surrounding ourselves with artwork depicting breathtaking sunsets, idyllic country landscapes, or beautiful people smiling without a care in the world, will somehow give us peace and make us just as happy as they are. In my experience, I've found just the opposite to be true. For years I listened to my patients expressing their intense feelings of loneliness and isolation. Repetitively, different voices spoke the same words. They felt that they were the only souls that had endured such devastation in their lives. I wanted so much to help them. I just didn't know how."

Lydia paused and gave her a quick smile before continuing. "Then one day, a patient brought in a book with illustrations from the Civil War. He shared that he felt the soldiers almost talked to him. He understood their pain and didn't feel quite so alone when he looked at them. His feelings inspired me. I hired a local artist to paint those watercolors for me. By displaying those illustrations on my walls, I've tried to let my patients know that they're not alone. Others have walked down similar paths. Others have healed, and so can they." She looked right into Maggie's eyes again and softly said, "So can you, Maggie. There's so much hope. Each time you come into my office, I want you to study those portraits, look through this glass, and feel the hope. Shall we go to work now?"

Together they walked across the wide pine floor and that faded braided rug to the easy chairs. They sat down across from each other. Just as she expected, Maggie found the chair to be quite comfortable. She felt so at ease with Lydia, a feeling she hadn't experienced for a long time. Moreover, for the first time in years, she felt a breath of hope.

CHAPTER EIGHT
Jason

The ticking was becoming louder. Maggie glanced across Lydia's office to the far-left corner where the grandfather clock relentlessly counted off the seconds of their silence. She began to tap her right foot softly against the dull pine floor and to twirl her hair loosely around her index finger in nervous anticipation of the onslaught of Lydia's probing questions. Meanwhile, Lydia sat comfortably in the faded easy chair directly across from her, looking at her with that relaxed facial expression that told her absolutely nothing. "Don't you want to ask me some questions about my past?"

"No, Maggie. Remember this is your hour. You, alone, determine what will or will not be said. I won't send you naked into the streets, as you fear, because you'll only shed clothing that you no longer need. We may continue to sit here, enjoying the quiet comfort that only a good friend offers, or, if you choose, you may share something about yourself with me. Rest assured, I'll never ask you grueling personal questions."

Lydia's words soothed her. Again, she felt safe sitting there with her. Her foot stopped tapping. Her hand fell relaxed to her lap. She took a deep breath, then began speaking. "All this discussion of the Civil War, this war among brothers, has reminded me of my own brother and our personal battles. I miss my brother, Jason. On some days more than others. I regret that he never met my daughter, Katie... I see him every day in her eyes. I often wonder if she'll have some of his personality traits as well. I guess we'll know soon enough..."

Her thoughts drifted into a comfortable silence.

After a few minutes, Lydia asked softly, "Is there anything more you want me to know about Jason?"

Maggie smiled. "I think you would have liked him. He sizzled with life. I'm afraid a little too hotly for Mom. She just never knew how to handle him. He was a gorgeous, cherubic-looking toddler with Shirley Temple style, blond curls, a chubby face and enormous, almond-shaped blue eyes. Looking into his innocent little face, you expected only angelic behavior, but Jason often exploded with emotion, charging headfirst into everything he did. I could tell by Mom's facial expressions and her tones of voice that she often found this aspect of Jason exasperating, but I thoroughly enjoyed the chaotic excitement that he created. Most of the time. One of my earliest memories of him was from the spring that he was three and I was seven."

...Dad left right after Jason was born, so it was just Mom, Jason and me. My mother worked in a factory. Every evening she came home quite tired. Even so, after the supper dishes were washed and put away, she often drove us to a little park, a few miles down the road from our trailer. It was quiet, wooded haven with swings, slides and monkey bars scattered along the banks of a small river. Mom brought old bread for us to throw to the ducks that were perpetually floating along that river. Jason and I loved to watch the ducks fight over the bread we tossed to them. In the spring, it was even more fun because of the adorable little ducklings. I was fascinated by how protective those mama ducks were, snapping at anybody or anything that even came close to their little ones. I remember thinking that they must really love their young.

Well, on this particular spring day, Mom forgot to bring bread and Jason was furious. He lay on the ground and cried, kicked, and screamed. I laughed at him and called him 'Baby Pants' and other equally childish names. Mom just walked away from him with an embarrassed, tired expression on her face. As Mom walked away, I watched Jason's face become red with rage. He picked up some small rocks and started throwing them furiously into the water. I think it was accidental. After all he was only a little kid who still had a pretty poor aim. But some of the rocks hit the ducks. I screamed for him to stop and for Mom to come help.

Before she could get to him, Jason picked up a much larger rock and flung it hard into the river. The rock hit one little duckling on the head. The duckling's head dropped down and it floated so awkwardly and still. Its mother squawked, a piercing, soulful sound, louder and more intense than I had ever heard a duck squawk before. She gathered all her other ducklings around her and they floated away rapidly. Mom looked at the dead duckling that was left behind, then picked up Jason and threw him, like a sack of grain, over her shoulder.

"You're just like your father," she screamed. "It's bad enough you have to look like him, but do you have to turn into him, too?" She was crying; something I had never seen her do before. She didn't say another word as we walked to the car and drove home. She stopped along the way at a little country market and bought a six-pack of beer. When we got home, she didn't bathe Jason or get him ready for bed; so I did. She just sat there all night, on the sofa, drinking beer. It's the first time I ever remember Mom drinking."

...After Maggie stopped reminiscing, she briefly scanned Lydia's face. As usual, she couldn't read any emotion there.

"Why do you think you chose this incident to relay to me about Jason?" Lydia finally asked.

Maggie hesitated for a few moments, pondering the question, searching for the right answer. "I don't really know. Maybe because it still bothers me so much. I have so many unanswered questions about that day. I thought you might be able to help me understand. Do you think Jason really meant to kill that duckling? Was he really just like my father? Do you think my mother still loved Jason after that night?"

Lydia looked thoughtfully at Maggie for a few moments before responding, "I think you know the answers to all your questions. The truth is always written across our hearts, but our minds don't always choose to read those words, mostly because we fear the truth will cut too deeply into our souls. But I promise you this. Over time, if you continue to refuse to face the truth, no matter how painful it is, the wounds from that denial will be more paralyzing to you than the truth. It's time that you answer your own questions. It's the only way you can recover from the pain."

Maggie started to twirl her hair around her index finger again as she thought about her words for a few minutes. "I'm sorry. I know you want me to do some soul-searching and give you the answers. But I can't. Not now. Maybe you'll understand why if I tell you a little more about Jason and my mother's complicated relationship."

...Everything changed so much after that evening. Mom drank more often. She never took us back to that park again. She stopped singing while she did the dishes and rarely laughed with us. She still brushed my hair at night and listened to my prayers, but she wouldn't do much of anything for Jason. I felt guilty about it, but never knew what to say to her or Jason. I just continued to care for and protect Jason. I bathed him, read him stories, and tucked him into bed at night.

Jason was extremely intelligent, but I don't think Mom was ever aware of it. He was reading before he even went to kindergarten. He really taught himself. Whenever I read to him, he would point to this word and that and ask me what they were. Once I told him, he never forgot. He was just as good at math. By the time he was six years old, he was adding whole columns of numbers. His favorite activity was writing with chalk all over our driveway. Sometimes he drew pictures, but mostly he wrote words or solved simple addition and subtraction equations.

I doubt Mom knew that it was Jason's work on the driveway. She would so often say to me, "Why do you fill the driveway with so much junk every day, Maggie?"

I tried to tell her that it was Jason who was so smart, but she wouldn't listen. I was afraid she would be mad at Jason if she knew it was him drawing all over the driveway, so I never pursued it further.

In early July, a few days after my ninth birthday, Mom started smiling a lot more and began singing again when she washed the dishes. She stopped drinking quite as much and she even read stories to Jason. When she read to him, Jason didn't try to impress her with his own reading ability. He just sat there, peacefully in her lap, with a smile on his face, not saying a word. I had never seen Jason quite so content. We found out the reason for the sudden change in her behavior a few weeks later. Mom had a new boss, Mr. Kenneth Harper, and apparently, he was smitten with our mom.

Mom planted petunias in front of our trailer and made new curtains for the kitchen and living room. She painted the bathroom walls a light yellow and put up new wallpaper, a delicate floral pattern, in the kitchen. Everything in order, she invited Mr. Harper to dinner one Friday evening. She still had to work during the day, so I offered to vacuum, dust, and clean the bathroom for her. I sent Jason out to play while I worked.

Around lunchtime, with the trailer fully cleaned, I proudly admired my work, then went outside to check on Jason. He was sitting in the middle of Mom's petunias. He had pulled most of them up and they were scattered around him, withering in the hot sun. His chubby fingers were wrapped around another petunia. I screamed at him to stop, but he still yanked it out of the ground then looked up at me with a face streaked with tears and dirt.

"Mommy hates me," he said in a husky voice. "She doesn't like you anymore, either. She only loves Kenny now."

I didn't know what to say to him. How could I be mad at him when he was so sad? "Come here, Jason," I said, holding my arms out to him. He obediently got up and came to me. I hugged him for a minute while thinking about our options. Mom would be furious with Jason when she saw her ravaged petunia bed. There had to be a way of preventing that. I looked down at the dead petunias at our feet. They were well beyond salvation. Mom paid me fifty cents every time I babysat Jason. Maybe it would be enough. I pulled away from Jason. "Go wash your hands and face now. We have to go to town for a little while."

I emptied the contents of my piggy bank into my pocket then put Jason into his little, red wagon. He was heavy and the sun so hot, but I still had to walk at a brisk pace to fix everything before Mom got home. Thirty minutes later, we arrived at Smith's Greenhouse located about a mile up the road. We went inside and I used most of my life's savings to purchase two dozen petunias. I put them carefully in the wagon.

"You'll have to walk home, Jason. You can't fit in the wagon with the petunias."

"I want to pull the wagon."

"Please, be good, Jason. It's a long walk home. You'll get tired pulling this heavy wagon."

"I can do it myself!" he said loudly, while jumping excitedly up and down.

"Fine. Have it your way. Pull them yourself."

The sun relentlessly beat down on us. My feet felt like they weighed fifty pounds. I worried about Jason. I didn't know what I would do if he gave out on me. His cheeks became beefy red and his blond curls matted tightly against his head. However, much to my surprise, Jason pulled that wagon of petunias all the way home without tiring or complaining. I hugged him and gave him a big glass of lemonade when we arrived back home.

"Would you like to play a game with me now?"

"He nodded his head. "Yes, I want to play!"

"OK. Why don't you put all the dead petunias in the wagon and hide them in the woods for me to find tomorrow while I plant the new ones? Only it's a secret game. You can't tell Mommy about it."

After the petunias were planted, I showered and gave Jason a bath. We had just finished dressing when Mom drove up. I was relieved when she didn't even seem to notice the new petunias.

"Thank you, Maggie," she said hugging me. "Everything looks beautiful. I need to start supper now." She hummed to herself as she prepared spaghetti and meatballs for dinner, looking up frequently to smile at us. I smiled back at her but Jason went to his room and slammed the door shut.

Mr. Harper brought a bottle of wine and some red roses for mom. The roses were beautiful, but I thought he shouldn't have brought the wine. Mom didn't need that. They had a glass of wine before dinner and Mom gave me some soda.

"Jason, do you want to come and have some soda with us?" she called.

"No!"

"Could you at least come and say 'hello' to Mr. Harper?" she cajoled.

"No!"

She got that embarrassed look on her face.

"It's OK, Tricia," Mr. Harper said. "Don't force him out on my account."

Mom smiled gratefully at Mr. Harper, then drank some more wine. I set the table while she finished cooking supper. "Maggie, will you please get your brother for dinner?"

Jason came out of his room for me and sat at the table for dinner. He stared angrily at Mr. Harper for a while, then looked at Mom.

"Aren't you going to eat your dinner, Jason?" she asked.

"No."

"Come on. Be a big boy. Eat your dinner."

"No! You can't make me. You can't make me do anything I don't want to. You never do anything for me!"

I watched both of their faces becoming flushed and angry and I knew neither one of them would back down. I wanted to intervene, but, like all the other times, I didn't know what to do or what to say to silence the storm.

"I'm not going to ask you again, Son. Eat your dinner."

"I hate you!" Jason screamed then picked up his plate and threw it at Mr. Harper. The plate splattered his crisp, white shirt with red sauce before falling to the floor, breaking into jagged pieces and spewing spaghetti sauce across Mom's clean kitchen floor.

I watched Mr. Harper's face change from surprise to shock to anger. He stood up, dabbing at his shirt with his napkin, but his attempts to clean it only made the stain expand. He looked at Mom and said in a low, tight voice, "I'm sorry. I can't stay here, Tricia. Not like this."

Mom walked him to the door. I don't know what he said to her, but she was crying when she came back to the kitchen. She took the bottle of wine into the living room and sat on the couch, drinking and crying at the same time. When the bottle was empty, she went outside. I looked out the window and watched her stomp on the petunias in a crazed frenzy. My stomach hurt. I couldn't watch her any longer. I pulled the curtain shut then went to find Jason. I put him to bed, then went to bed myself, pulled the covers over my head and cried myself to sleep.

...Maggie tapped her right heel against the pine floor and nervously played with the ring on her hand. Finally, she looked at Lydia again. "I'm not sure I've answered any of my questions yet, but perhaps you understand a little more about our family dynamics now."

"What do you think I should understand about them?"

"I don't know. We weren't a normal family. There was always something missing. I never understood why they tore each other apart. They were both nicer to complete strangers than they were to each other. After a while, I avoided being home with the two of them. The trailer just wasn't big enough for all their anger. By the time I was twelve years old, I was spending most of my time with my best friend, Kate, and her family. In my fantasy world, they were my real family."

A bittersweet memory of her mother suddenly jarred into her consciousness. Its emergence troubled her and suddenly it seemed very important that Lydia understand a little more about her mother.

"For a period of time, in my early teenage years, I remember thinking that I hated my mother. I found fault with everything about her, especially her parenting skills. After all she was an adult and should have taken much better care of Jason. But my hostile feelings towards her completely changed the day my eighth-grade class went on a field trip to the factory where she worked in Santa Clara."

"I hadn't told her that we were coming. We walked into a huge steel building that had only a few windows. There were lights, but not enough of them. It was dismal inside. I remember that it was a warm, comfortable spring day but without any air conditioning, it was stifling hot inside. But even more overwhelming than the heat was the noise. Huge machines, ugly steel monsters, filled that room. Grinding wheels of all sizes were moving along between the machinery on conveyor belts. My eyes adjusted to the lighting. I studied the workers, searching for Mom. Finally, I spotted her, standing between conveyor belts. She looked so small surrounded by all that machinery. Beads of perspiration adorned her forehead and I could tell by the tight curls sticking out below her kerchief that her hair was damp as well. Her face tensed as she bent over a wooden pallet that contained grinding wheels. She glued a round label to the outside surface of each grinding wheel, then had to lift each one and turn it over to attach a different label to the backside. I could tell that they were heavy because she grimaced as she lifted them. She barely had enough time to wipe the sweat off her brow before another pallet arrived and she began the process all over again.

Maggie was unable to tell Lydia anymore, because her throat tightened, just like it had back then. Lydia respected her silence.

After a few moments, Maggie regained her composure. "It hurt so much to see her there. I couldn't believe that she had to work like this for ten hours a day. I think I loved her more at that moment than I had ever loved another person. Before she could see me, I turned and walked out of that dirty, horrid factory. I would never forget the lesson she had taught me. I told myself that I would never work in a place like that. I think that it was seeing her working there that inspired me to go to nursing school. For a while, I tried to spend more time at home with her, but she and Jason were always at each other's throats.

It didn't take long for me to drift back to my old habits of spending all my free time with Kate and her family. I loved my mother and brother both dearly. I just couldn't stand being in the same room with the two of them." Maggie finished speaking and they sat together silently for a few minutes.

After a time, Lydia asked softly, "Is that everything that you want to share today?"

It would have been so easy to simply say, 'yes,' but something deep inside of Maggie tugged, pulled, and clawed itself to the surface. For some unknown reason, she felt her survival depended upon Lydia knowing the whole story today.

"I know that I've told you that Jason was super smart. He excelled at school, but he was a loner. I don't remember him ever having any close friends. I guess he just shone too brightly to be a part of this world. He was destined to feel all of life's pain and rarely experience its joy. I knew that Mom couldn't afford to send him to college and I was terrified of what Vietnam would do to his fragile soul. When he turned eighteen, I volunteered to join the army so that he couldn't be drafted. I thought he would be relieved but when I told him, he was outraged by my actions."

"'I'm a man! How long are you going to continue to protect me from life? You have no right to place yourself on the line for me. I would never ask you to do this. It's not right,' he said. And then, his ranting stopped as suddenly as it had started. He walked over and hugged me tightly. Before he let me go, he whispered to me, 'OK, Maggie. Thank you. I guess I'm not really surprised that you would do this. You have always been there for me. Don't worry. I won't let you down now. I love you, big sister.'"

"I remember feeling tremendous relief. I was grateful he had accepted my decision. I told him that I loved him and that I hoped he understood why I did it. I left for Kate's house less than thirty minutes later. It was the last time I saw Jason alive. After leaving a note for me on my bureau, he hung himself from a tree in the woods behind our trailer."

"I can still see each word so clearly in the note he left for me. 'Maggie, I can't let you sacrifice yourself to protect me. Thank you for being the perfect big sister. I just can't let you do this. Now you can stay home. I'll always love you, Jason'"

"But I couldn't stay home, Lydia. Everything in that trailer screamed his name. I felt as if I had hung that noose around his neck myself. I needed to get as far away from that trailer as I could. Gratefully, I left for Fort Sam two weeks later. I don't know. Maybe I should have stayed home to help Mom. But God help me, I just couldn't. I remember receiving so many letters from her when I was in Nam. They were filled with endless questions about Jason. Why this and why that. On and on. I never asked her, but I cried myself to sleep many nights wondering 'Why Mom? Why? When Jason was alive and you could have asked him anything, you never asked him even one question to try to understand him.' Why did they live like strangers? I often wept for all of us and everything we had lost."

Maggie realized that she had told Lydia so much more than she had initially intended to share. Somehow, sitting across from her, she had just felt obliged to tell her everything. Now, Maggie felt as if she had revealed too much. She looked down at the floor, suddenly afraid to meet Lydia's eyes.

Lydia allowed her to sit for several minutes, before speaking. "Maggie, I think you've answered all your questions, but by doing so, you may feel exposed and vulnerable. I want you to just lay your head back against the easy chair now and breathe slowly. Feel the love they both had for you. Breathe their love into your whole being. That's right. Breathe in slowly. Exhale fully. With every breath you take, feel their love filling you so completely, from the top of your head to the tips of your toes. Hold them close with each breath you take. Feel the peace."

She did what Lydia asked. With her eyes safely closed, her mother and Jason came clearly into focus. She prayed that, away from the brutal intensity of this world, they had finally discovered each other's true identity and could finally love one another as much as she had always loved them.

CHAPTER NINE
Lullabies and Fairy Tales

The gentle peace that had bathed her soul in warm, soothing waters following the release into Lydia's capable hands of so many years' worth of bottled pain dissipated instantaneously when she pulled into the driveway and saw Adam's pale-blue Mercedes. Knowing that it would be so much easier to just drive away, she got out of the car, walked slowly to the front door, and stepped inside. Adam was sitting on the living room couch, holding Katie, speaking baby-talk to her. It saddened her to recall a time, not so long ago when nothing had made her happier than watching them together like this. Adam looked up at her with bitter eyes; their coolness stirred her. Instinctively, she tensed, preparing for battle.

"Have you come home, Darling?" she asked sarcastically, knowing full well the answer to her own question.

"No, not quite," he said with agitation. "I found I just couldn't stay away from Katie any longer. I missed her too much." He looked down at his daughter. "Daddy just missed you so much, didn't he Sweetie Pie?" he said, giving Katie a big smile and gently tickling her belly before looking back up at Maggie. "There's no doubt in my mind that she'll always be what keeps me going, my reason for living. And it's important to me that she knows she can count on me. That I'll always be here for her and I'll never leave her." His tone hardened suddenly, "Even if I've been forced to leave her mother." Maggie was surprised to see his eyes and voice soften slightly just as quickly. "I'm sorry, Maggie. I shouldn't have said that." He paused for another moment before continuing. "I came back today, hoping you might consent to Katie spending a few days with me. If it helps you say 'yes,' I'd be happy to take Camille along to help me keep Katie on her schedule."

"I don't know, Adam. You haven't even given me any warning. You just showed up today, out of the blue, and are now expecting me to say it's OK for you to take Katie for the entire weekend. What if I had plans? Fortunately, I don't. But that's not really the point. I could have… But I suppose she's your daughter, too. And I do agree with you that it's important for you to have time together." Maggie twirled her hair loosely around her finger and stared down at Adam and Katie together for a moment, just allowing her thoughts to run freely. She knew it was an important decision and she came to realize there was really only one choice. She said grudgingly, "I guess it will just have to be OK. Let me go talk to Camille about it." She turned away from him and ran up the stairs, refusing him the satisfaction of seeing her fall apart. She knew he respected strength and she was determined he would see only steel in her.

Maggie found Camille in the nursery changing Katie's crib sheets. Slightly out of breath from running up the stairs, Maggie took a deep breath before explaining the situation fully to her.

"I would be happy to help Mr. Prescott with Little Miss Katie for a few days," Camille said. She could see tears just beginning to form in the corners of Maggie eyes. "Don't you worry, Mrs. Prescott. She'll be fine. We'll be back before you know it. Now, if it's all right with you, I just need a few minutes to throw together a few personal things to take with me for the weekend."

"Of course. "Take your time. I'll pull together some essentials for Katie while you do that." Maggie placed Katie's Winnie the Pooh blanket, some tiny outfits and sweaters, diapers, wipes, and a few of her daughter's favorite toys into the diaper bag. While she packed, her thoughts ran wildly again. Her anger with Adam clashed with her protective mothering instincts. *After walking out of Katie's life without so much as a goodbye hug, he thinks he's entitled to her at the drop of a hat. Why did she even listen to this ridiculous request, let alone consent to it? It was bound to have some harmful effect on Katie's delicate psyche. She wasn't a toy to be played with or discarded at whim. She was a child… Her child. And it was her responsibility to protect her. But he was her father. Her father not only loved her, but wanted her in his life. Was there anything more joyous than to be cherished by your father? She could think of nothing and, with relief, realized she had, indeed, made the only correct choice for Katie.*

When everything was packed, Camille and Maggie walked downstairs. Maggie went to the kitchen and added some of Katie's baby bottles to the diaper bag. She then grabbed a dozen small baggies of her expressed breast milk from the freezer and placed them on top of ice packs in a small cooler, before returning to the living room. Adam was still sitting on the couch with Katie in his arms. "Adam, I just realized this will be the first time Katie has been away from me since she was born. May I hold her for a moment before you leave?"

"Sure. Believe me, I understand," Adam said, rising from the couch and handing Katie to her.

Maggie hugged her tightly against her chest then cradled her in her arms, taking a photograph of her perfect, delicate features with her mind. She kissed her gently on both cheeks. Katie smiled and batted wildly at her with both of her small arms.

Maggie looked into Adam's eyes. "Please, bring her to a pediatrician. Her immunizations are due this week. A local pediatrician is fine for her shots."

Adam seemed irritated and started to speak, then clamped down his jaw, turned his head toward the window and said nothing. Maggie handed Katie to Camille, while Adam gathered up Camille's suitcase and all Katie's paraphernalia. From the foyer, Maggie watched the three of them getting into Adam's car. Her throat tightened and tears formed in just the corners of her eyes. "I'll miss you Precious Little One," she whispered.

After the engine noise from his Mercedes faded into lonely, intolerable silence, she walked through the house, searching for something, but, as usual it eluded her. She walked into the nursery and picked up Katie's large, white teddy bear. She curled up in the rocking chair, hugging the bear tightly to her chest, somehow comforted by its softness. She closed her eyes and subconsciously began humming a lullaby. Suddenly, she became aware of that melody, but couldn't place it. *Where have I heard it before?* She searched through the pages of her past until she recalled the first time, she had heard that soothing lullaby.

...After surviving four nightmarish months in Vietnam, the only thing that Maggie knew for certain was that she felt an intense hatred of the Viet Cong. With every wounded American soldier carried through the doors of their ER, her hatred intensified until she knew that if she were ever confronted with a Viet Cong soldier, she wouldn't hesitate to wrap her hands around his neck and choke out every breath of his life. She had learned that, while her feelings of sympathy and sorrow for her own American soldiers weakened her, her newfound feelings of hatred and outrage for the Viet Cong seemed to strengthen her. She allowed her mind and soul to become an agar dish for the growth and proliferation of these intense negative emotions.

Sometimes, Vietnamese women and children were wounded by this war that raged in their backyard. If their injuries were critical, the Dustoff pilots didn't hesitate to evacuate them to the 71st for treatment. A tiny, three or four-year-old boy was one such evacuee. He arrived unaccompanied by his parents so Maggie didn't know his story. Judging from the gunshot wounds to both his abdomen and back, he evidently had wandered into crossfire. He had lost a lot of blood. His face was so pale that his brown eyes, in contrast, seemed to fill it. Those brown eyes followed Maggie around the room, but his facial expression never changed, not even when she started two IV lines on him, drew blood and prepared him for surgery. If he were in pain, he gave no indication. As she began transfusing him with his first unit of O negative blood, she looked into his enormous eyes and became aware, for the first time, that they weren't the eyes of a child. These eyes belonged to a man, who after enduring a lifetime of pain, still had the will to survive. Maggie knew these eyes well, but had never before seen them in a child. A feeling of helplessness washed over her as she stared at this delicate child of stone, for she knew there was nothing she could give him, not hugs or bandages, not songs or love that would ever change those eyes. He was a child who, after living with war, had been forced to either grow up immediately, bypassing his childhood all together, or die. For a moment, she worried about his chances of surviving surgery, something she hadn't done for a few months. He lost consciousness just before he went back to the OR.

He was still comatose when he came out of the OR three hours later. "How is he, Dr. B?" Maggie asked.

Dr. Bennett removed his surgical hat and mask, sighed wearily, then brushed his fingers through his thick, black hair. "I just don't know. I'm not convinced we were able to fix the little fellow. One of the bullets was lodged deeply in the lower lumbar portion of his spinal column. I was able to remove all the fragments, but there's bound to be some degree of residual damage. It's simply a matter of how much. He'll be in spinal shock for several weeks. We'll just have to wait and see. We'll know more when his post-operative edema subsides. Best I can give him is fifty-fifty. He'll walk or he won't."

"Will he wake up, Dr. B?"

Dr. Bennett sighed again. "Yeah, he'll wake up. Probably in just a few hours. But I'm not sure that's a blessing either. You know how these Vietnamese feel about handicapped children."

She nodded. She had heard the stories. After surviving hours of surgery and weeks of rehabilitation, many Vietnamese children with lasting, permanent injuries had been sent home only to be sympathetically sacrificed by their caring village.

Dr. Bennett smiled wearily at her again. "What are you still doing here? It's not that busy and your shift must have ended a few hours ago? You know the rules of survival. You can't let yourself get attached or you'll never be able to let him go."

"I know the rules. However, I'm afraid it's too late in this case. He has no one. I thought he might remember me. I was hoping seeing my face when he wakes up might comfort him just a little bit." She looked down at his tiny body on the stretcher. "He's so small. I hate this damn, ugly war."

Dr. Bennett put his arms around Maggie's shoulders. "I hear you. Just don't get hurt any more than you have to."

"I'm a big girl."

"I know, but sometimes, it's the big people that get hurt the most. Be careful."

Maggie watched Dr. B walk out of Post-op, then focused all her attention back on this fragile child. Around 2200 hours, he began to stir. She looked into his big, brown eyes and smiled, but his face remained as unresponsive as earlier. His body was rigid. She knew he must be in pain. As ordered, she gave him a small dose of morphine. Only after the narcotic had induced sleep in him did she leave him to the care of the night shift nurses and return to her hooch.

Over the next few days, Maggie visited him on the Post-op unit as much as she could. Although she was no longer responsible for his care, something always drew her back to him. On the third day following surgery, she was surprised to find a small man, sitting cross-legged at the foot of the boy's bed just watching him sleep. His eyes never left the child. He spoke softly in Vietnamese and occasionally sang a lullaby to him.

When the child awoke, the bond between the two became strikingly obvious. The boy still didn't smile, but his eyes screamed with a love and adoration that were mirrored in his father's eyes. Maggie's throat tightened watching them. She ran out of Post-op cursing her own father who had discarded her like trash when she was about the same age as this boy. *You bastard! She thought. What gave you the right to walk away from me? Didn't you care that I needed you? I needed you.*

Never having experienced it herself, she was captivated by the father-child bond; she continued to be drawn back to them, like a moth to the flame. In broken English, the man spoke to her about his son. Cuong was his youngest child and only son. Every time that she visited them, he thanked her again for helping Cuong. Looking into his grateful eyes, she couldn't muster up the courage to tell him that Cuong may never walk again. To overcome the guilt she harbored for keeping the secret of

Cuong's uncertain prognosis, she gave him some clothing for Cuong and a small white teddy bear. The nurses at the 71st collected used clothing and toys like this from family and friends back in the States. These items were given often as gifts to a local orphanage.

Cuong's father returned the favor by giving Maggie a special gift. Knowing that she was fascinated by the lullabies he often sang to his son, one day he presented her with a Vietnamese children's book filled with poems and songs. The cover was cracked and the pages worn, but she cherished his thoughtful gift. Often, when her shift was over, she would sit next to Cuong's father at the foot of Cuong's bed and he would translate some of the poems for her. Her thoughts became preoccupied with prayers for Cuong's recovery.

Ten days after his surgery, Cuong moved his legs and Dr. Bennett predicted a full recovery. Maggie hugged Cuong. His father's joy was intoxicating so she hugged him as well. The next day, Cuong was transported to a Vietnamese hospital and she never saw him again. As she cared for the wounded soldiers in the ER, she hummed the lullabies that Cuong's father had taught her. Somehow it soothed them all.

One month after Cuong was discharged from the 71st, his father returned, on a stretcher in critical condition. He had taken a round from an M-16 after he had thrown a grenade at a platoon of marines, killing three of them and severely wounding two others. His stretcher was within eyesight of these wounded marines. They shouted to her, "Kill that Gook! Don't you dare help that bastard."

Maggie knew that she was supposed to hate this Vietnamese man. Hadn't he just killed and mutilated her boys. But she couldn't. God help her, she just couldn't. She knew he was the enemy; he was a Viet Cong guerrilla. But all she could see was him sitting cross-legged at the foot of Cuong's bed, humming that lullaby to his sleeping son.

She didn't remember much else about that day. She recalled wanting to ask Cuong's father so many questions to try to understand the nightmare that was unfolding around her. She knew that she didn't really want to hear his answers. She worked like a mechanical nurse, blocking out everything but thoughts of Cuong, his father, and that haunting lullaby. They had shattered her agar dish into hundreds of pieces, destroying her value system, leaving her weak and vulnerable.

Where would she find the strength to care for these broken soldiers, day after day, if not from her hatred of the Viet Cong? Yet, how could she ever truly hate them again, knowing that they weren't monsters after all, but fathers who adored their children as fiercely as many Americans? This Viet Cong guerrilla was a better man than her own father. How could she hate him?

...Sitting in the rocking chair, she couldn't think about Vietnam anymore. Thoughts of that world always tore into her soul creating so much confusion and anguish. *Wasn't she lonely enough without drudging up painful memories that were better left safely buried in her past?* She stood up and placed Katie's teddy bear back in her crib. *Do you miss her as much as I do, Teddy?*

She felt restless. Hoping a few hours of sunbathing by their pool might relax her, she put on her bathing suit, grabbed a towel, and walked to the pool. They employed a gifted gardener, Mr. Matei, whose Japanese heritage had helped him become the most sought-after landscape artist in Carmel Valley. Their gardens, cobblestone walkways, lawns, shrubs and trees were landscaped to symmetrical perfection and immaculately maintained. Mr. Matei had planted a variety of flowers, flowering trees and bushes to ensure that year-round, they never went without color from their blooms. The shrubs were sculpted with Japanese grace and the old-fashioned lampposts, positioned precisely every ten feet along their walkways, provided the final brush strokes to the picture of charm.

Despite the undeniable beauty of their private, man-made paradise, nestled among Pacific Mandrone, rugged Monterey Cypress, cedar, and white oak trees, she never knew how the surroundings would affect her. Sometimes, the inherent peacefulness caressed her like warm, tropical waters. More often, she felt as she did today, guilty for having so much in a world where so many had so little. As usual, she attempted to combat these feelings of guilt by convincing herself that it was OK for her to lounge in luxury, enjoying the sun's sensual rays against her skin, because she had paid her dues. She had lived most of her life balanced precariously on that tightrope between poverty and the lower middle class. Only for the past five years had she lived in this wonderland, thanks to Adam carrying her off on his magnificent white steed.

    Maggie closed her eyes and concentrated on the sun, feeling its warmth seeping into every pore. *I don't recall Cinderella ever lamenting about being chosen by Prince Charming. Don't they say 'if the glass slipper fits, wear it'?* She chuckled to herself, enjoying her wit. Then, another thought provoked her into a state of anxiety. *No one ever talked about the possibility that Cinderella may be thrown out of the castle, glass slipper and all. What would become of her when her fairy tale screeched to a halt?*

CHAPTER TEN
Shade of Gray

Throughout the rest of the weekend, Maggie was lonely and restless, missing Katie so much more than she had expected. She found herself constantly wandering into her nursery, sitting in the rocking chair, and clutching Katie's white teddy bear. She missed Camille as well. This surprised her. Perhaps for the first time, she realized what a friend she had in Camille. She thought of ways to let her know this when they came home.

Far worse than her loneliness, however, was her anxiety about Adam. She knew that she couldn't hang out on that cliff much longer. She had to know where her life was headed. She realized that when Adam brought Katie home, she must face him like a rational adult. *Lydia would be proud of me, she thought. Didn't she advocate confronting the truth no matter how painful it might be?*

Late Sunday afternoon, Maggie heard Adam's Mercedes in the driveway. Her heart quickened its beat and she began to breathe a little faster, as from the foyer, she watched them approaching the house. She opened the front door and smiled down at Katie, still sleeping in Camille's arms. She kissed her softly on the head. She wanted desperately to grab her out of Camille's arms and hold her close, but knew she had to do something else first.

"I'm so happy you're home, Camille. I don't want to wake Katie. Would you mind settling her in her crib while I talk to Adam? I'll be up in a few minutes."

Adam looked questionably at her. "I don't have much time, Maggie. I've made plans for this evening."

She wanted to scream, *This is important! Don't you realize we're important?* Instead, she just smiled at him and promised, "This won't take long. Let's go to the kitchen." They walked down the hallway and into the kitchen. "Can I get you a cup of coffee or something cool to drink?"

"No thanks," he replied as he settled into a wooden chair at the kitchen table. "Remember, I can't stay long."

She sat across from him and nervously began rubbing her right hand back and forth across the table's smooth surface. Feeling that wood somehow calmed her nerves. "This is hard for me to say. But I think it's important that we talk together about our marriage. I can't go on much longer, not knowing how you feel about me... About us." She looked into his eyes, relieved to see most of the coolness was gone.

"I hope you know I'll always love you, Maggie," he said softly. "At least, I'll love the person I thought you were. With that said, I honestly don't think that I can ever live with you again. As hard as I try, I just don't trust you anymore. I can't help but wonder what else you've done and never told me."

She wanted to cry, but knew that would be too easy. She looked angrily into his blue eyes. "Everything is always so crystal clear, so black and white for you. Isn't it? I guess that keeps things so safe and simple. Everything is always in its right place. I'm sure, in your mind, anyone who served in the Vietnam War is wrong or evil; while anyone who demonstrated against that war is right or good. But I was there. I felt it here, in my heart. That war wasn't fought in black and white. Gray and red were the colors of Nam. Uncertainty was splashed in large, gray letters across everyone's faces- doctors, nurses, corpsmen, pilots, and soldiers. Every one of us had doubts and anxieties. Questions ate away at our sanity every day. Why was this horror continuing? Who ordered this nightmare? How many more are coming through those doors? What are they dying for? Was it worth the cost? Our questions went on endlessly. They could have filled an encyclopedia. The funny thing is that no one, not one of us, had the answers. I guess that's because you and your fellow demonstrators had them all."

She looked away from him for just a moment, struggling to calm herself enough to continue. She took a deep breath then looked back at him. "Even more devastating to me than the gray was the red. A river of red surrounded us, overflowing with blood, pain, and death. To this day, I refuse to wear that color because it hurts too much to remember. Oh, Adam, can't you see? There was never any black and white in Nam. There aren't any now and there never were any clear-cut answers."

Adam seemed quite agitated by her words. He stood up and walked out through the French doors onto the deck. She followed hesitantly behind him. He rested his arms on the railing and looked out towards their pool with an unsettled look upon his face, something she had rarely seen. After a grueling few minutes, he finally responded to her. "I'm trying to understand. Believe me, I'm trying. But I just can't see it your way. You're absolutely right. I do feel that anyone who volunteered to serve in Vietnam was wrong. I don't think I would go as far as to say that they were evil, but I do know that they were misguided or confused. Perhaps, this is the gray you are referring to. The war aside, what bothers me the most is that you didn't tell me the truth. I feel that was unconscionable on your part. There's no gray here. Without an inkling of doubt, I see only black and white on that matter. If you truly loved and respected me, you would have told me this about your past. Don't you see how your past collides with my principles? And what is left of a man when he is stripped of his principles? No matter how steep the price I must pay to maintain my integrity, to me it's worth it. I am nothing without my principles."

Sadly, she watched the confused, unsettled look leave Adam's face. He was as strong and determined as ever. She realized that there was now little hope that he would listen to her again, but she also knew she had to try. "Don't you see, Sweetheart," she said softly. "You're seeing us in black and white, too. But no man can be completely right and another completely wrong. We humans can only achieve shades of gray. I see now that I may have been wrong not to tell you about my service in Vietnam. I say 'may' because I'm not completely certain of that." She stepped closer to him and looked directly into his eyes, speaking in an almost-whisper. "The war ended twenty years ago. Are you really going to condemn me for something I did that long ago?" She looked away from him before he could answer and continued speaking. "I didn't participate in that war. I participated in the healing from the war. I was saving lives, not taking them. Don't you see? We were really on the same side."

Adam looked coldly at her. "Are you saying then, that not one of the soldiers you helped ever went back to kill some more?"

She had to look away from his intense, blue eyes. "No, I can't say that. They went back. But I would have done anything to prevent it. We hated to send them back. It made all our efforts seem futile." She looked back at him and spoke with even more desperation in her voice. "Adam, can't you see the gray? It's so clear to me. We were both doing our part to survive that nightmare."

"No. That's where you're wrong. You were trying to survive it, but not me. I was trying to stop it with all the strength I could muster. To me, our efforts were worlds apart."

They were both quiet for a few moments. "I guess it all boils down to one point," he said. "Why didn't you tell me? I can forget and forgive almost anything but that."

She looked at him with tears in her eyes. "Do you really need to ask me that question? Do you think Katie would be here today if I had told you five years ago about this piece of my life? I knew that you would have condemned me then, just as you're doing now. I loved you and hoped you would never have to know about Nam. And, if by chance you did find out about it, I prayed you would love me for who I am now and not for someone I was twenty years ago-"

He interrupted her. "You're missing the most important point. Don't you see? It's what we do that determines who we are. Our lives aren't just a series of unrelated incidents. Everything we did yesterday, do today, and will do tomorrow is based upon our principles. And it's these principles that determine our true identity. That's why, after learning that you served in Vietnam, I said that I don't know you anymore. That information shattered my entire image of you." He looked back in the direction of the pool before continuing. "I'm sorry, but I just don't want to get to know this new you. Probably because I'm afraid that I may still love you. And that, well that scares the hell out of me, because if I still loved you, I would be totally abandoning my principles. I refuse to do that. I will never do that."

After listening to him repeatedly put his lofty principles above her, she became angry. She actually felt sorry for him. "You'll never get past your damn black and white," she said bitterly. "I just can't listen to this anymore. To me, people are so complicated. So intricate. So unique. Their principles are just a small part of who they are. In fact, under certain circumstances, I have seen their principles change. They need to, if they are to survive." She turned away from him and walked back towards the French doors. "I'm going to check on Katie," she called over her shoulder. "You can let yourself out."

She walked back into the house without turning around. She just couldn't handle any more of his philosophical bullshit today. For the first time, she realized how unalike they really were, and didn't regret, quite as much, that their futures would now be taking separate paths. Perhaps, she might even be happier on her journey without him. She had been walking on egg shells in his world for five long years. He spoke the words of a pampered, selfish man who had never experienced the cold brutality of the real world. He was a man who could see only black and white. After living with poverty and war, hunger and death, she knew the gray and red. These colors were a part of her very soul. She couldn't condemn Adam. She knew he wasn't completely at fault. So, enthralled by his black and white world, instead of introducing him to the real Maggie Taylor five years ago, she had transformed herself into the white lily that he needed to complete his canvas. Now it was time for her to paint her own self-portrait with a whole rainbow of colors.

Maggie walked into the nursery and gently lifted her daughter from her crib. She sat down in the rocking chair and cuddled her warm, sleeping body against her chest. "I promise you, Sweetheart," she whispered. "I won't keep any secrets from you. Your mama may not be a white lily, but she's no dandelion either. I still have so much to learn. We'll just have to teach each other."

CHAPTER ELEVEN
The Lone Ranger

She was running barefoot in the sand, laughing so hard that her steps mimicked a drunken fool. Every few strides she glanced back over her shoulder. Her heart raced. Rapidly, he was gaining on her.

"You'll be sorry when I catch up to you, Maggie Darling," he called out to her.

His words thrilled her. She laughed harder, causing her steps to become even more erratic and slower in the sand. Suddenly, she felt his arms around her as he lifted her off her feet, cradled her in his strong arms, and swung her around in circles until they collapsed laughing in the sand. They kissed long and passionately, enjoying the warm softness of each other's mouths.

She looked up into Jake's deep-blue eyes. "I love you, Sweetheart," she said, knowing the words were totally unnecessary. They sat up. She nestled her body comfortably between his legs and leaned her head back against his chest. They watched the waves of the South China Sea break onto shore, momentarily oblivious to the war that raged around them.

…Maggie awoke and sat up in bed, smiling as she remembered her dream about Jake. Their love affair, fueled by the heat of the Vietnam War, had been so intense that twenty years later dreams of Jake were still common. On many lonely nights, she would have given anything to see his face, hear his soothing voice, and feel his arms around her again. So often, she regretted that she had left him. *Regrets. My whole life is saturated with regrets, she thought.*

She heard Katie beginning to stir. She walked into the nursery, lifted her out of her crib, and hugged her. She stopped fussing and nuzzled against her mother. "Good morning Little Sunshine," Maggie said, kissing her on the head.

Camille was already up, preparing Katie's oatmeal, when Maggie walked into the kitchen with Katie in her arms. "Good morning, Camille. Did you have a good night's rest?"

"Why yes, Mrs. Prescott," she said, smiling shyly at her. "It's so kind of you to ask."

"You've been with us for over four months now. Please call me 'Maggie.'"

"Oh no, Mrs. Prescott," she said, looking down at her feet. "I couldn't do that."

"I understand," Maggie said, squeezing her shoulder gently. "But I hope someday you'll feel comfortable enough with our friendship to call me 'Maggie.'"

"Maybe someday, Mrs. Prescott. Do you want me to feed Katie her oatmeal this morning? I know that you've got to get ready for your appointment with Dr. Rothschild."

"That's right. I'd completely forgotten about that. I'd be lost without you." She handed Katie to Camille, grabbed some toast and coffee, and then ran upstairs to shower and dress. Forty-five minutes later, she was driving to Lydia's office in Salinas. It was a gorgeous day. The sun streamed through the windshield and warmed her, spirits and all. She picked up two coffees from the Dunkin' Donuts Drive-Thru on the corner by Lydia's office, drove down Lydia's long, winding dirt driveway, then parked her car and walked into her practice, carrying the coffees.

"I brought you a treat today," Maggie said, smiling at Lydia and handing her a coffee. "Here's some extra cream and sugar for you. I wasn't sure how you liked it."

They settled comfortably into the easy chairs and sipped their coffees. Lydia smiled at Maggie. "Thank you. I appreciate this. I can't help but notice that you seem unusually happy today. Is there anything in particular you want to share with me today?"

Maggie chuckled. "You're right. I guess I am feeling quite content today. I'm not completely sure why. However, I do think you would have been proud of me this weekend." She took another sip of coffee. "Let me see if I can explain. I faced the truth. And you're so right. It is easier to confront it than to be paralyzed by nagging doubts. I'm sure you remember me telling you that my husband left me. The truth is that I didn't actually know where our marriage stood. And that was tearing me apart. I just couldn't take one more day of not knowing. I talked with Adam about it on Sunday, and, although it's not totally resolved, I can read the writing on the wall now."

"And what do you see on that wall?"

"In letters ten feet high, it says 'Why did you ever marry him?'"

"I'm actually surprised by your reaction to what must have been a difficult weekend, so I surmise that the answer to your question is also written on that wall?"

"Yes, in a manner of speaking. I lay awake for hours last night, trying to piece together my years with Adam so I could understand how I really felt about the end of our 'fairy tale.' I'm wondering if you'll be as surprised as I was last night when you hear what I found out. But I actually don't think any of it will make sense to you unless I tell you a little more about our relationship first."

"You know that I'm a nurse. But coming home from Nam, I just couldn't go back to that profession. I tried, but it was too hard. There were just too many memories that would creep into my work day; and I found I had absolutely no control over them. I couldn't do my job effectively like that. Those memories hurt too much. So, I spent a decade looking for the right job. I discovered that I liked being with people that were happy and comfortable and whole."

"Five years ago, I found the perfect job. I worked as a hostess at a posh restaurant, overlooking San Francisco's Fisherman's Wharf. A lot of suits came through that restaurant. I catered to their every whim, but their artificial, egocentric words, mannerisms, and requests were sometimes difficult to stomach. Then, I met Adam. His sincerity was refreshingly different. He stood out like a rose among weeds. Apparently, our atmosphere agreed with him because he became a frequent flyer. Each time he came back to dine with us our conversations lengthened until one day he asked me out. Adam introduced me to his world of elegant dining, opera, theater, and romantic get-aways. I savored every minute with him. Who wouldn't enjoy receiving roses on a weekly basis, candle-lit dinners, or unplanned, exotic weekend trips? I sincerely believed that I had fallen in love with him."

"It is difficult to explain this next part to you, or even for me to completely understand it myself. Although Adam, in my eyes, was different from the other executives who frequented our restaurant, he also belonged with them. I didn't admit it to myself back then, but, in retrospect, he was really more similar to them than he was different. Looking back, I think that I became infatuated with his world and desperately wanted him to accept me into it. And so, clothed in a hostess's elegant wardrobe, I gave up my true identity as Maggie Taylor, the former nurse battling poverty and memories of Vietnam, and transformed myself into a woman capable of becoming the future 'Maggie Prescott.' I made Adam's thoughts, dreams, and desires my own. I agreed with every opinion he ever expressed. I laughed at all his jokes. I pretended to not only admire, but to actually like his pretentious friends and to care about their trivial problems. And all the while, I walked on eggshells, so afraid Adam might see the real me beneath the facade I had erected. Only last night did it dawn on me that I have lived a nightmare while convincing myself that it was a fairy tale. Finally, I can look back at my years with Adam for what they really were."

Maggie sighed deeply, placed her coffee down on the side table, stood up, and walked towards the window. She looked out through the glass and saw a group of children playing a game of tag. A part of her wanted to join them; to become a child again so she could relive her life, making better choices this time. Lydia respected her silence and need for space. After a few minutes, Maggie returned and sat back down in her easy chair. She picked up her coffee and took a few sips in contemplative silence.

"This must be very difficult for you," Lydia said softly.

Maggie nodded, comforted by the fact that Lydia understood. "Do you think it's possible that I married Adam to protect myself? I chose to marry a man with whom I would never be able to share a single, meaningful memory of my life. I knew he wouldn't have been able to accept my impoverished upbringing, my mother's alcoholism, or my service in Vietnam. So, I couldn't tell him about any of it. By marrying him, I could block out so much of the hurt in my life."

"And did that work, Maggie? When you were with Adam, were you able to forget about all your painful memories?"

"No. Not really. I think it worked well enough during my busy, wakeful hours. But it never helped in the middle of the night. I've never found a way to stop my dreams from taking me down those painful roads I traveled on so long ago." Suddenly, she could see the point Lydia was trying to make in her own, gentle way. "You're right. How could I have thought that I could just throw away my past and never think about it again? What's even more absurd is that I actually thought that he loved me when I didn't even feel safe enough to tell him anything about myself that really mattered. After all, shouldn't your husband be your soul mate? Adam told me not so long ago that he didn't know me. At the time, his words hurt me deeply. Now, after hours of reflection, sadly, I think he was right. I never allowed him to see the real me, so how could I believe that he ever truly loved me? Adam is right. He doesn't know me."

"You've shared many thoughts about your relationship with Adam with me. But what about your feelings? How do you feel about your marriage ending and the fact that Adam may no longer be your husband?"

"I feel like I've finally been freed. Like a great, crushing weight has been lifted from my chest and I can breathe again. I've lost Adam, yet I feel relief, not regret, because I may finally be able to become myself again."

"I'm sorry to disappoint you, Maggie, but I've found that life is rarely that simple. It is never tied up in such tidy, little packages. Are you certain that you have no regrets?"

"No. Just the opposite is true. I have many regrets, but none about Adam leaving me."

Lydia looked questionably at her. "I'm not sure I understand."

"Do you know why I seem to be in better spirits today?"

"Perhaps, some of the reasons, but I think there may be more to the story?"

"There is. When I woke this morning, I remembered a dream about Jake. Thoughts of him always make my day a little happier, or at least a bit more bearable."

"You've never mentioned Jake before. Who is he?"

"Why Dr. Rothschild, I can't believe you're actually asking a personal question. If you don't watch out, I may see you as a shrink instead of as a close friend."

"I'm sorry. I didn't mean to probe."

"It's OK. I'm just teasing. You have nothing to apologize for. Jake was a major in the army, a Dustoff pilot. He was with me in Nam. It seems like just yesterday when we first met."

...Major Bradshaw looked coolly at Maggie. "Lieutenant Taylor, you've been here almost four months. It's time you learned how to triage. You're assigned to the helipad with Captain Pollard this week."

Despite her anxiety about learning to triage, Maggie didn't really mind her new assignment. It was a warm June morning in Pleiku, and, although their elevation would prevent it from becoming unbearably hot, she knew the ER would become quite steamy by midafternoon. She felt fortunate knowing most of her day would be spent outdoors where there was a breeze and it wouldn't feel quite so muggy.

While waiting for the Dustoffs, Captain Pollard reviewed the principles of triage with her. Maggie listened to her words, but she found them overwhelming. She couldn't picture herself making the split-second decisions Captain Pollard stated that they must make during a push when heavy fighting has occurred and the Dustoffs come in non-stop for hours at a time. The 71st

THE PRECIOUS WENTLETRAP

might get one hundred and fifty wounded in just a few hours. If the battles really heated up, large Chinooks, helicopters capable of transporting up to fifty wounded at a time, were used instead of the Hueys that generally carried eight, but could be stretched to hold up to sixteen wounded. She prayed there would be no pushes this week.

"Are you listening, Lieutenant? Your mind seems elsewhere."

"I'm trying to process all the information, Captain. But there's a lot to learn. Can I be honest with you? I just can't picture myself doing it. I just don't feel qualified to decide who goes where. We're talking about life and death, living and dying, all determined by these decisions."

Captain Pollard looked at her with a warmth she hadn't seen in a lifer's eyes before. "If it makes you feel any better, Lieutenant, none of us ever feel comfortable doing it. No one wants to make those decisions. With that said, we all know it has to be done or we wouldn't be able to save any of them. Our docs need to be operating, not out here categorizing patients. So, it's up to us nurses to get the patients to them in the best order to save the most men and in good enough shape that they can survive surgery."

Maggie never imagined that anyone but herself felt this uncomfortable with the responsibility of triaging. Knowing that most found it difficult, she felt calmer and relaxed enough to comprehend what Captain Pollard was sharing with her about triage.

"Lieutenant Taylor, forget everything you ever learned in nursing school about triage. This is war, not a stateside ER. We know we can't save everyone, but we save a hell of a lot of them. We're proud of our survival rate here at the 71st. Ninety-eight percent of the boys who come through our doors will make it. I attribute this record to our solid triage system. We can't get tied up trying to save a soldier so mangled that it would take hours to put him back together. The price tag is too great. We may save him, but how many others will die in the process? We only have so many operating tables, so many doctors. No matter how many wounded come through our doors, we're not getting any more of either resource. And we never ask the Dustoffs to stop coming. We must keep accepting the wounded. That's why we're here. We've developed a triage system to cope with any circumstance. No matter how many they send us, we can deal with them efficiently and competently.

"I'm sure you know by now the three categories to our triage classification system. Class One we call "Expectants." These are the boys beyond hope of salvaging. They're the poor souls with multiple, extensive wounds, requiring over four hours of surgery or head wounds with fixed, dilated pupils. We put these soldiers to the side, behind the screen whenever possible. I know that you've worked with these boys before, Lieutenant."

Maggie nodded, remembering Chris Haskins. There had been many others since Chris, but that first one had left an indelible imprint on her heart.

"If any of the soldiers in this Expectant category are still alive after all the other wounded have undergone surgery, then we'll send them back to the OR. But, as you know, this rarely happens. Regardless, we never leave these dying boys alone. Someone is always with them, holding their hands and whispering to them as they die. They gave everything for us. We won't let them forget how much they're loved."

Maggie knew that Captain Pollard was speaking truthfully. Her mind wandered in sad reflection of these soldiers. She had stood beside them, looking into their terror-filled eyes, so many times over the past four months. She could still see every face. Time had never made it any easier for her as some of the other nurses had promised it would.

Captain Pollard's words forced her to refocus on triage training. "Class Two is the 'Immediates.' They have a good chance of surviving surgery, but they are critically wounded and need to go to the OR as soon as possible. They must be stabilized and sent to the OR stat. Finally, Class Three is the 'Walking Wounded.' They may or may not need surgery. At any rate, their wounds are less severe and they can afford the luxury of time.

They must wait until the more critically wounded patients have been treated before going back to the OR themselves. Captain Pollard stopped explaining and looked at Maggie. "Any questions so far, Lieutenant?"

She had thousands, but didn't know how to ask any of them. She was more afraid than she had ever been in her life. Captain Pollard had made triage sound so simple, so concrete. Supposedly, there were only three classes of patients, but she had been at the 71st for four months. Each patient seemed so unique to her. She knew triage would be very difficult. Suddenly, the steamy ER seemed so much more appealing. Over the past four months, she had become very adept at stabilizing patients while maintaining an emotional distance from them.

In the distance, they could hear Dustoffs approaching. "Oh, a few more things I forgot to mention," Captain Pollard yelled above the noise of the landing Dustoffs as they walked closer to the helipad. "The cardinal rule is multiple wounds. Almost no one has just one injury. Be damn sure you find every wound. The Dustoff crews do a remarkable job of stabilizing the patients. They've saved so many boys' lives. Listen to their reports, but be sure to re-evaluate each soldier yourself."

She started to say something else, but the choppers drowned out the rest of her words. Maggie followed her to the helipad, sweating profusely. The morning went by quickly. Captain Pollard was an excellent teacher. Maggie relaxed enough to take in most of what she was teaching her about triage, but it required so much concentration on her part.

A strange looking helicopter landed in the early afternoon; its side was splashed with silver paint. Unusual as it appeared, the medic and crew chief emerged from the Huey, carrying a litter bearing a wounded soldier just as the other Dustoffs had done all day. They deposited the soldier on a stretcher, gave a quick status report, and then went back to the chopper to bring more wounded out. Maggie bent over the soldier and quickly began examining him, while Captain Pollard observed her.

"Are you always this serious?"

Maggie looked up, surprised to hear his question. "Excuse me," she said to a tall, ruggedly handsome man with enormous, dark-blue eyes and sandy-brown hair.

"You need to smile now and then," he said with a hint of a Southern drawl. "Don't get me wrong. The boys feel ninety-five percent better just seeing your pretty face, but they'll relax even more if you smile at them. Tell them a joke. Laugh with them. Try it. You'll be surprised how much better you all feel."

Maggie was irritated by his comments. And yet Captain Pollard stayed in the background, saying nothing to this major who continued to distract her as she tried to triage the patients. Soon, all four wounded from the chopper were on the ground around her, but she still hadn't been able to move past the first patient.

He seemed amused by her nervous attempts to examine the wounded under his watchful eyes. "See you all later," he chuckled before heading back to his chopper. Maggie looked up as his chopper lifted off. He was grinning and waving at her.

After he left, Captain Pollard helped her triage the patients. After they were settled safely in the capable hands of their ER nurses, Maggie asked her about the pilot.

"That was Major John Allen Kelleher, or the Lone Ranger. Use whichever name you prefer. He answers to both."

"I suppose he calls his chopper 'Silver,'" she said sarcastically, remembering the splashes of silver painted on the side of his Huey.

"That's right," Captain Pollard said, but there was no sarcasm in her voice. "I can't tell you how many boys that man has personally saved. He's dedicated to our soldiers like nothing I've ever seen. He'll fly in any weather and I've heard there's no such thing as an unsecured landing zone to him. If there's a critically wounded soldier out there, he'll pick him up no matter how many Viet Cong are firing at him. He hasn't earned the Medal of Honor yet, but it's only a matter of time."

She stopped talking and turned to leave the ER. Maggie followed sheepishly behind her, feeling foolish for saying anything against Major Kelleher. Two hours later, Silver landed again and Major Kelleher got out to observe Maggie work. She looked up at him and smiled, but stopped immediately when she noticed a fair amount of blood on his left shoulder.

"You've been hit Major Kelleher. Why don't you sit down and let me take a look at you?"

"You're just dying to get your hands on me. Aren't you?" He laughed but didn't sit down. "I honestly would love to stay and chat, but I can't. We have one more run to make, then I'll be back and I'll be all yours." He tipped his head to her with a silly, boyish grin on his face that infuriated her.

"Now, just a damned minute, Major Kelleher. You can't fly your chopper until you've been patched up. I know I can't technically give you orders, but please listen to me."

"I hear you. I'll be back in just a few minutes. By the way, I'm impressed that you cared enough about me to find out my name." He winked at her, then turned and headed back towards his chopper.

She grabbed a dressing and some tape then ran after him. "I've heard you're a dedicated fool," she called out to him.

Abruptly, he stopped and turned around with just a flicker of anger in his eyes. "You heard wrong. I may be dedicated. But I'm no fool."

"Then stand still for a minute and let me dress your wound. You'll still have time to save your boys."

"Damn, you're a feisty one," he said, and stood still for one minute, exactly, while she put on a pressure dressing.

Her hands trembled slightly. She was nervous standing so close to him and she could feel his eyes on her while she worked. With relief, she saw that it appeared to be just a surface wound. She knew he would be OK. "See you soon, Major," she said when she was done, then saluted him.

"It's a date." He grinned at her, but didn't return the salute.

She watched his chopper lift off, but his face remained behind. She smiled frequently over the next hour, recalling his dark-blue eyes and his boyish facial expressions. He was a man that she would love to get to know better, but she realized this was probably just another impossible dream. After all, he was almost a hero and she was just a new nurse.

True to his word, Major Kelleher touched down forty-five minutes later. He only had two wounded soldiers with him this time, but they were both in the Immediate Class. They transported them to the ER quickly so that they could be stabilized for immediate surgery. Finally, she was free to focus all her attention on the major.

"Please, lie down on this stretcher, Major Kelleher."

"I know I'm wearing an army uniform, but I don't actually consider myself a military man," he said as he lay down on the stretcher. "I'm just here for the flying experience. I would really like it if you called me 'Jake;' if it doesn't bother you too much. You're not the gung-ho military type, are you?"

She smiled shyly and shook her head. She extended her hand out for him to shake. "You can call me 'Maggie' if you like, too."

To her surprise and pleasure, Jake held her hand for much longer than is customary for a handshake. He gently stroked her hand with his fingers and looked right through her with his intense, blue eyes before letting go of her hand. Slightly embarrassed by his gesture, she looked around, but no one was watching them. She looked back at Jake. "Please, remove your shirt so I can dress your wound properly."

"You make it sound so official, Maggie. I know that you're just dying to get a good look at me," he said, grinning at her with that lovable, boyish expression on his face.

Back home, under normal circumstances, she probably would have been offended by Jake's boldness. But somehow, here in Nam, the rules were different. She believed him and knew his words were sincere; he genuinely was attracted to her. Perhaps, too, it was because she was drawn to him with such intensity. The pleasure and excitement that she felt as he removed his shirt was unmistakable.

She gently cleansed his wound with antiseptic solution, then applied a new dressing. She took longer than she needed, without exaggerating the time too noticeably. But she knew he must be aware of her dalliance.

As she applied the last piece of tape, he grabbed her hand with both of his and looked right into her eyes. "Maggie," he said almost in a whisper, "I would very much like to get to know you better. Someone needs to teach you how to laugh properly. Would you consider spending time with me?"

She looked into his dark-blue eyes, fighting a strong urge to kiss him. "Yes, I would like that very much."

"Good." He smiled and tenderly kissed both of her hands before putting back on his shirt. This time, she didn't look around to see if anyone saw their inappropriate behavior. At that moment, she didn't care about anything else but him.

...Maggie stopped reminiscing about her first encounter with Jake. "You know, Lydia, so many days I would gladly go back in time and endure another day in Vietnam, just to see him again. God, I miss him."

"Do you know where he is now?"

"I don't know. But I'm pretty sure he didn't survive the war. He was still in Vietnam and had signed up for another tour when I came back to the States."

"Would you like to know if he made it back home?"

Maggie didn't answer Lydia's question. Instead, she got up and walked across the room to her display case. She peered down through the glass at the doomed Confederate soldiers. Lydia followed her across the room and stood beside her. Maggie looked into Lydia's eyes and somehow found the strength to share her thoughts. "I know if Jake had been alive during the Civil War, he would have been marching right up front, up this hill. He was such a lovable, brave bastard. Everyone else was always more important to him than himself. I've never met such a selfless person in my life. I know I'm supposed to see hope when I look through this glass, but all I see today is fear. I'm so afraid Jake died just as courageously and needlessly as all these poor Rebels did." Maggie began to cry unashamedly.

Lydia hugged her. Maggie clung to her, feeding on her

strength. After a few minutes, Lydia spoke softly to her. "You know, Maggie. We could find out if Jake is still alive."

She pulled away from Lydia, walked to the window and looked out. The children were gone. She felt as abandoned and alone as that deserted, dirt driveway. After a few minutes, she turned back towards Lydia. "I know that you're absolutely right. You don't know how many times I've thought about finding out about Jake myself. It would be so easy, too. He comes from a very large family in Monticello, Georgia. But the same thing stops me every time. Everything would be wonderful if he were alive. But what if he didn't make it back? I need that hope, Lydia. By not knowing the truth, I can always hope our paths will cross again. Someday... That 'someday' keeps me going."

Lydia looked sadly at her. Maggie was surprised to actually be able to read her expression. "You know the last thing I would want to do is to take all your hope away, Maggie. But remember what I've been trying to teach you. You have to face the truth, no matter how painful it is, or you'll never fully recover."

"I understand, Lydia. I'm trying so hard to do that because I trust you. But I can't do it. Not this time. I'm just not ready to cross that bridge yet. I don't know what I would do if I found out that Jake was dead, too. I need him to be alive. Even if it's only in my dreams."

"It's all right. I understand. When you're ready, we'll cross that bridge together."

CHAPTER TWELVE
The Bonfire Still Burns

Lydia and Maggie walked back to the easy chairs and sat down. Maggie looked across the room to the Grandfather clock, saddened to see that their hour was almost half over. She smiled at Lydia wondering if Lydia was even aware of how much comfort her disheveled appearance brought her, those endearing wisps of gray that hung down loosely around her face, her warm, inviting, brown eyes smiling through those old-fashioned dark glasses, and her wrinkled, dark suit. Maggie was grateful for all the wounds Lydia had helped her bandage thus far. She felt close to her, but felt compelled to find a way to make their bond even stronger so that it could never be broken.

"I've known you for a few months now, Lydia, yet I know so little about you. It may not be appropriate for me to ask, but I'd really like to know more about you. Perhaps why you chose to become a psychologist? I think the profession suits you well."

Lydia quietly acknowledged the compliment. "Thank you. I do enjoy it tremendously. It can be challenging but I find it to be equally or perhaps even more rewarding. At one time, I adhered to a fairly simple rule, 'don't tell my patients anything personal about myself for any reason,' but I don't follow that rule anymore. You see, I've discovered that trust is never a one-way street; rather, it develops through a more equal sharing of thoughts including personal experiences between both individuals in the relationship. Even in a so-called patient-doctor relationship like ours. So, yes, I will tell you something about myself." Lydia looked directly into Maggie's eyes and spoke softly. "Understand, though, that what I'm about to tell you, I share only because I trust you. And I hope, too, that it will help you feel less alone with your grief."

"I understand," Maggie said, feeling proud to have gained her trust so completely.

"You've asked me why I chose to become a psychologist. It may sound strange to you, but believe it or not, initially, I chose the field of psychology, not to understand others, but to understand more about my past and myself. Like you, I experienced considerable trauma in my childhood. I was born in Berlin in 1928, the third daughter of Samuel and Josephine Rothschild. My mother, like most women of her time, didn't work outside our home. She was a soft-spoken, proper lady. She rarely laughed or even smiled, but my sisters and I never doubted that she loved us very much. My father was a professor of literature at the University of Berlin. We adored him. No matter how weary he was after his day's work, he would still read to us- my sisters, Anna and Ruthie, and me, every night. I remember that he would sit in his big, comfortable easy chair by the fireplace, while we would find a cozy spot with a pillow on the rug at his feet to listen. As he read, he would look up every few sentences to steal a glance at Anna, Ruthie, or me to see how his words were affecting us. I still remember how special I felt when his eyes fell upon me. Through him, we learned to love books. Sometimes, even now, when I read, I hear his voice in my head, speaking the words. We lived in a modest, third-floor apartment above a tailor's shop in a predominantly Jewish neighborhood, directly across the street from the University of Berlin. One of my earliest memories was a night in May 1933 when I was about five years old."

...Papa woke Mama, my sisters and me in the middle of the night and brought us to the living room where our windows overlooked a square. Partially concealed behind the drapes, we looked out for almost an hour, watching thousands of people swarming into the square, carrying torches. A huge bonfire roared in the center of the square, sending hundreds of sparks of red and orange into that night sky. It was breathtaking. Many people were hurling rectangular objects into the flames, but I couldn't discern what those objects were. My sisters and I began to speak loudly, excitedly, until Papa sternly motioned us to be quiet. That was unlike Papa.

"Papa, may we go outside, too?" I asked.

"Lydia, my child, don't you see what they are doing?" he said so sadly.

I shook my head. "No, Papa." I still didn't understand what was wrong. Why was Papa so very sad? The bonfire was so beautiful and I thought it would be fun to stand closer to it.

"They've made a bonfire out of books," he cried. "They're destroying great works of literature- books by Upton Sinclair, Jakob Wasserman, Albert Einstein, Hugo Preuss, and so many, many others." Papa's hands were shaking now, and, for the first time in my life, I saw tears running down his cheeks. "They're burning books. When they can perform such an unthinkable act, God only knows what will happen next."

He gently called my sisters and I to come to him. He wrapped his arms around us, almost like he was trying to shelter us from this life's event. "Don't ever forget this night my precious girls. Mark my words, the world will never forget or forgive us for what we've allowed them to do here tonight. For the first time in my life, I'm ashamed to call myself 'German.'"

"... I didn't understand then what my father was trying to say, Maggie. I was too young to share his shame, but still remember his words. And his pain. History tells me that the world changed so much over the next few years, but safely sheltered from it with my family in our apartment, I didn't see it. Not until I was ten did I realize what a dangerous thing it was to be a Jew in Germany during that era."

...In November of 1938, again, my sisters and I were wakened in the dead of night, this time by Mama. Quiet Mama spoke so loudly and shook us vigorously. "Wake up! Wake up. Anna! Ruthie! Lydia! Get up now!"

We woke to the smell of smoke and the terrifying sound of glass breaking.

"Hurry girls!" Mama screamed.

We jumped out of bed and started groping for our clothes in the darkness. Mama helped us. "Hurry, girls. Put on your socks and shoes quickly. Don't forget your warmest coat." The anxiety in her voice frightened us even more than the terrifying sound of breaking glass and the smoke.

"Come now, girls. There's no more time." She grabbed my hand yelling, "Follow us," to Ruthie and Anna.

We joined Papa in the hallway, holding my little brother, Joseph, in his arms. "Let's go out the back," he called to us. "We must all stay together."

As we walked down the back staircase, the smoke got thicker. My eyes burned and my throat hurt. I started coughing and choking. The sound of breaking glass was even louder and I could hear so many loud, angry voices. I tried to pull away from Mama. "Please, let's go back upstairs," I cried, knowing that we would be safe there.

"No!" she said sternly, squeezing my hand so tightly that it hurt. Then she let go of my hand and looked me in the eyes. She stroked the hair around my face for just a few seconds. "Try to be a big girl, Lydia. It's going to be OK. Cover your mouth and nose with your hand. Your mama and papa are right here with you. Don't be afraid." But Mama was wrong. It was never all right again after that night.

...Lydia brushed a few tears away that were forming in the corners of her eyes. Maggie wanted to help her, just as she had comforted her so many times in the past few months. "You don't have to tell me anymore today. I know how difficult it is to remember. I understand that you experienced a pain quite similar to mine."

"I appreciate your concern, Maggie, but I will tell you the rest. In a few minutes. I promised that I'd help you feel less alone. I intend to keep that promise today."

Lydia got up and walked to the window. Maggie watched her walk across the room, but didn't follow her. She knew that she just needed a little time to collect herself before she would be able to continue. Finally, Lydia returned to her chair and looked at Maggie. It saddened Maggie to see that all traces of tears had now vanished from her face. She, herself, had so rarely felt that gentle, blessed healing power of tears. Precious tears and the subsequent release of pain that the act of crying brought had been so fleeting in her life, too. She listened intently as Lydia began speaking again.

...Papa opened the back door. When we followed him out that door, our lives would forever be changed. I could see that our entire building was on fire. An angry mob of people, mostly men, swarmed towards us. They carried clubs and were screaming obscenities at us. They swung their clubs at the windows of our building. The noise was terrifying. Joseph was crying loudly. Papa handed him to my oldest sister, Anna.

"Run away, girls! Go quickly!" he cried, while gently shoving us away from him.

Too frightened to leave him, we didn't move.

"Go now!" he yelled. "You, too, Josephine. I'll stay and keep them from you."

But it was too late. The crowd surrounded us. They beat Papa with their clubs, until he fell to the ground. A few of them continued to strike at Papa even though he lay helplessly and still on the ground.

"Stop! You're killing him!" Mama screamed.

In response to her outcries, one man smiled hideously at Mama, then grabbed her by the arm and pulled her after him. He threw her to the ground and jumped on top of her. The crowd circled around them. We couldn't see Mama anymore, but we could hear her crying. Anna, still holding Joseph, Ruthie and I huddled around Papa. Ruthie called Papa's name and gently shook his shoulders. He didn't answer. He didn't move. I knew our papa was dead. But I didn't cry. I just knelt on the ground at his head, closed my eyes, and rocked back and forth, back and forth. "Please, God. Please, bring us home. Make them go away," I prayed.

I thought my prayers must have helped because the crowd soon moved on, leaving Mama behind, moaning on the ground.

Ruthie and I ran over to her. Her clothes were torn and her face bruised. She wouldn't open her eyes, but we could see tears rolling down her face. My sisters and I wanted to help her, but didn't know what to do. From across the street, we saw another, much smaller, crowd approaching us. I was terrified. As they got closer, I saw that it was our Rabbi and some of Papa's friends from the University. They gently picked up Mama and Papa.

"Your papa is alive, but he is badly hurt," Rabbi told us.

A stranger reached down and took my hand. "Come follow us. We'll take care of you." I looked into his eyes. They were gentle, like Papa's. I followed him.

The crowd brought us to a strange house and into a hidden room in the basement. It would be our new home for a few months. From that night on, we lived in fear, sometimes moving in the middle of the night, and always hiding in strangers' attics or cellars.

I didn't understand what had happened to us. I longed for home. "Mama, why do we have to hide?" I asked.

She only said three words, but repeated them bitterly, "Because we're Jewish... Because we're Jewish."

...Lydia looked at Maggie and said softly, "Perhaps, you can understand why I chose Psychology now. I just had to understand why. Why did so many people despise my family and me? What had we ever done to them?"

"I'm sorry that you and your family had to suffer so, Lydia. I don't know the answers to your questions either. I feel the world is often cruel and unfair for reasons that rarely make any sense. Did the study of psychology help?"

"Yes," she said bitterly. "I learned that there is never a valid reason for hate. It just is. It's an evil, ugly entity. But it's real. Just as real as love. And, after coming to terms with my past, I decided to help others come to terms with theirs."

Maggie reached out and clasped Lydia's hand. "Thank you... For everything. I wish I knew how to rid this world of that hate. I know it didn't end with your war. It was with us in Nam, too." Maggie dropped her hand and looked directly into her eyes. "I think you made the right decision when you chose to become a psychologist. I think you're really helping me."

"I'm glad. I think you're making wonderful progress, too. I'm proud of you. I know I promised that I would never ask you grueling personal questions. I'll keep that promise, but I do have an assignment for you for next week. I think, between the two of us, we've spent enough time on pain for a while. Therefore, I want you to look back over your life and remember three of your happiest memories that you feel comfortable sharing with me. Please, feel free to bring in photographs or keepsakes if it will help you to relay these memories. Use this week to recoup some strength. You'll need this reprieve before moving ahead with your healing."

Excited by Lydia's assignment, Maggie briskly walked to her car. She was anxious to get home and pull out all her photo albums and Vietnam memorabilia. It felt so good to be given permission to just sit down and pour over them. It had been years since she had felt safe looking at her past.

CHAPTER THIRTEEN
Qui Nhon

While driving home from Lydia's office, Jake danced in and out of Maggie's thoughts until he stood alone on center stage. For once, she didn't feel guilty about it. *Hadn't Lydia asked her to recall her happiest memories? Who could have conceived that they would find such happiness in that world of pain and death? Perhaps, it was the daily horror that enveloped them that caused their time together, in contrast, to seem so beautiful. After all, wouldn't a painting by Renoir appear even softer, gentler if it were displayed next to Picasso's hard, cold cubism? Or maybe, every era simply needed its Romeo and Juliet, Anthony and Cleopatra. She thought the most plausible explanation, however, was simply that they were two lonely people who desperately clung to each other in order to survive that nightmare.*

Whatever the reason, no one before Jake had ever touched her life with the same degree of passion. Regrettably, no one after him had ever fulfilled her needs so completely either. There were days when her mind, body, and soul, literally, ached for him. She thought perhaps we never fully recognize or appreciate the love we have until we've lost it; when we see it only from a distance. She remembered how ordinary, almost ugly, the colors of the Grand Canyon appeared when she was walking the Bright Angel Trail and she could reach out and touch its rock walls. It was only when viewed from the top that the breathtaking splendor created by the contrasting, exquisite colors of the canyon walls became apparent. Bold, vivid oranges melted into soft, subdued purple hues creating an awe-inspiring masterpiece so seldom seen by the human eye. Perhaps, it was the same for love.

Camille was pushing Katie in her stroller through their gardens when Maggie arrived home. She joined them. Katie laughed and reached out her arms towards her mother. Maggie smiled back and squeezed her tiny hands, before bending down and kissing the top of her head. "Was she a good girl for you, Camille?"

"Why of course, Mrs. Prescott. How could Little Miss Katie be anything but good?"

"We're so lucky to have you," Maggie said, reaching over and squeezing her shoulder for just a moment.

Camille blushed considerably and pushed the stroller a little faster.

"I'm sorry. I didn't mean to embarrass you. I just think it's important that you know how much I appreciate all you do. I don't know what I would have done without you for all those weeks when I was feeling so badly."

"Hush now. You're doing well now. And it makes my heart sing to see you smiling again. Don't ever worry about the past. It's gone and it's too late to change anything. My mother always told me, 'concentrate on today and tomorrow will take care of itself.'"

Maggie smiled at Camille. "I think your mother was a wise woman."

They both laughed, then walked together in silence for a few minutes.

"Mrs. Prescott, I have a question, but I'm afraid to ask. I don't want to hurt or offend you."

Maggie reached out and pulled Camille's hands off the stroller, bringing it to a complete stop. She held Camille's hands and looked into her eyes. "You're my friend. You can ask me anything."

"All right. Please, don't be upset... I know that you and Mr. Prescott talked yesterday, and now today, you're so happy. Is Mr. Prescott coming home soon?"

Maggie dropped Camille's hands and looked away from her.

"I'm sorry. I shouldn't have asked."

"Don't be sorry. It's OK. I was going to tell you soon. I just wasn't prepared for the question today." Needing something to do, Maggie began to push the stroller before continuing. "No,

Mr. Prescott isn't coming home. I seriously doubt that he'll ever come home. Sometimes, things happen between people that even time can't heal. But please, don't feel sorry for me. I think I may be OK without him. I guess who we should be feeling sorry for is Katie. I feel like a monster for breaking them apart."

Camille reached out and touched Maggie's shoulder. "Now Mrs. Prescott, you're doing it again. You're worrying about things you can't change. Mr. Prescott loves Little Miss Katie very much. I'm certain that he won't let her out of his sight for more than a few days at a time. You haven't done anything to permanently separate them from each other."

"I hope you're right." She looked down at Katie who had fallen asleep in her stroller. "Doesn't she seem even more angelic when she's sleeping?"

"She's something else. I suspect the Lord, Himself, can't be much more beautiful that a sleeping child. To me, it's the loveliest sight in the world." They both gazed down smiling at Katie for a few moments. "Shall I put her in her crib for her nap now?"

"That would be perfect. Can you believe it? Dr. Rothschild has given me a homework assignment. I feel like I'm in school again. It would be great to start working on it."

"You seem to like Dr. Rothschild. I'm so happy it is working so well for you," Camille said, before leaning over Katie's stroller and gently picking her up to bring inside.

Maggie followed behind Camille, but reached out and tapped her right shoulder before they reached the door. "I don't remember ever properly thanking you for introducing Lydia to me. By doing that, you may very well have saved my life."

Camille stopped walking and turned around to face Maggie. She said softly, "Go on now. I just did what any human being would have done if they saw another suffering so."

"No. In my eyes, it was a lot more than that. I won't ever forget your part in helping me. I know I still have a long way to go, but with Lydia's help, I may get there... Someday. May I ask you a personal question now?"

"Why of course, Mrs. Prescott."

"I've always been curious. How did you learn about Dr. Rothschild?" Maggie watched Camille's eyes sadden. "I'm sorry. I shouldn't have pried."

"It's OK. It was just so long ago. Way back then, I was married to Carlos. I knew him all my life. We grew up together. We always knew we would be married. And we were- at fifteen. I lost three of his babies. They just kept dying inside of me. Then I lost him. Two months after he turned eighteen, we got a letter. My Carlos was going to Vietnam." Her voice grew just a tad stronger but much more bitter. "The government said that he was too young to drink, too young to vote, but he wasn't too young to carry a gun and kill for them. Does that seem right to you?"

Maggie shook her head. "No," she said softly. "It wasn't right. Did he come home from Vietnam?"

"Yes, he came home. One year later. But it wasn't my Carlos that they sent home to me. He drank too much. And he was angry. So very angry. He broke so many of our things. He just couldn't stop throwing and punching and hurting. So often, too, he screamed and cried in the middle of the night. Sometimes, when I tried to calm him, he would wrap his hands around my neck and squeeze so hard. He would almost choke me to death before he would wake up enough to recognize me. He stopped eating. He half-starved himself. Then he bought a gun. It was big and black and ugly. I hated that evil thing. He would sit for hours with it in his lap, just staring at it, not saying a word. He really frightened me. That's when a friend told me about Dr. Rothschild."

"So, Dr. Rothschild helped Carlos?"

"Yes, for a while. But not everyone accepts help. You have to reach out and grab that hand when it's extended out to you. Then you have to hold on to that hand and not let go until you can stand on your own again." Katie began to fuss in her arms. Relief seemed to fill Camille's eyes. "I must bring her in now, Mrs. Prescott. Perhaps, we'll talk again later?"

They walked inside. Camille brought Katie to the nursery

while Maggie went into her bedroom. She thought about Camille and Carlos for a few minutes. She wondered what had happened to him. She could guess. Perhaps, Camille would tell her someday but she wasn't confident of that. Finally, her thoughts returned to her assignment. She pulled down two large photo albums from the bookcase and put them on her bed. She then retrieved the large, manila envelope from her bottom dresser drawer. She slipped out of her canvas shoes and stretched comfortably on her stomach across the bed. She was about to open the first photo album, but she stopped her hand midair. Remembering that she had nothing tangible by which to recall the happiest week of her life, she laid her head down on a soft pillow and closed her eyes. Concrete images couldn't have been any clearer. She would never be able to forget a single moment of her week with Jake in Qui Nhon.

...She leaned her head on Jake's shoulder and prayed they would be landing soon. Sitting next to Jake in the first row of a tiny turboprop U-21, a plane that the army used for transporting up to seven passengers during the Vietnam War, she felt cramped and was becoming so nauseous from the turbulence. As always, Jake sensed her mood without her needing to say anything.

"We're almost there, Darling. I think our week will make this bumpy ride well worth it."

She smiled at him and kissed him lightly on his cheek. "Don't worry about me. I'm OK."

He squeezed her hand a little tighter in response, and then turned his head back to talk with the co-pilot again. Sometimes, Maggie thought Jake knew everyone in Nam. No matter where they went, soldiers, marines, nurses, medics, pilots- everyone it seemed to her- walked up to Jake and shook his hand or slapped him across the back. "Lone Ranger, is that really you? Damn good to see you, Sir. How many boys did you save this week?' Admiration, respect and love were always clearly expressed in their voices and on their faces. Jake took it all in stride. He accepted their warmth gracefully, giving them back just as much sincere appreciation in return. She felt privileged to be dating a man the entire world seemed to love.

Fifteen minutes later, they were approaching the Qui Nhon airfield. In the distance, Maggie could see the brilliant turquoise waters of the South China Sea and its powdery white sand beaches, dotted with abundant, graceful coconut trees. Adding to the splendor of the tropical setting were stunning rocky cliffs that surrounded Qui Nhon Bay and countless rock formations of various shapes and sizes, jutting out from those azure waters. Suddenly, her entire body tensed as the pilot made his rapid, steep descent. Although Jake had prepared her for this, telling her that it was the only safe way to land when there may be enemy fire, it still took her by surprise and frightened her.

Jake smiled at her, squeezed her hand, and said under his breath, "It's a good thing that you're a nurse. You'd make a lousy pilot."

She laughed and slapped his shoulder in mock indignation. Then it was all over. The plane slowed to a stop. They quickly disembarked and grabbed their duffel bags. Jake shook the pilot's hand. "Thanks for the lift. I owe you."

"Lone Ranger, you know the debt has already been paid in full. We considered it an honor to taxi you and your little lady here. Have a good break. No one deserves it more than you." He saluted Jake and Maggie was surprised to see Jake actually return the salute.

She teased him as they walked away. "I don't know, Jake. You're not turning into a military man on me, are you?"

"No," he laughed. "Don't worry about that. You have to understand though. He would have been insulted if I hadn't returned his salute. He meant to show respect. I would never do anything to jeopardize that. He's a damned good pilot. I admire him."

She smiled to herself. Jake was such a humble man. She didn't think he was even aware of how much he was loved. "Tell me more about where we're going," she said as they rode together in the back of an army jeep.

"I think I've mentioned before that my last assignment was with the 54th Medical Detachment in Chu Lai. It's up the coast about seventy-five miles from here. I used to spend a lot of my down-time at an orphanage right outside Chu Lai. Those kids helped me forget about the war, for a little bit anyhow. And there's one I can't wait for you to meet, a sweet, little Vietnamese girl named Thanh. Her entire family was burned to death inside their hooch when our coordinates were confused and we dropped napalm on them."

"Oh my God. So heartbreaking. The poor child. Was she hurt also?"

"No. But if she hadn't been drawing water from the village well at the time, I'm sure she would have died as well. I think it was her eyes that drew me to her. They never smiled. I was determined to make her laugh." He smiled tenderly at Maggie. "I guess that's my mission in life, to bring laughter into the hearts of lonely, little ladies."

"Well you do it very well Major Kelleher. Just remember though, you're still working on this assignment. You can't move on until your mission is completed."

Jake laughed and hugged her across the shoulders. "Don't worry. I'm all yours."

"I think we've gotten sidetracked. Please, finish your story. Did you ever get Thanh to laugh? I know how difficult that can be because I became quite attached to a sad, little Vietnamese boy myself."

"I would like to take all the credit, but I don't think that's the case. I know some French nuns are responsible for her really breaking out of her shell. You see, a few months after I started going to the orphanage, Thanh developed skin lesions on her hands and feet. Soon, they became quite numb and she experienced muscle weakness as well."

"Not leprosy?"

Jake nodded. "That's right. Unfortunately, when she contracted that dreaded disease, she was evicted from the orphanage in Chu Lai. I refused to let her be abandoned to the Vietnam countryside where she probably wouldn't have survived for very long. I asked around and learned of the Ben San Leprosarium here in Qui Nhon, run by French nuns. I borrowed a chopper and brought Thanh down. The sisters are truly remarkable. I visit whenever I can to help and to check on Thanh at the same time. We'll be spending the week with them."

"How is Thanh doing now?"

"We'll see soon enough. It should be a great week for us. The view is incredible. The Leprosarium was built on a bluff overlooking Ky Co beach on Qui Nhon Bay. The building was originally built by the French to house some of their top commanders when their forces were still in Vietnam. One of the children of the French commanders developed Leprosy. No one would help his child except a French priest and some nuns. When the French pulled out of Nam, he gave the building to the French sisters to continue their work. And so Ben San Leprosarium was born. At that time, lepers were shunned, cursed and feared by the Vietnamese. They were living in cemeteries and anywhere else they could find that no one else wanted to be. This leprosarium was so badly needed. I'm afraid time hasn't changed much about leprosy. Lepers are still forced to live in social isolation. Even the Viet Cong are afraid of contracting leprosy, so we don't have to worry about them all week. French sisters are still here today caring for the leper colony. Which reminds me. They are Catholic sisters and I didn't want to offend them. I told them that we were married. Is that OK with you, Mrs. Kelleher?"

In response, she snuggled a little closer to him. "Nothing would make me happier than to be Mrs. Kelleher... Even if it's only for a week."

Jake squeezed her shoulders a little tighter and smiled down at her with his lovable, boyish grin. "Look," he said pointing excitedly. "You can just start to see the South China Sea. We're almost there now. Did you know, because of the beautiful beaches in this area, before war tore this country apart, Qui Nhon was a resort town?"

She could clearly picture this. The homes, nestled among lovely gardens, were quaint with beautiful, red clay roofs. After meandering about five miles through the outskirts of Qui Nhon, their jeep pulled up in front of the Leprosarium. They got out with their duffel bags.

"Thank you for the transportation, Sergeant. You got us here safe and sound."

"That's what I was aiming for. I'll be back for you in one week, Sir. You all have a good time now."

As the jeep pulled away, they stood quietly, side by side, allowing their senses to take in fully the pastoral scene before them. The main building of Ben San Leprosarium stood quietly, majestically on a hill, a lonely centurion far above the South China Sea. Like so many of the homes they had passed along the way, this two-story building was of unmistakable French design with fresh, white stucco walls and a red clay roof.

Jake pointed to a fairly large structure to the right of the main building. "That's their chapel. They use it for mass and prayer of course, but it also functions as a school house during the week. Believe it or not, Sisters Yvonne and Theresa teach all the children to read, write and speak in French, English and Vietnamese." Jake pointed further to the right. "And just beyond their chapel you can see their barn. They have a few pigs and some cows."

"And chickens and goats," Maggie laughed, delighted to see so many chickens and goats scattered across the grounds.

"That's right. Their chickens and goats roam freely. They provide eggs and milk for the entire community. Now, if you look behind us you can see where the colony lives. I know it may look like a lot of room to you, but if anyone develops Leprosy, their entire family is welcomed to live here together with them."

Maggie turned around and saw four large, identical hooches. They were built in the style of a military complex, quite similar to her nursing quarters at Pleiku. "I guess you didn't want me to miss home too much. You're always so thoughtful." She laughed then turned back around to view the graceful main building again. She noted that lush gardens surrounding this building further enhanced this idyllic setting. Their greenery and blooms somehow accentuated the spectacular view of the South China Sea. Far below, the South China Sea beckoned to them to come and walk on its powdery, white sand beaches and to bathe in its warm, turquoise waters. "Oh Jake, it's lovely," she said joyfully, while reaching out for his hand and stifling a strong urge to pull him down the path to those warm waters. But she knew, first and foremost, she must meet his 'family.'

Soon, smiling French sisters and Vietnamese people of all ages emerged gracefully from the front door and gathered around them. Jake introduced Maggie to Sisters Simone and Jeanne who were both nurses, Sisters Yvonne and Theresa who taught the children, and Sisters Marie and Cecile who worked alongside the leper colony in the gardens and tended to the livestock. As Jake finished introductions, Maggie noticed a beautiful girl with long, dark hair and luminous, solemn, brown eyes standing patiently in the doorway. Maggie saw that her right hand was misshapen, having the appearance of a claw, and that some of her fingers were missing. She touched Jake's shoulder. "Is that Thanh?" she asked softly.

He turned in the direction that she pointed, smiled broadly, and then raced towards the child. Maggie watched her entire face light up as Jake scooped her tiny body into his arms and spun her around and around. It was the first time that Maggie had ever seen a Vietnamese child smile so fully. Her smile exploded into laughter, but Maggie couldn't tell who was laughing harder, Thanh or Jake. Even the sisters were smiling and laughing now watching their joyful reunion. And somehow, seeing the pure love and joy in Jake's eyes for this beautiful, little girl, Maggie's love for him deepened. *She thought, this is the man I want holding my heart forever.*

One of the sisters looked shyly at Maggie. "Thank you, Madame Kelleher for bringing Jake back to us. He has been gone too long. Thanh asks for him every day. She cries on the inside but never on the outside. She is a very brave girl."

"I'm happy to be here, Sister. I'll try not to keep Jake away so long next time." Maggie smiled down into gentle, brown eyes peeking out of her white habit. "Would you mind telling me your name again? I apologize for my poor memory."

"Certainly, Madame Kelleher. I am Sister Simone. I'm a nurse, just like you." She reached out and squeezed Maggie's hand. "It's so kind of you to promise to bring Jake back to us more often."

A few minutes later, Sister Simone and the other nuns ushered them inside where an unbelievable French luncheon had been prepared for them. It was easy to forget they were at war when they saw the table laden with such splendor. Quenelles do brochette- made from milk, butter, bread crumbs, eggs and finely ground fish, mixed, poached and served with a cream sauce- fluffy biscuits, rice, peas, and roast pork were all set before them. They dined, conversed, and exchanged smiles with the sisters. Maggie couldn't remember a more charming and inviting environment. Little Thanh happily ate her lunch sitting next to Jake. She didn't have to say a word; her eyes spoke for her.

After lunch, Sister Simone took them up to their room on the second floor. It was tiny but so cozy. The furniture was sparse, consisting of a double mattress on the floor covered with a faded, handmade quilt, one small dresser, and a night stand on which stood a chipped ceramic basin filled with fresh water. The room had only one small window, but it overlooked the South China Sea. Sister Simone opened it, allowing a strong sea breeze to fill their room.

"Thank you, Sister Simone," Maggie said. "The room is lovely."

"You're most welcome, Madame Kelleher. We hope you and Jake have a wonderful stay. I will let you rest now. You must be tired after your journey back to us." Smiling shyly, she turned and walked out of the room, softly pulling the door shut behind her.

Jake smiled across the room at her. "Well, Mrs. Kelleher, what do you think? Was this worth the uncomfortable ride?"

"This is heaven. I would have gladly ridden across the Sahara Desert on a camel to spend a week here with you."

Jake walked towards her, lifted her into his arms and carried her to their bed on the floor. Gently, he unbuttoned her shirt and caressed her. He kissed her softly, gently at first, but with increasing strength and urgency as the minutes passed. They made love in their newfound paradise, drowning out the war with their passion. Neither remembered that they were in Vietnam. For that moment, all they were aware of was their love exploding within their souls. Exhausted, they slept for several hours.

Maggie awoke first, momentarily confused by her surroundings until she felt the ocean breeze on her skin and saw Jake sleeping so peacefully next to her. She smiled and gently stroked his cheek before slowly, carefully getting out of bed. She used the ceramic wash basin on the night stand to sponge herself off, then changed into a bathing suit and shorts. Jake opened his eyes as she was brushing her hair. She smiled across the room at him. "Would you like to walk down to the beach? Perhaps, Thanh can join us?"

Jake jumped out of bed and walked across the room to her. He gently pulled the hair away from her face, then softly cupped her face with his hands and kissed her. He looked into her eyes. "So, you're willing to share me already? You're a remarkable woman. Now, I remember why I love you so damned much."

Twenty minutes later, they were walking down the steep, narrow path to the beach with Thanh in tow. The water was bathtub temperature, or at least what she remembered bathtub temperature to be. It had been almost seven months since she had enjoyed the luxury of a bath. They jumped through the waves together, each of them holding tightly onto one of Thanh's hands. Jake chased them along the shoreline, through the breaking waves, until they got mad enough to gang up on him. He was man enough to let them dunk him several times. They laughed, frolicked, built sand castles, and lounged on the beach for several hours, satiating their senses with the sweet sounds, sights, and smells of their tropical paradise.

As the afternoon progressed, Thanh inched closer to Maggie until she was sitting right beside her. "Madame Kelleher," she said, looking at her with her big, solemn brown eyes. "I think you're the prettiest lady I have ever seen."

Maggie hugged her. "Why thank you, Thanh, but I think you should look in a mirror, Honey. You're very beautiful yourself."

Thanh smiled shyly at Maggie then grabbed her hand. "Will you come and look for seashells with me?"

"I'd love to. But first, you have to do one thing for me."

Her eyes became solemn again. "I will do anything for you, Madame Kelleher."

"OK. Please, call me 'Maggie.'"

Her eyes brightened. "That is an easy thing to do. Please, come and look for seashells with me, Maggie."

Jake smiled at them. "Do you ladies mind if I join you? Or is this a purely female expedition?"

"What do you think, Thanh? Should we let this disheveled gentleman accompany us?"

"Oh yes, Maggie. I think we better or he may throw us out to sea again!"

Jake and Maggie laughed. "She's so precious," Maggie whispered to him as they each grabbed one of her hands. The three of them walked along the soft sand beach, looking for seashells.

They walked slowly, stopping frequently to allow Thanh to scoop up her treasures from the sea. As they headed back in the direction of the Leprosarium, Thanh suddenly became quite excited. She let go of both of their hands and squatted down in the sand. Carefully, she extracted a cream-colored spiral shell, approximately two inches long, which had been partially buried in the sand. She gently brushed off the sand then laid it in the palm of her hand for them to see. The tip of it had been broken off, but, even with this tiny flaw, its delicate loveliness was unmistakable. Maggie had never before seen such an exquisitely beautiful shell, even with all the summers she had spent shelling on her California beaches.

"It's beautiful, Thanh. Do you know what it is, Jake?"

"Let me see here. May I hold it for a minute, Thanh?" He carefully placed it in his hand then gently turned it over, studying it closely from all angles. His facial features became quite animated. "It can't be. It can't be. I think it is though. Yes, I'm positive now." He looked up at them with an excitement in his eyes Maggie had rarely seen. "It's a Precious Wentletrap. Or if you prefer the scientific name, an Epitoneum scalare." He sat down in the sand and continued to examine the seashell, turning it over and over again in his hand. Finally, he looked up at them and smiled broadly. "Sit down with me for a minute in the shade of this coconut tree," he said, patting the sand next to him. "I want to tell you ladies a story about this seashell."

Maggie sat down across from Jake, gently pulling Thanh next to her. When they were settled comfortably on the sand, Jake began. "When I was a kid, every summer, the first two weeks of July, my parents took us to same little cottage on Hilton Head Island in South Carolina. I spent most of my days exploring our private beach, carrying a red plastic pail, searching for seashells unique enough to gain my father's admiration. Day after day, bucketful after bucketful, I would carry my treasures back to my dad's lounge chair, hoping that just one of them would meet with his approval. My father, an astronomer by profession and a traveler of the seven seas by choice in the adventurous days of his youth, possessed eyes that had seen all the wonders of this world and beyond. Those eyes never got excited over any of my discoveries, no matter how unique or special they appeared to mine. Each time, after looking quickly, feigning only mild interest, he would always say the same thing. 'They're nice, Son. Why don't you run along and play now?' But I didn't give up. Not me. I kept searching and hoping and believing, by some innate, childhood faith, that I, his lowly eight-year-old son, would find something on that lonely barrier island beach so unusual that my father would be awed."

Jake paused for a minute to examine the seashell again then

looked back at them, smiling excitedly. "One day, after a fairly large storm, I found a shell, partially buried in the sand, colored just like this one, with the same intricate, spiral design. It appeared to me that someone with rock-steady hands had frosted each spiral to symmetrical perfection. Funny thing, I almost tossed that shell away because it had been cracked by the storm. I thought my dad would ridicule me for it. But this time, I didn't care. I thought it was still the most beautiful shell I had ever found."

Maggie smiled at Jake, totally enthralled by his childhood tale.

Jake smiled back at both of them before continuing. "My dad quickly looked through my bucket of shells with me. He started to say, 'They're nice,' but stopped midway through the sentence and picked up that beautiful, broken shell. 'It can't be,' he said, turning the shell around in his hand, staring at it so intently. I was so proud. I had never found or done anything in my life that captivated my dad for so long. After a few more minutes of careful examination of my seashell, my father looked right into my eyes and spoke so softly. I felt as if he were telling me the greatest secret in the world.

"'This is the Precious Wentletrap, Son,' he said. 'Its name is Dutch for spiral staircase. I've only seen one other like it, when I was in the Philippines. Local Filipinos told me that back in the 18th century, the Wentletrap was the most valuable seashell in the world because Catherine the Great, a powerful Russian czar had one.' He went on to tell him that Catherine was the daughter of a German prince. At fifteen years of age, she went to Russia to marry Peter III, ruler of Russia. Catherine was a beautiful, but strong woman. Her marriage had been planned for her. There was no love between her and Peter. So young, so beautiful, and full of life, she fell in love with Grigori, the brother of one of her army officers. Grigori gave Catherine a Precious Wentletrap, just like this one, as a symbol of his love for her. He wanted her to know that she was precious and that he would always love her. Peter found out about their affair and, in rage, threw her

Precious Wentletrap across the palace courtyard. Catherine, too strong for tears, simply bent down and began picking up the shattered Wentletrap, piece by piece, collecting the fragments in her handkerchief. Less than one week later, Peter was murdered and Catherine became the empress of Russia. Tradition tells that, after Peter's murder, Grigori gave Catherine another Wentletrap, larger and more beautiful than the original, but Catherine still held on to the pieces from the first one.'

"The Filipinos told my dad that ever since Catherine and Grigori's affair, the Precious Wentletrap has been a symbol of love. Other royalty have cherished it as well. They claimed that Emperor Francis I of Austria bought one for his wife, Maria Theresa, in 1750, paying four thousand Austrian guilders for it, or almost twenty thousand American dollars."

Jake's story excited Maggie. "This shell has only one tiny flaw. Are they still priceless?"

Jake laughed. "I see that you think we may have found our fortune. Unfortunately, that's not the case. Recently, shell collectors have discovered lairs of Wentletraps near Sumatra and Australia and other parts of the Indo-Pacific, right around here. They aren't rare anymore and accordingly; their material value has decreased significantly. In fact, they can be bought now for as little as five dollars." He paused and looked directly into their eyes. "But I like to remember back to the 18th century. Back to when they were so very rare, when they symbolized love for someone as powerful as Catherine the Great."

Jake stood up when he had finished his tale. They stared at the Precious Wentletrap for a few more minutes, each of them taking a turn to hold it in the palm of their hand while imagining Catherine the Great cherishing one just like it. Finally, Jake looked right at Thanh and handed the seashell back to her. "Thanh," he said softly. "Keep this Precious Wentletrap. Whenever you hold it, remember how much Maggie and I love you and will always love you. You are so precious to us."

The week raced by. Jake and Maggie spent hours helping the sisters with the leprosy patients, working in the gardens, caring for their livestock, and assisting Sister Yvonne in the chapel with the children's classes. And no matter what they were doing, Thanh was usually right beside them. Maggie and Jake managed to steal some time to enjoy quiet, romantic moments alone as well. They talked so freely. Jake knew Maggie so completely, inside and out, even more thoroughly than Kate did. She felt so comfortable, so content, and so completely happy in the role of Mrs. Kelleher. She felt as if this is what she was destined to become all along. She prayed the week would never end, but she knew her prayers would again fall on deaf ears.

Maggie and Jake spent most of their last day at Qui Nhon by themselves, probably because they were both saddened to see their week drawing to a close, so afraid of losing the intimacy they had established. In the early afternoon, they laid next to each other on the soft sand in the shade of a coconut tree, holding hands, watching the waves break on the shore. Sound, sight, smell and touch all worked together, a perfect symphony orchestra, to completely soothe them. A peace washed over them as tangible as the waves themselves. They fell asleep in each other's arms.

Maggie found herself so cold, so very cold. She was walking through that thick fog. It was choking her. Where was Jake? She needed him, but he wasn't there. She tried to run but she knew she was too late. He was gone. "Jake!" she cried. "Wait for me. Jake!" she screamed louder. She began to cry. She tried desperately to run, but it was impossible. She couldn't breathe in that thick, tenacious fog.

"Wake up, Maggie. What's the matter?"

She opened her eyes and looked into Jake's concerned, gentle eyes.

He softly stroked her face and kissed her hair. "I'm right here. Are you OK?"

"Have you ever read 'Gone with the Wind?'"

He smiled down at her. "Are you kidding? I grew up in Georgia, less than fifty miles from Atlanta. It was required reading for all seniors at Monticello High School."

"Did you like it?"

"Forget the book," he said firmly squeezing her shoulder with concern still showing in his eyes. "Tell me what's bothering you. You sounded really scared."

"I'm trying to," she said impatiently. "Do you remember at the end of the book when Scarlet finally realizes she loves Rhett? She's trying to run back to him through all that cold fog. She runs after him, but it is too late. She has already lost him. That's what I'm afraid of Jake. I've looked for you all of my life, yet I know that I'm going to lose you in that cold Pleiku fog."

"Oh, Sweetheart," Jake cradled her face in his hands and tenderly kissed her. "You're not going to lose me. This is real life. Not fiction. I promise I'll never be 'Gone with the Wind.' I love you too much." He stood up, bent over and picked her up. He held her in his arms, looked down at her, and laughed. "I think such dreadful thoughts deserve a punishment." He ran towards the sea, carrying her in his arms

"No," she screamed, laughing and kicking wildly. "Put me down! Did you hear me? Put me down this minute!"

He ran until the water was up to his waist then flung her into the South China Sea. She came up sputtering, laughing and furious.

"It looks like you need to be dunked again," he called out to her.

She splashed water into his face, then ran away from him as fast as she could. Soon her feet were on dry land again. She ran barefoot in the sand, laughing so hard that her footsteps mimicked a drunken fool. Every few strides, she glanced back over her shoulders. Her heart raced. Rapidly, he was gaining on her.

"You'll be sorry when I catch you, Maggie Darling," he called to her.

...In the distance, Maggie heard Katie's muffled cries. She didn't want to open her eyes because Jake only lived in her dreams, but her daughter needed her. Regretfully, she opened her eyes, got off her bed, and walked into the nursery.

CHAPTER FOURTEEN
Photographs and Memories

Maggie sat down in the easy chair in Lydia's office, placing her photographs, a joke book, and a small box beside her.

Lydia looked at her collection of memorabilia and smiled. "I see you took your assignment seriously. Was it difficult for you?"

"Yes and no. I learned a lot about myself." She looked across the room at Lydia's display case of the Battle of Gettysburg. *Where was that evasive hope that she tried so hard to instill in my soul? Why can't I reach out, grasp it, and reel it in? Would it ever become a part of my life?* She looked back at Lydia. "It was difficult for me to accept that for every happy memory I recalled, there was a sad moment of equal or greater intensity. In the last few years, I think I've become an expert at blocking out my past so I wouldn't have to remember that pain. I know you've told me many times that this might have been a mistake." She smiled, looking into her warm, brown eyes. "I believe you now. I just let my thoughts run rampant this week, remembering everything, grain and chaff alike. Those precious memories brought me such pleasure and soothed me beyond words."

Lydia nodded. "I've learned through the years that the most difficult step is always the first one. It's often hard for people to trust and believe in one another. They would rather cling to their old, comfortable belief system, even when it's not working. It makes me happy that you're willing to try. I think that you'll heal more quickly now."

"I hope you're right. I know I do feel quite rejuvenated today. I have one confession though; I found it challenging, almost impossible, to choose just three memories. Selecting ones that

I feel comfortable sharing with you complicated matters further. I discovered that I have some memories that are just too private to share with anyone. Even someone I trust as much as you. I hope that I haven't offended you."

"Maggie, for shame. I thought you knew me better than that. Think back to your first visit. I told you that I only want you to tell me that which you're comfortable sharing with me. I encourage you to keep your deeply personal, happy memories to yourself. Painful memories, however; are a different story. With time, I hope you'll feel safe enough with our relationship to unburden yourself from all of them." She paused and smiled at Maggie. "Enough said. Now, I'm looking forward to hearing your stories."

Maggie pulled out some photographs and the small box. She handed the photos to Lydia, but kept the box on her lap. "Feel free to look through them. They're all from my thirteenth birthday expedition to San Francisco."

"Is this your mother?" Lydia asked, holding up a photograph.

"No, actually my family isn't in any of them. Once I turned thirteen, my mother said that I was too old to celebrate birthdays anymore. I told Kate, and the next thing I knew, she had invited me to celebrate my birthday with her and her parents in San Francisco. It was such a perfect trip. If I were asked to change even one moment of that day to make it better, it would be an impossible task for me. It's uncanny how vividly I remember it. That day is so clear that it's almost as if it happened yesterday.

...I didn't think that my mother would allow me to go if she knew my birthday was the reason behind the invitation, so I didn't tell her why they wanted to take me. I was thrilled when she gave me permission to go. Although San Francisco was less than fifty miles from our home, I had never been. Understandably, because of nervous anticipation, I didn't sleep well the night before. I woke up that morning feeling tired but happy. Jason acted funny at the breakfast table. I assumed he was just sad because he would be alone with Mom all day.

"When are you coming home, Maggie?"

"Not sure. Probably around nine o'clock tonight. You're not going to miss me, are you?"

"Do you promise to be home by nine?"

"Cross my heart and hope to die," I said solemnly then laughed. "You're too much, Jason. It's Saturday. There's no school. Why don't you play you're a world-famous explorer in the woods or something? You always love that game."

"It's only really fun with you." His eyes were beginning to brim over with tears.

"Come on Jason. It's only for a day. Cheer up." Hearing Kate's car in the driveway, I jumped up. I looked over one last time at his sad, little face. Almost instinctively, I reached over and tousled his blond curls.

"Remember, Maggie," he said, pushing my hand away. "You promised to be home by nine."

"I remember. See you in twelve hours."

I ran out the door and began the happiest day I had ever lived in my thirteen years. Doc and Mama O'Brien kicked off the day by taking us to a little boutique in the heart of San Francisco. They bought Kate and me matching chiffon dresses, ones we 'just had to have.' Kate's was lilac and mine primrose. I remember all the fun we had twirling and giggling in front of the mirror, watching the pastel fabric billowing out around us. Doc wouldn't let us stop with just the dresses. He bought us purses, pillbox hats, and white gloves to complete our ensemble. The boutique manager consented to our tearful pleas. We wore our new outfits out of the store.

One of my most memorable moments of the day was walking, alone with Kate, across a small span of the Golden Gate Bridge. Doc and Mama O'Brien remained in the car at the Visitor Plaza Parking, but I'm sure their eyes never left us as we pranced in our new dresses across the burnt-orange bridge. I remember the top of the bridge was so high that it was buried in swirling, white clouds and strong wind gusts blew across the bridge forcing Kate and I to hold our hats tightly against our heads to prevent them from blowing away.

The rest of the day passed much too quickly. We ate dinner in an elegant restaurant at the top of a skyscraper. In my eyes, we were in heaven itself. I had never been in such a magical world. I didn't even know that such places existed. After dinner, it was off to a movie, followed by ice cream sundaes, then finally, the long drive back home. Sitting so tired, yet so contently beside Kate in the back seat of Doc's Oldsmobile, I fantasized that I was Kate's sister again, but just like for Cinderella, my dream ended at the stroke of midnight.

I walked into our trailer, humming softly to myself. I twirled around the kitchen in my new dress. That's when I saw it. On the counter was a double layer chocolate cake, clearly made by Jason. The layers were lopsided, the frosting splattered with crumbs, and the lettering could only have been done by a child. I walked into the living room. Jason was curled up in a ball on the sofa, snoring softly. I bent over and easily picked him up. He was so tiny for his age.

His eyes fluttered open. "Maggie, is that you?"

"Yes, Silly. It's me. Sh now. Go back to sleep. I'll bring you to bed."

"No, Maggie. Is it nine o'clock now? I waited for you forever."

"It's way past nine, Jason. It's even after twelve. I'm sorry I'm so late."

"It's OK. But put me down. I have something for you."

I put him down and he retrieved a small box, hidden under the sofa pillow. He handed it to me, smiling shyly. "Happy birthday, Maggie."

I hugged him and then opened the box. His present meant more to me than any of the expensive gifts I had received from Kate and her family that day. Suddenly, I was overwhelmed with guilt for coming home so late and with shame for wanting Kate to be my sister instead of having him for my brother."

...Maggie opened the box on her lap and pulled out a beautiful, turquoise Indian bracelet. "See Lydia, this is Jason's gift. I think he used every penny he had ever saved in his nine years to buy it for me. To this day, I've never received a more beautiful birthday present. I still love it so much that I refuse to wear it. I would fall apart if anything happened to it. Especially now when it's the only thing I can actually hold on to in remembrance of Jason." She gently placed the bracelet back into its box and softly closed the lid. "I miss him so much. Why did such a perfect, giving human being have to live such a horrible life and die so needlessly?" Tears began to flow, but this time she didn't care and didn't even attempt to stop them. "Do you see what I mean? For every joyful memory, there's so much pain and sadness. Sometimes, I wonder if it's all worth it."

Lydia brought a box of Kleenex over to Maggie and sat down in the chair closest to hers. She waited a few minutes before speaking. "Maggie, not all of Jason's life was horrible. I'll bet if we could ask him, giving you that present was one of the happiest moments of his life. Imagine the pride he felt presenting his big sister, whom he adored, with such a beautiful gift."

"Do you really think so?"

"I know so. Jason may have been little, but I'm certain he felt the same happiness and joy we all feel, watching someone we love open our carefully chosen gifts."

Maggie laughed. "He did smile an awful lot. Then he actually grabbed my hand and pulled me into the kitchen. I acted surprised to see the cake. He sang 'Happy Birthday' to me, then at twelve-thirty at night, Jason and I each ate a huge piece of chocolate cake. It may have been Jason's first attempt at baking, but I'll guarantee it was the most delicious cake either one of us had ever eaten."

Lydia reached over and squeezed Maggie's hand tightly for just a moment, then looked right into her eyes. "Jason sounds like a very special person. I think the world lost a great deal when he died. I'm truly sorry for your loss and all the pain his death has brought you, but never forget why he died. Jason wanted to ensure that you didn't get hurt or suffer. Imagine how devastated he would be if you ever did anything to hurt yourself. Whenever you're feeling like it's just not worth it, remember that Jason thought your life was the most important thing on this Earth. If for no other reason, take care of yourself for him."

Maggie looked down at her hands, clenched tightly in her lap, then glanced back at Lydia. "I promise I will. I never thought about my life from Jason's perspective. I would never want to do anything to hurt him."

Lydia smiled at Maggie. "That's good to hear. Now, do you have another memory you want to share with me?"

CHAPTER FIFTEEN
The Stars of Texas

Maggie held up the joke book that had been lying beside her. "This is the only concrete thing I have to relay this story, but I think it's enough."

Lydia read the title *1001 Jokes to Make Even Mona Lisa Laugh*. She smiled. It was the only encouragement Maggie needed to begin.

...July 10, 1968 was my twenty-second birthday and it was hot and humid in Pleiku. The war seemed to intensify in that heat. The sound of Dustoffs approaching was as constant and relentless as the stifling heat itself. There weren't enough wounded yet to classify it as a push, but we were rapidly approaching that point. It was so busy that we simply worked by territorial boundaries. The rules were simple. Anyone who was placed in your general vicinity was your responsibility. Austin, David J. was an enormous boy that was deposited on a stretcher in my territory.

He grinned up at me. "Howdy nurse. I ain't seen anyone as pretty as you for months. Hell, maybe years." His smile widened. "I did it, Nurse. I made it! It's my birthday today and I'm still kicking. My buddies said I wouldn't live to see my nineteenth birthday on account of my feet. Said they covered too damned much Gook, booby-trapped ground when I walked. What do you think, Nurse? Have you ever seen such big clunkers?"

I smiled back at him. He had such an infectiously happy personality. "You know we have a lot in common, Private Austin. It's my birthday, too. Just a minute here. I'll let you know." I peeked beneath the sheet. Both of Private Austin's legs were twisted grotesquely and almost totally severed from his body at the level of his knees. Tourniquets were wrapped tightly around each leg just above the knee to stop the bleeding. He also had a large abdominal dressing that was completely saturated with blood. I was surprised that he was still so coherent. If he had any chance at all, he needed to go back to the OR stat. Despite feeling fearful for his life, I pulled the sheet down quickly and gave him my best smile. "I don't know, Private Austin. It's a close call but I would have to say your feet are definitely in the running for the biggest I've ever seen. And believe me, I've seen a damned lot of feet over the past five months. I need to hang another pint of blood on you. I'll be right back."

"OK. Take your time, Nurse. I ain't fixing to go anyplace right now. And call me, DJ. DJ's the name." He closed his eyes.

I ran and got the blood, then looked for Captain Pollard, the charge nurse of our ER that day. I was not envious of her position. The responsibilities of her job were enormous, requiring her to get a complete report from the triage nurses on every patient as they entered the ER. She had to process this information quickly to manage the flow of patients so that they made it to the OR as close as possible to the order indicated by the triage team. She had to stay abreast of major changes in our patients' conditions and in the OR's. It didn't take me long to spot her. Her uniform was soaked with sweat and blood. She was rubbing her forehead with the back of her right hand and her face seemed more strained than usual. I wasn't sure if her increased anxiety was a symptom of the choking heat and humidity or from the pressure of the split-second decision-making she had already endured over the past eight hours. Part of me wanted to walk away from her and just let her do her job. She was one of our finest. Then I thought of DJ. I just had to say something. Anything I could do to give the kid more of a chance of beating these odds.

"Captain Pollard," I said loudly, on the verge of losing control.

She immediately looked in my direction. "Lieutenant Taylor. What can I do for you?"

"My patient, Private Austin, needs to go back to the OR stat.

He won't make it otherwise. You have to help me with this."

"Calm down, Lieutenant. I'm well aware of his status, but, believe it or not, there are actually a few other Immediates more critical than him. The OR will be tied up for at least two hours. You remember what triage entails. Let me do my job and you do yours. Go keep him stabilized until it's his turn."

I clenched my fists tightly at my sides and turned away abruptly before I said something to her that I would regret later. *I don't give a damn about your triage system, I thought. All I care about is my soldier... This soldier that shares a birthday with me. If I'm going to make it to be another year older, he is too. And I know what his status is better than you. My soldier doesn't have two more hours of life in him. Hell, I don't know if he even has one hour.*

I didn't really want to curse her, but I desperately wanted to curse this system, this triage that allowed us mortals to act as gods. But I remained the 'good' officer. I held my tongue and went obediently back to work. In retrospect, maybe I shouldn't have. Maybe my words could have had an impact on Captain Pollard and allowed DJ to move up the triage ladder. I still wonder if I erred in not fighting harder for DJ's life.

I ran back to DJ and hung the pint of blood. I reinforced the pressure dressing over his abdomen. He was still bleeding so heavily. I took a set of vitals. His pressure was down to 80/40 and his pulse was 120, weak and thready. I knew he was becoming shocky. He opened his eyes when he felt the pain of the catheter entering his right arm as I inserted another IV line to infuse more fluids in hopes of bringing his pressure back up.

He smiled up at me, but it wasn't the big, boisterous grin from earlier. I knew everything was a struggle for him now. "Oh, it's you Nurse. I thought I was back on our ranch."

I smiled down at him. "You don't have to talk now. Why don't you just rest and save your strength? You'll be going back soon for your operation."

"I know I should rest. But I can't right now. Would it be all right with you if I just talked with you for a few minutes? You don't know how much you remind me of my girl, Victoria. Most of my buddies said their girls left them when they got orders for Nam. But not my Victoria. It's been so long since I've seen her. I miss her... I miss home."

"Where's home, DJ?"

"Waco. Waco, Texas. Only state in the union worth a damn."

I smiled at him as I finished taping up his IV line and tubing to secure it. "You know, I've heard that about Texas."

"You heard right then. I was just thinking how great it would be to be there now riding my horse. Victoria and I liked to ride at night beneath the soft light of a full moon. We could ride for miles and still not leave my father's ranch. Have you ever seen the stars in Texas?"

I shook my head. "I can't say that I have."

"There can't be anyplace in the world that has as many stars as in our Texas sky. After riding for a bit, we would tether our horses and spread a blanket on the ground. We would lie back, look up into that starlit sky, and talk forever. Every once in a while, though, those stars would just take all our words away. God, what a sight. Life seemed to hold so much promise, to be full of infinite possibilities when we looked up at them. We felt that the whole world without limits was ours to experience. I miss that feeling... I haven't felt that way since I left home."

DJ stopped talking and looked right into my eyes. They seemed to penetrate deep into the fiber of my soul. "I know I joke a lot. But I'm serious now. You have to be honest with me. I know I'm in pretty bad shape. I just have to know though. Can the docs fix my legs so that I can ride with Victoria again when I get home? She's waiting for me and I don't want to disappoint her."

My throat got so dry. My thoughts raced, searching for something to say that would be truthful but still give him some hope. I never wanted to take away all their hope. God help me, I just couldn't think of a good answer. I knew he would lose both of his legs. They would be amputated above the knees. Looking into his eyes again, I read something different this time. I got the feeling he already knew about his legs. Perhaps, he wanted me to answer something else for him; something more important than if he would ever ride his horse again. I was so confused. The harder I tried to think of something prophetic to say to him, something he could cling to that would help him hold on another hour, the more the right words eluded me.

"It's all right, Nurse," he said softly, looking away from my eyes. "I understand only the docs can answer my questions. I wasn't being fair to you. Don't worry about me. I'll be fine." He closed his eyes.

The soldier's respirations on the stretcher next to DJ's had become quite noisy and irregular. He was fighting to get enough air into his lungs. I turned to assist him.

DJ must have sensed somehow that I was leaving because he reached up and grabbed my arm. "Don't leave me, Nurse. Please, don't leave me. Not now." Intense fear was written across his face and in his eyes.

I patted his hand. "Try not to be afraid. I'll be back in two minutes. See your buddy over there. He's having trouble breathing. I have to help him. I'll be right back."

He looked over at the stretcher then back up at me. "OK. I understand. I want you to help him." He closed his eyes again.

I quickly walked over to the next stretcher. Lieutenant Sander's face and arms had been burnt by napalm, leaving his skin charred, torn, and bloodied. As hard as I tried to follow Kate's advice, I just couldn't look into his eyes. Fighting off a strong urge to gag, I placed my stethoscope on his chest and concentrated on his respirations. Movement across the aisle suddenly caught my eye. I glanced over at Kate. She, too, was tending to a napalm burnt soldier but she was looking directly into his eyes and appeared to be having a pleasant conversation with him. Feeling guilty and inadequate, I sighed, then turned back to his chest and completed the auscultation of his lungs.

I briefly looked at the Lieutenant's face. "Your throat is swelling making it difficult for air to get into your lungs. Are you having trouble breathing?"

He nodded.

"OK then. Here's what we're going to do. I'm going to insert a little, plastic airway into your mouth that will help keep your airway open. You'll be able to breathe a lot easier. Does that sound good to you?"

Again, he nodded.

I grabbed an airway and gently inserted it, then placed a roll behind his neck to help keep it properly aligned. His respirations quieted and became more relaxed. "You'll be more comfortable now. We'll keep a close eye on you. If you have trouble again, we may need to put a different kind of airway in called an endotracheal or 'ET' tube. Worst case scenario, you'll need that and a ventilator to help you breathe for a little while. But don't worry about anything now. Just know we'll be watching you closely. Why don't you just rest now?"

He smiled in appreciation, then closed his eyes.

With two extremely critical patients, I needed Sergeant Powers' help. I had to find him now. "Sergeant," I said, somewhat out of breath from running around the ER looking for him. "I'm out straight. I'm worried about Lieutenant Sanders. His airway is barely open. Can you find Dr. Anderson for me and ask him to assess the need for an ET tube? I need to get back to Private Austin. He's really getting shocky. I need to stabilize him for surgery."

"Don't worry. I'll find Dr. Anderson for you. I'll keep you posted."

"Thank you," I said, then turned to go back to DJ.

Kate called out to me as I walked by her. "Maggie, can you please hang another liter on Corporal Hunter over there? I'll be tied up with this dressing for a while yet and his solution is just about out."

I nodded. "I'll take care of it." I quickly hung another liter of crystalloid solution before finally running back to DJ. *I'll have to check his blood pressure again*, I thought as I walked towards his stretcher. *If it's still down, I'll try to get orders for a dopamine drip to stabilize him until it's his turn in the OR.*

DJ's chest wasn't moving. I grabbed his wrist and felt for his radial pulse. I couldn't palpate anything. I moved my fingers to his neck to feel for his carotid pulse. It, too, was glaringly absent. Frantically now, I placed my stethoscope on his chest and listened for his apical pulse. Silence. I moved the stethoscope to a new location and strained harder to hear. Silence. *Maybe it was just too damned noisy in here, I thought. I wanted to scream, Shut up! Everyone shut the hell up! Can't you see I need to hear DJ's heartbeat? But I knew, even in a soundproof room, I wouldn't be able to hear his apical pulse.*

"You're not going to die on me!" I said with conviction as I yanked the sheet off of him revealing his blood-soaked abdominal dressing and his twisted legs with the two tourniquets still tightly in place. I tilted his head back and gave him two quick, full breaths watching his chest rise with each one, then quickly climbed onto the stretcher, straddled his hips, and began chest compressions. "Code blue! We have a code blue here," I yelled loudly. "I could use some help."

"One and two and three." I counted off the rhythm as I pushed my hands down, firmly locked in place on his chest in the correct position. Down and up. Down and up. Tears froze in my throat. My heart pounded in my chest. I wanted to scream. *Open your eyes DJ. Damn it! Talk to me again. Don't you know you're not supposed to die alone? We don't let anyone die alone.*

Kate and Sergeant Powers were the first to arrive. Sergeant Powers tilted DJ's head back correctly, then placed an ambu bag over his mouth and nose and coordinated ventilating him with my compressions. Kate placed her fingers on his neck to palpate for a pulse. Dr. Anderson arrived next with Captain Pollard right behind him.

"How long before the OR is available?" Dr. Anderson said, looking at Captain Pollard.

"It will still be at least another hour."

"He doesn't have another hour," Dr. Anderson said sharply. "There's only a slim chance we can bring him back. But if we do, he needs to go back to the OR immediately to repair his internal injuries. We'll never be able to stay ahead of his blood loss out here."

"I don't know what you expect me to do, Doctor. They are all tied up now. It's the best we can do."

Dr. Anderson sighed and rubbed his forehead with the back of his right hand. "I'm sorry. This makes no sense. Stop CPR." He removed the stethoscope from around his neck and placed it on DJ's chest. He listened for a full minute, glanced at his watch, then looked at me. "Time of death 1624 hours. I'll sign his death certificate after you complete it." He turned and walked away with Captain Pollard.

I slowly climbed down off the stretcher, fighting with all my strength not to cry. Kate stayed for a few minutes. She cradled my right shoulder and back with her arm. "Are you going to be OK? Do you want me to stay and help?"

I looked around the ER. We were still so swamped. We easily would be going full force for another five or six hours. "No. You'd better go check on your patients." I looked into Sergeant Powers' eyes. "I'm sure Sergeant Powers will help me."

"You got that right, Lieutenant."

"Thank you, Sergeant. Can you quickly check on Lieutenant Sanders' respirations then come right back?"

After Sergeant Powers walked away, I looked down at DJ. I stroked his head for just a moment. *I'm so sorry, DJ. I never should have left you. I just didn't know you were going to leave us so soon.* Gently, I removed his two IV lines then completed his documentation. I was in the middle of completing his death certificate when Sergeant Powers returned.

"I see you're finishing up. I'll go grab a body bag."

I had completed everything when Lance returned. We placed DJ in the body bag, then wheeled him to the morgue. Lance and I had become close friends, as close as possible for an officer and an enlisted person. The rules were a little grayer in Nam than with stateside assignments. Something about the shared pain brought us all closer together. Lance could read me almost as well as Jake and Kate could. It might have been my walk, or my lack of words, or simply my facial expression. Somehow, Lance just knew that this loss was different for me.

He hugged me and allowed me to cry on his shoulder for a few minutes. "It's not your fault, Maggie. You did everything you could for him."

I wanted to believe Lance; but I knew I never would. The rest of my shift lasted forever, the way all nightmare days in Pleiku did. We worked almost nonstop for the next several hours. I forgot it was my birthday. All I remembered was DJ's face and his infectious smile. By 1930 hours, the last patient had passed through our ER. Somehow, among the chaos, we had maintained our ninety-eight percent survival rate. I was one of the last nurses to leave.

Captain Pollard walked over to me. "Maggie, I'm sorry we couldn't get to Private Austin in time, but you understand triage a little bit more now. We have to follow the rules or we wouldn't have been able to save as many as we did today."

I knew the humane thing to do would be to tell her it was OK, that I understood and that she had done a great job on a difficult day. But it would have been a lie. At that moment, I didn't give a damn about her numbers. I just wanted DJ to still be alive to celebrate his birthday. I turned my back to Captain Pollard without saying a word and walked out of the ER. Nothing seemed more appealing to me than a shower and some sleep to forget about this damned place for a while.

I opened the back door to our Hooch. Balloons lined the center hallway which ran the entire length of the hooch. "Happy birthday, Maggie!" Kate and the other eight nurses who shared our Hooch called from the doorways to their rooms. I didn't want to disappoint them so I smiled and played the role of a happy, excited birthday girl.

"There's more, Maggie. Hurry and get changed."

The nurses tossed pillows at each other, laughed, and clowned around while I obediently showered and changed into clean fatigues. I even smiled so they wouldn't guess how I was really feeling.

"That's much better now," Kate said, giving me a quick hug.

"Now turn around so I can put this blindfold on you." She laughed when it was in place and grabbed my hand. "Come on now. No time to waste."

I knew we must be headed to the Bastille, our party room. Some of the doctors had renovated a hooch next to ours and protected it by piling sand bags one third of the way up on all sides and on the roof, so even when we were being shelled, a nightly ritual at the 71st, our parties could continue. We used any small excuse to party. It helped us all survive that war.

Kate removed my blindfold.

"Surprise! Happy birthday, Maggie," everyone cheered.

As I had suspected, we were in the Bastille. Miraculously, someone had managed to find a cake in the middle of the war. Beer flowed. The radio was tuned to "Voice of America" broadcast. Someone turned it up as it blasted our favorite song 'Draft Dodger Rag' by Country Joe and the Fish. We formed a huge circle around the room with our arms on each other's shoulders. We swayed back and forth to the music screaming out the words.

For it's one, two, three, what are we fighting for?
Don't ask me, I don't give a damn,
My next stop is Vietnam.
For it's five, six, seven, open up the pearly gates.
Well there ain't no time to wonder why
Whoopee, we're all gonna die.

The love we felt for each other, borne out of our camaraderie from enduring such pain and heartache together, day after day, was unmistakable. It was so tangible that you could almost reach out and touch it. We couldn't let go of each other. When the radio stopped playing that song, we sang it again ourselves, finding the energy to sing even louder the second time around. Jake walked into the Bastille in the middle of the song. Although it was only a few weeks old, our affair was no secret. The 71st was worse than a small town. Everyone knew your business. He walked over to me when the song was over and put his arms around me. Everyone whistled, clapped loudly, and stomped their feet.

"Any objections to me kidnapping this little lady?"

"Hell no!" They screamed.

Kate stopped us. "Hold on a minute, Major. Maggie needs to cut her cake first."

Jake walked me over to my cake. Before blowing out the candles, I wished for something that I knew could never come true. I wished DJ were in the room with me, helping me to blow them out. My hands were shaking when I tried to cut the cake, so Jake helped me. Everyone whooped it up as Jake gently fed me a bite of cake then kissed off the crumbs.

"Any further objections?" Jake asked. Loud stomping, whistling and clapping answered his question. We turned to walk out of the room.

We didn't get far when I noticed Captain Pollard standing alone. "Just a minute, Jake. There's something I need to take care of before we go." I walked across the room to Captain Pollard and extended my hand to her. "You did a tremendous job today. I don't know how you do it, day after day." We shook hands firmly.

Her face showed just a hint of a smile, but her eyes softened tremendously. "Thank you, Lieutenant Taylor. I understand what a tough day it was for you, too. We've all been there. It's never easy to let go of them. It's not anyone's fault. Sometimes, they still die despite all our good intentions and efforts."

My throat began to tighten, so I simply nodded my head in agreement then turned and walked back to Jake. We walked arm in arm to my room in the hooch. With the party in full swing, we would have ample time alone in the hooch. We lay down next to each other on my bed and kissed until our hunger subsided.

Jake gently pushed the hair back from my face and looked into my eyes with deep concern. "You seem unusually subdued tonight, Maggie. Especially for a birthday girl. Is there anything wrong?"

Safely cradled in his arms, I told Jake about DJ. When I had finished the story, I lamented, "I never should have left his side. It's my fault that he died alone."

"Oh, so you were out powdering your nose and shooting the breeze with Kate when he died?"

"No!" I said with a mix of anger and irritation in my voice. "Weren't you listening to me? I was helping another soldier who was in respiratory distress and hanging an IV solution for Kate."

"Yes, I heard you. But did you hear yourself?" he said softly before cupping my face in his hands and looking into my eyes. "We all want to be perfect for them. We all try to make the right decisions... Every time. But we can't. It's impossible to do. We're not gods. We're just human beings, and, hard as we try, that's all we'll ever be. If you're going to survive over here, Sweetheart, you have to stop beating yourself up. You're taking things harder than you need to." He let go of my face and pulled a small package from his pocket and smiled at me. "I have just the present to help you with this."

...Maggie handed the joke book to Lydia. "This is the present Jake gave to me that night. I love the inscription he wrote on the inside cover. Reading it helped me get over so many nightmare days in the ER."

"May I read it?" Lydia asked.

Maggie nodded.

Lydia read it aloud. "My dearest Maggie, laughter really is the best medicine. When you've had the kind of day that you would give anything to forget, but know you'll always remember, open up this book and read a few pages. And laugh. Forget you're here. For a few minutes anyhow. Then read between the lines and see how I adore you. I love you, Maggie Taylor. I know I always will. Forever yours, Jake."

Lydia looked up at her and smiled. "That's beautiful, Maggie."

She nodded in agreement. "I loved receiving it. It was the first time Jake ever told me that he loved me. I often slept with this book tucked under my pillow. It made me feel that he was there with me."

"Do you still sleep with it under your pillow?"

"No, not for over five years. Not since I met Adam. But maybe I will again someday soon." She pulled out her last group of photographs and handed them to Lydia.

Lydia looked through them, smiling broadly. "These children are precious. Obviously, they're Vietnamese or Asian? More memories from Vietnam?"

She nodded. "Besides the book to help me get by, Jake also encouraged me to participate in Medical Civilian Action Patrols or MedCaps for short. These programs provided American health care to Vietnamese civilians. Jake was stationed in Chu Lai prior to Pleiku and, through MedCaps, had frequently visited an orphanage right outside of Chu Lai. He shared with me that it really helped him block out some of the daily horror of Nam. With Jake's encouragement, I convinced Kate, Dr. Bennett, and a few other nurses to participate with me. On our off-days, we started visiting an orphanage called 'Hanh Phuc' which loosely translated means "happy together' in Vietnamese. Hanh Phuc was located about an hour's drive southwest of the 71st in the Ia Drang Valley."

Maggie pointed out a few Asian women in the photos. "Hanh Phuc was run by these two women. Phuong was South Vietnamese and definitely in charge. An was a Montagnard. The Montagnards, or mountain people, were thought to be the original inhabitants of Vietnam. Sadly, they were driven to the less fertile lands of the Annamite mountain highlands by the invading peoples of mostly Chinese origins, similar to how we drove the Indians off their lands in our country. Understandably, the Montagnards despised the Vietnamese and visa-versa, but since there were so many Montagnard children living in the orphanage, Phuong needed An. Somehow, these women learned to live together peacefully for the sake of the children."

Lydia held up a photo of some children standing in front of a Quonset hut. "They are so sweet. Were there a lot of children?

And it looks like the orphanage was quite rustic."

"When we first started going to Hanh Phuc, there were approximately twenty-two children, but the number seemed to grow weekly as the war continued to rob them of their parents. The orphanage was composed of six Quonset huts with grass roofs, bamboo walls, and dirt floors. There were no doors or windows, just spaces cut into the sides of the huts for those purposes. They were without plumbing or electricity."

"I can see what you mean. They appeared to have lived in extreme poverty. Was that difficult for you to see?"

She nodded. "Not just for me. For everyone. The children were all barefoot and their clothes torn and ragged. Images of those children are still crystal clear today. I remember how polite they were. They lined up quietly. There was no pushing or shoving or name calling. Each one carried his or her own little metal bowl and just waited patiently for it to be filled with such scant amounts of rice and tiny bits of chicken. They rarely smiled. Their world was devoid of manufactured toys. Sticks, stones, bamboo and other naturally-occurring materials became their toys. Even at play, they were so solemn. I desperately wanted to make them laugh. We all did."

"Now, just a minute. I think you were successful," Lydia said, holding up a photograph. "I think this little fellow definitely has a smile on his face. And is that a hula hoop this little girl has around her waist? I love her smile, too."

"Yes, we were successful, now and then, but those moments were too rare. We wanted to have more of them. So, one of our first projects was to write home to our families, friends, and community churches. We asked for used clothing, books and toys to be sent to us. When we had collected enough so every child would receive a toy and an outfit, we brought it all to Hanh Phuc." She pointed out a few photos to Lydia. "In these photos, you can see the children in their new outfits. We expected some smiles, but they never came easily to their faces. I think they were happy with their new clothes and toys. I know that we were thrilled. After the initial day when we brought them, however, we never again saw them wearing the clothes we had given them or playing with the toys. They vanished from their lives as quickly as they had come."

Maggie paused speaking while Lydia looked through a few more photos. "Are these children holding toasted marshmallows?"

Maggie nodded and smiled. "Yes. By far, my happiest memory of Hanh Phuc was our bonfire. It was Kate's idea. She remembered how much fun she and I had camping out in her backyard when we were kids. Again, we asked for help from our families and friends back home. They sent us marshmallows. We brought three fifty-gallon drums along with the marshmallows to Hanh Phuc. We filled the barrels with bamboo and wood, then lit them in early afternoon. It would have been too dangerous to have fire at night because they may have inadvertently drawn enemy fire. We showed the kids how to toast the marshmallows and taught them some fun campfire songs. We even did the Hokey Pokey around the fires."

"What a wonderful idea Kate had. It looks like everyone, including you, had a wonderful time. So your visits to Hanh Phuc were mostly social in nature? Do I have the right impression?"

"Not quite. Our visits were actually more medically oriented. We gave the kids physicals, administered limited medications, de-wormed and de-liced them, and taught them English. It's just the social aspects were much more enjoyable and every trip had a certain amount of that wonderful social interaction with the kids. Jake had been so right. I loved to go to Hanh Phuc. Although the children were orphans, they were mostly whole. Many were malnourished and sickly, but we had the means to cure them. After seeing so many broken bodies, incapable of being completely healed, no matter what we did for them, it was so refreshing to be working with whole human beings again. Our efforts reaped tremendous results, which in turn, brought such satisfaction. I looked forward to my respite at Hanh Phuc. A day spent there nourished me for another week at the 71st."

"Even now, I think Hanh Phuc must be rejuvenating for you. It's the first story you've shared with me that didn't have an accompanying sad side."

Maggie looked down at her hands, clenched in tight balls against her rigid body. While she didn't verbally respond to Lydia's remarks, her entire body screamed out the fallacy of that statement. Maggie didn't dare look into Lydia's eyes for fear she would probe deeper. And she wasn't ready for that... Not today... She wasn't sure she would ever be ready to share that story.

CHAPTER SIXTEEN
Keeping Secrets

Autumn passed with all its glorious colors, leaving in its wake a frigid world stripped of its finery. For years, seeing the wind blow through the bare branches had evoked feelings of loneliness in Maggie, but this year was different. She had Lydia and Camille beside her to warm her spirits even on the most brutally cold winter's day. Each week, her trust in Lydia deepened and she was able to reveal to Lydia more harsh memories from her past. Lydia never judged her. She listened. She played the devil's advocate, just as Jake had done so many times before her, enabling Maggie to see the events and her responses to them in a different light. So gradually at first, then with an ever-increasing tempo, Lydia skillfully showed Maggie that neither her hurt nor her painful emotions needed to permanently scar her. She learned from Lydia and grew stronger as her twenty-year-old wounds were soothed and bandaged. Still, there was one story she couldn't tell Lydia. She wasn't sure she would ever be able to shed those last few articles of clothing.

Adam and Maggie remained civil towards one another. Occasionally, when he brought Katie back home after one of their weekends together, they talked together at length about their daughter. They both seemed to possess the same degree of parental pride. It was fun to share notes. As Katie approached her first birthday, she began to take her first steps. She started saying a few words. She laughed frequently and smiled even more. She appeared to be a normal, happy, well-adjusted toddler. For the first time, Maggie let her hair down and breathed a little easier. Perhaps, their failed marriage wouldn't have a harmful effect on her daughter, after all.

By mid-May, flowers and trees in full bloom, her spirits brightened further. Adam would be bringing Katie and Camille back late in the afternoon. She planned a surprise for all of them. The hours dragged by, as they always do when you're waiting. Finally, at four-thirty in the afternoon, they arrived. Maggie walked out to the car to greet them.

"Adam, it's such a gorgeous day. Would you like to stay for dinner? We're having our first barbecue of the year. I've prepared steak, your mother's potato salad, and corn on the cob. I even remembered your favorite. We'll be having strawberry shortcake for dessert." She smiled at him, but was surprised when Adam didn't return the smile and avoided her eyes.

"Camille. Would you please bring Katie inside so I can talk with Maggie?" He said Maggie's name with just a hint of anger and his face looked drawn and tense.

After Camille walked away with Katie in her arms, Adam said curtly, gesturing in the direction of their pool, "Let's go sit for a few minutes. I need to talk with you."

Maggie speculated about the contents of the large manila envelope Adam was carrying as they walked towards the pool. They sat across from each other at the poolside glass table. He placed the envelope on the table in front of him, folded his arms across it, before looking at the water for a few moments while she nervously brushed her hands across the glass surface of the table. Finally, he looked back at her.

"I'm sorry if it disappoints you, but I can't stay for dinner. I've already made plans for this evening." He paused for a few seconds, exhaled deeply, then handed the envelope to her. "I think we both know it's over, Maggie. I've filed for divorce and worked out a very fair divorce settlement for you to look over with your lawyer. I didn't want to hurt you by having it served. You can pull a few strings when you're part of the system. You'll see that everything is quite generous. You're welcome to stay right here with Katie and Camille. You can keep the house and almost everything in it, your car, your jewelry, everything. I'll continue to pay for medical bills. There are hefty amounts for both alimony and child support. I am only asking to have Katie three weekends a month."

She couldn't listen to anymore. "Just stop, Adam. Stop!" She got up quickly, leaving the envelope untouched on the table and fled down the cobblestone walkway. She heard his footsteps behind her.

"Please, Maggie. We have to talk about this."

She turned around and faced him, not caring this time if he saw her tears. *Why am I crying? Haven't I told Lydia hundreds of times how glad I am that our marriage is over?* Her tears and feelings made no sense to her. "I'm sorry, Adam. I don't know what's wrong with me. I knew this was coming. I guess I just didn't think it would be so soon. I thought we would all be sitting out on the deck right now enjoying a barbecue. Can't we talk later? Maybe after dinner?"

Adam looked away from her and rubbed his forehead with his right hand as he often did when he was agitated or uncomfortable. "I'm sorry. I can't stay. As I've already said. I have plans for this evening."

It suddenly became quite clear to her. She looked at him coldly. "Oh, so our divorce isn't even finalized yet and you already have someone waiting in the wings? I guess I really meant a lot to you. You bastard!" She slapped him hard across the face. She was prepared to hit him again, but he grabbed her arm.

"Stop it, Maggie. I refuse to fight with you. You will behave as an adult and not a damned child. We've both known it was over for the past nine months. I've nothing to apologize for."

"That's right. How could I forget? You're a man of impeccable principles. Everything was done by the book then? Nothing could possibly be out of order. Right, Adam? Well, I hate to break it to you, Darling, but it's immoral to date someone when you're a married man. And, as far as I know, you're still married." She pulled free from his hold on her arm, turned around, and began walking away from him.

"Maggie, please. Just look at the divorce agreement. I'm giving you everything. I wouldn't do anything to hurt you or

Katie."

She stopped and turned around abruptly. "No, Adam. Tell me then, why are you leaving us?" She turned back around and ran as hard as she could down the cobblestone walkway, hoping he would give up and leave.

He called after her. "I'm leaving the papers on the table by the pool. After I bring in Katie and Camille's belongings from this weekend, I'm leaving. Have your lawyer contact my lawyer if you have any questions. Obviously, I was mistaken when I thought I could talk to you."

She lay down on the grass beneath a Pacific Mandrone tree, folded her arms under her head, and looked up at the deep-blue sky which was marred by only a few puffy, white clouds. *How could everything look so perfect yet be so wrong?* She closed her eyes and listened as the sound of Adam's car faded in the distance. The engine noise was replaced by the gentle chirping of birds in the branches above her, the early evening choir of crickets rehearsing, and leaves rustling in the soft breeze. Everything sounded so peaceful, while a storm raged inside of her. She couldn't understand why their impending divorce was affecting her like this. *Wasn't this what I wanted all along? Why then was she fighting such a strong urge to rip the papers into a million pieces and throw them into the pool?* She didn't know the answer and soon tired of searching for it. She stood, walked back to the pool, picked up the envelope, and went back to the house.

Camille was sitting on the living room floor with her arms outstretched towards Katie who was walking unsteadily across the carpet on her chubby, little legs with a broad grin on her face. Camille smiled at Maggie when she entered the room. "Isn't Katie doing wonderfully?"

Maggie nodded. "She is doing great," she said as enthusiastically as possible, but it sounded forced, even to her own ears. She turned and walked into the kitchen. The steaks, potato salad, and strawberries were still spread across the counter. She slowly walked towards them, becoming progressively angrier with each step until she boiled over. She picked up the steaks and hurled them across the room. "Damn you, Adam!" she screamed. She threw the potato salad followed by the strawberries, until finally, out of ammunition and energy, she sat down on the kitchen floor amongst the strawberries with her back resting against the kitchen cabinets. She laid her head down on top of her arms, folded across her knees, and cried. She couldn't stop her tears and, for once, it just didn't matter. She stopped trying to fight the storm and simply let it escape.

"Mrs. Prescott, are you all right?" Camille cried, running into the kitchen with Katie in her arms.

She looked up at Camille, with tears still running down her face, and just nodded.

Camille sat down next to Maggie with Katie in her lap. She brushed through Maggie's hair with her fingers, then put her arm around her shoulders. "I'm so sorry, Mrs. Prescott. But don't worry. I'll stay right here with you."

They sat like that for some time. The storm quieted. Her tears subsided. Slowly, she got up and began picking up strawberries. Without a word, Camille joined her. Suddenly, Maggie started laughing and couldn't stop herself.

"What's so funny, Mrs. Prescott?"

"Oh, Camille, just look at what I've done. I can't believe it. You see this kind of thing in movies. But have you ever seen it in real life?"

She shook her head and joined in Maggie's laughter. "You're a bad one all right. I guess I'm going to have to supervise you more closely in the kitchen."

Camille's humorous attempts to scold her caused Maggie to laugh even harder, making it impossible to pick up the strawberries. She collapsed into a ball on the floor where, for some unknown reason, her laughter turned back to tears again.

Camille put Katie down and hugged Maggie tightly. "Hush now, Mrs. Prescott. Everything will be OK."

With Camille's comforting touch, Maggie regained control. She sat up on the floor and surveyed the kitchen. "What have I done?" She looked sorrowfully into Camille's eyes. "I'm so sorry."

"You hush now. This is nothing. I'll have it picked up in just a few minutes. Can I fix you something for dinner before I start cleaning up?"

"No, thank you. I'm not really hungry."

"All right then. Why don't you go upstairs and rest? I'll feed Katie for you and take care of everything here."

"No. It wouldn't be fair to leave you with this mess that I created." She bent down and started picking up strawberries again, until Camille gently pulled them out of her hands and touched her shoulders, pushing her gently in the direction of the stairs.

"Please, Mrs. Prescott. I think you should rest now. I can manage everything."

She smiled gratefully at Camille, then walked slowly up the stairs to her bedroom. It sickened her to see their room. She knew she couldn't sleep in that bed anymore, not the one she had shared with Adam for almost five years. She walked over to her dresser. Adam smiled back at her from their wedding portrait. She wanted to throw him across the room; instead she picked up their portrait and gently touched his face. She looked at herself smiling so radiantly and looking adoringly at him. "Oh Adam, what happened to us?" she whispered. "Where does all that love go when it dies?"

She placed their portrait face down on the top of her dresser, then changed into a nightgown. Desperately needing to talk to someone, she pulled out Kate's journal from the bottom drawer of her dresser and brought it with her to the guest room. She stretched across the bed and began reading in hopes Kate would have some answers for her. She read one of the last entries in Kate's journal, trying to memorize every word.

Forgive me my Friend

I know your eyes will follow me
If I ever leave this place.
I've held your hand

And stroked your head
Yet, the pain won't leave your face.

I've sat next to you
Dressing your wounds,
Bandaging your heart with my ears.
But you refuse to share
What's eating you
So, even I can't calm your fears.

I desperately want to help you, my friend
To forget this world where we live
Try as I may,
I know in the end
It's myself I must learn to forgive

I know I've let you down-
Let them all down
When they just needed a hand to hold
But sometimes the pain
Incapacitates me
Why at twenty-two
Have I grown so old?

So I'll look in your eyes
And utter this plea
Forgive me, my dear, dear friend
I've tried to be strong
For too damned long
But even Fire burns out in the end.

Maggie was crying uncontrollably by the time she finished reading Kate's poem the third time through. *Oh Kate, you didn't let me down. You never let any of us down. I'm the one that hurt you. It's because of me that you're dead. Oh, God! Why did you take her? I need her. I need her now.* Maggie drifted to sleep with her head resting on Kate's journal.

She was running in that dense Plieku fog. She would remember its unmistakable coldness always, how it seemed to penetrate so deeply inside of you. She knew Kate was up ahead. She recognized her tiny figure and her red hair.

"Wait for me, Kate!" She called out to her.

"I'm sorry. I can't wait, Maggie. Can't you see? There's so many of them. I have to help them!"

"Please wait, Kate. I'm coming. I'll help you." She ran harder, but couldn't reach her. She lost sight of her in that damned fog. "Kate. Where are you? Answer me! Kate!"

Finally, after minutes that seemed like years, she saw a glimpse of her red hair again. She ran towards that hair and caught her. She touched her shoulder. It felt wet. "I'm here, Kate. Let me help you."

Kate turned around to face her. Maggie screamed when she saw her face. It was smeared with blood. Her entire body was mutilated and bloodied. Maggie looked down at her own hands. They were covered with blood, too. She wiped them vigorously on her clothing, but the blood wouldn't come off. She looked up. Kate had vanished in the fog again. Maggie began to sob.

"Maggie, are you all right?"

She recognized his voice. It was Jake. "No, Jake. I'm not. Where are you? I need you."

She ran through that thick Pleiku fog calling Jake's name. She could hear his voice but she couldn't find him. She grew weary of running. Physically unable to take another step, she stopped to catch her breath. She looked at her hands again. Blood was pouring from them. She sobbed uncontrollably and screamed, "Jake! Jake! Where are you?" But there was no answer. Just as she had feared all along, she had lost both Kate and Jake in that cold Pleiku fog.

Maggie woke up on the guest room bed, crying and shaking, with her nightgown soaking wet. She turned on the bedside lamp and screamed in terror. Her hands were dripping with blood. She ran to the bathroom sink, turned on the faucet, and placed her hands under a full stream of water. Still, the blood wouldn't come off. She wrapped them in a hand towel and ran sobbing into the hall.

"Camille! Camille!" She screamed. "Please, wake up, Camille. I need your help." She sat down in the hallway and leaned against the wall, crying. She looked down at her hands. Blood was beginning to seep through the hand towel. "Oh, my God. Oh, my God."

"I'm here, Mrs. Prescott. Please, stop crying now. I'm here."

She looked up at Camille, leaning over her. "What am I going to do? My hands won't stop bleeding. Help me, please."

Camille sat on the floor next to her and gently removed the towel from her hands. 'Let's have a look now, Mrs. Prescott. See. There's no more blood."

Maggie looked down at her hands with the blood oozing from all surfaces. "What are you talking about? Are you blind? Can't you see the blood? Oh, make it stop. Make it go away!" She wrapped her hands back up in the bloodied hand towel and pressed down hard, trying desperately to stop the bleeding. She cried in terror.

"Please stop, Mrs. Prescott. There's nothing wrong with your hands. Look again."

"You're either crazy or blind, Camille! Are you just going to let me bleed to death? Please, help me. Please, please, help me." She closed her eyes and began sobbing, rocking back and forth, back and forth. Camille got up quickly and went downstairs, leaving Maggie alone and terrified.

CHAPTER SEVENTEEN
Thanh

Not able to face seeing the blood again, Maggie didn't open her eyes when Camille returned a few minutes later. Camille sat down next to her and put an arm around her. She hadn't been this frightened for years.

They sat together in silence for a long time until they heard the front door open and footsteps coming up the stairs. Maggie's body stiffened.

"It's OK, Mrs. Prescott," Camille said softly. "It's just Dr. Rothschild. I called her for you. Everything will be all right now."

They heard Lydia's quick footsteps on the stairs. She stood directly in front of Maggie, looked down at her and said firmly, "I'm here, Maggie. Please, open your eyes and look at me."

"I'm sorry, Lydia but I just can't do that. I don't want to see my awful hands again."

"Tell me about your hands. What's wrong with them?"

With her eyes still tightly closed, Maggie held up her hands. "Look at them! Can't you see all the blood? It's never been this bad before. I've tried but I just can't get the bleeding to stop. I'm afraid it will never stop. Oh, Lydia, what are we going to do?"

"I understand, Maggie. I promise I won't leave until you're OK." Lydia looked at Camille. "Camille, would you be able to find a large bath towel and bring it to me right away?" After Camille scurried off, Lydia sat down next to Maggie and spoke softly to her while stroking her hair. "It's going to be OK, Maggie. I'm going to wrap your hands in the thick bath towel so you won't be able to see the blood anymore. Is that OK with you?"

Maggie nodded. "But how are you going to make them stop bleeding? Should we go to the hospital?"

"That's always an option. But I pray we won't have to. I hope that, together, we'll be able to stop the bleeding."

Camille returned and handed the large bath towel to Lydia who gently wrapped it around Maggie's hands. "It's OK to open your eyes now, Maggie."

She slowly opened her eyes and looked down at her hands, grateful to see that, as Lydia had promised, the towel had covered the blood completely.

Lydia turned towards Camille. "I'm going to take Maggie downstairs now. I think she'll be all right now. I'll call if I need anything else."

For the first time, Maggie noticed that Camille had tears in her eyes. "Thank you for coming, Dr. Rothschild. I just didn't know what else to do. Please, help Mrs. Prescott. It breaks my heart to see her this way. I'm so afraid that I'll lose her, too."

"Don't worry, Camille," Lydia said. "It's different this time. Maggie isn't Carlos. And I've changed, too. Sometimes, I wish that I could go back in time. With everything I've learned over the years, I think I might have been able to help Carlos now."

Camille was no longer crying. She looked down intently at Lydia. "Now, Dr. Rothschild I will always be grateful for you. You did help my Carlos. My mother taught me the past is done. There's nothing any of us can do about it. It would make me happy just to know that you learned something from my Carlos's dying. Something to help Mrs. Prescott now."

Lydia stood up and hugged Camille, then released her and looked into her eyes. "I did learn something from Carlos. Many things. I promise you that I'll use that knowledge to help Maggie tonight. You get some sleep now. I know it's been hard on you."

Camille padded down the hallway to her bedroom, entered her room, and closed the door softly behind her. Lydia reached down and helped Maggie to her feet. "Come with me now, Maggie. Let's go downstairs. We have a lot of work to do."

Maggie obediently walked with Lydia down the stairs into the living room and sat on the couch.

"Shall I make us some tea?"

Maggie shook her head, holding up her hands, still covered with the large bath towel.

Lydia nodded and sat down in a beige armchair across from Maggie. "I understand. I guess it would be difficult for you to drink tea right now. Instead, why don't you close your eyes and rest your head back against the sofa. Just listen to my voice and try to relax."

Maggie did as she asked. Her voice alone, the one she had come to trust and know so well over the past nine months, soothed her tremendously.

"Concentrate on your breathing, Maggie. Breathe in and out slowly. That's right. Breathe in two, three, four. And out, two, three four. In, two, three, four. And out, two, three, four. Now, each time you breathe in, I want you to imagine that you're breathing in oxygen, relaxation, and everything good that your body needs. And each time you breathe out, think of ridding yourself of tension, fear and anything harmful to yourself. Just concentrate on your breathing. In and out. In and out. Slower, Maggie. Really relax now. With every breath out, let go of the tension in your forehead, your face, around your jaw, in your neck and shoulders, in your arms and hands, in your chest and abdomen, in your hips, in your legs and finally in your toes. All your tension is leaving your body. You're feeling much more relaxed. That's right. Good job, Maggie.

"Now, we're going to try a little imagery. Keep your eyes closed and continue to breathe in and out, slow and easy. Just listen to my words and try to picture what I'm saying. It's a warm summer day. It's not too hot. Just perfect. There's a gentle breeze. You're walking slowly in the sand, barefoot. The sand feels warm and soft against your feet. Like a gentle massage. You can hear the sound of sea gulls and the waves as they continuously, rhythmically break on the shore. Their repetitive sound soothes you. You hear the soft voices of people sunning on the beach, but they're far enough away that their voices don't detract from the peacefulness that you feel. Walking up ahead is a figure that you recognize. Your steps quicken. You need to talk to them. Who is it? Who do you need to talk to? Without opening up your eyes, answer me."

"It's Kate. I can tell by her red hair."

"Why do you want to talk to her? You've almost caught up to her. What do you want to ask her? You've reached her, Maggie. She's turning around to look at you. She's smiling. She's so happy to see you. You hug for a long time. 'I've missed you, Maggie,' she says. She's crying because she's overjoyed to see you. How do you feel, Maggie?"

Maggie was crying, making it difficult to speak, but she knew she needed to answer Lydia's questions. "I missed you, too, Kate. Why didn't you ever let me help you? Why did you suffer alone? I'm sorry you were the one to die. I know it's all my fault. It's my fault." Maggie couldn't speak through her tears any longer.

"Maggie, listen to me. Kate is waving and walking away. She says not to worry. She says that she's OK and that she's happy. Kate is happy, Maggie. Concentrate on your breathing again. In and out. In and out. That's it. Nice and easy. Now, open your eyes and pull the towel off your hands. It will be OK. The bleeding has stopped."

Maggie did as Lydia instructed. She sighed, letting go of some additional, residual tension when she saw that the bleeding had, indeed, gone away.

Lydia looked at her with concern and gently said, "I know I've promised you that I would never ask you probing questions. With that said, it's important that you are aware that, if you continue to keep so much pain locked inside of yourself, I don't think I will be able to help you much longer. I think it's time you trusted me with all your painful secrets. Do you think you might be strong enough tonight to share with me what happened to Kate in Vietnam and why you blame yourself for it?"

Maggie looked down at her hands, clenched tightly at her sides. She felt like crying again but fought off the tears. "I don't know. I just don't know if I can tell you. How can you help me? Nothing I say now can change what happened. It's done. Kate is gone and she's never coming back. No matter how much I need her to."

"You're absolutely right, Maggie. Kate can never come back, but I still think that I can help you. Haven't we been through a lot together these past few months? Can you honestly say that you haven't healed from many of your wounds? Remember the Battle of Gettysburg. You, too, can recover from anything."

Lydia walked over to her and sat beside her on the couch. She gently unclenched Maggie's right fist and placed Maggie's hand in her own. She squeezed tightly. "I'm right here with you. I'm not leaving until you've let go of some of your pain. It's suffocating you. You can't get better until you let go. I'll stay right here with you until you're ready."

They sat in silence for about five minutes. Maggie concentrated on her breathing, trying to relax as Lydia had taught her. And she knew she would tell her. Lydia was right, after all. She had helped her so much. Maggie knew she couldn't continue down this road any longer. She didn't want to live another day like today. She collected her thoughts, trying to arrange them coherently so Lydia would understand everything completely. Lydia was still sitting next to her, providing gentle comfort when Maggie finally began to speak.

... Thanksgiving of '68 was the first holiday that we actually enjoyed in Vietnam. For once, it was quiet. For once, we didn't hear the distant drone of approaching choppers. For once, we could just sit, talk, sing, hug, and drink. It was almost as if the war was on hold, allowing us catch our breaths, for the entire day. After finishing our Thanksgiving dinner, Dr. B, Kate, Jake's best friend, Spencer McGrath- the Dustoff pilot with whom he flew most often, Lance, Jake and I gathered in a small circle in the Bastille, drinking beer, listening to music and just conversing. These simple, ritualistic get-togethers comforted us more than any other therapeutic measures we had discovered in Nam. We so needed to bathe in the bonds of close friendship to recover from our personal battle scars. Our wounds were gently bandaged by the warm touch of our friends.

Dr. B pulled out his wallet. "Did I show you the latest picture of my girls?"

Dr. Bennett was the only married individual among our tightly knit circle. We adored him and cherished the pride he always displayed so unabashedly for his wife and two small daughters. While his girls were sweet, we enjoyed watching his endearing facial expressions as he showed us their photographs or shared a story about them with us. Somehow, seeing his face transform as he forgot about the war and thought about his family and home instead, brought us all hope. For a brief moment, we were all one with him in another world thousands of miles from the hellhole we presently inhabited.

"Let me see those photos," I said, reaching for his wallet. "How sweet, Dr. B. How old are they now?"

"Jennifer is six and little Vanessa just turned three. God, I miss them."

"I like this one of Jenny on her bike. She looks so tiny on that big two-wheeler."

"She was. That's from last August. We gave it to her for her fifth birthday. It had training wheels then. How she hated them! She was something else. She rode it up and down the sidewalk a few times, while Sandy and I took pictures and clapped. After just a few minutes, she stopped in front of me with such a frown on her face. 'Daddy,' she said. 'You've got to take the training wheels off.' Sandy and I laughed. We explained that she needed them to keep from falling but our words and laughter only seemed to make her angrier. 'Oh, Daddy,' she said. 'You just don't understand. I'm the wind. These training wheels are holding me back. I want to fly!'"

We all laughed.

"How adorable," Kate said. "What did you do?"

Dr. B ran his fingers through his hair and smiled. "Somehow, we managed to come to an agreement with her. Against my better judgment, we took the training wheels off the next day. Within hours, Jenny was riding unassisted, generally very fast. What a daredevil she turned into. I worry about Sandy handling her alone without me. She's such a little spitfire."

"Takes after her daddy, does she?" Kate teased.

We laughed again then sat quietly, nursing our beers.

Spence broke the silence. "Has everyone been enjoying the quiet these past few weeks? Do you think we're even averaging two evacuations per day, Jake?"

"Barely, and most of them aren't wounded. They just have that damned Hong Kong flu."

"I always thought the flu was pretty mild," Lance said. "But it's sure hitting us hard this year. Everyone seems to be catching it."

"And it's not always so benign," I said. "We have three marines in Post-op still on ventilators because of it. They're not doing well. I'm afraid they won't all make it."

"I think it's only dangerous if complicated by pneumonia," Kate said. "We don't seem to have any medication that really helps. Antibiotics don't work against it because it's a virus."

"It's interesting that you should bring that up, Kate," Dr. B said. "I don't think I ever told any of you this, but I almost went into research medicine because of my great respect for Dr. Vernon Knight at Baylor University in Texas. He was my mentor in every respect of the word. We've kept in touch over the years. In his most recent letter, he told me the National Institutes of Health established a clinical research unit at Baylor that he's responsible for. They asked him to concentrate on immunology and respiratory viral infections. He says he plans to focus a lot of his attention on the Hong Kong flu. He's really quite excited about it especially because there's a brand-new synthetic drug, Amantadine Hydrochloride, developed by DuPont a few years back. Vernon says it may prove to be the first drug with antiviral capabilities. Unfortunately, it's not available for use yet. It's still in development and trials."

"How do we treat it then?" I asked.

"Not very damned well, I'm afraid," said Dr. B. "All we have to rely on are our traditional supportive measures- aspirin for fever, bed rest, and lots of hydration. And fortunately for us, you're 100 percent on target, Fire. It's really only dangerous when complicated with pneumonia. But then, the stakes are too high for me. Flu complicated by pneumonia carries a fifty percent mortality rate, even with the best supportive treatment."

His ominous words had a strong impact on us. After a few minutes of our silence, Dr. B continued. "I strongly suspect that you're right. It's been unusually quiet because both sides are down with pretty nasty cases of influenza. I hear it's currently affecting one in five and this ratio is climbing."

We nodded in agreement with his assessment.

"On a more positive note," I said. "Phuong has finally agreed to allow us to administer polio inoculations for the kids at Hanh Phuc."

"Anybody care to place bets on that happening?" Dr. B laughed.

"Oh, come on now." I chastised the group. "She has only changed her mind five times. I'm convinced that this time is the real McCoy. Tomorrow, I'm bringing the inoculations, syringes, the whole shebang."

"OK, Maggie," Dr. B said. "I've got to admire your perseverance. If you'd like, I'll go with you tomorrow. Maybe she won't be able to refuse both of us."

"Thank you. That would be great."

Radio Telephone Operator, Private Sanchez, approached the group. "Major Kelleher, I just received a message for you," he said, handing Jake a slip of paper.

I nervously sipped my beer, watching Jake's facial expression tense as he read the message. I could feel my heart pounding in my chest. I didn't like him flying at night. Having him fly in the fog and clouds of central Vietnam's monsoon season frightened me even more. Jake stopped reading then looked up at me. Tension was drawn across his face in deeper lines than I had ever seen before.

"What's wrong, Jake?"

"It's Thanh. There's an influenza outbreak at the Leprosarium.

So far, no one has died, but a few, including Thanh, have pneumonia now. Thanh has been in and out of a coma for three days." He stood up and squeezed the paper into a tight ball in his hand. "Don't ask me why the sisters waited three days to send this message. I thought I made it clear that I wanted to be contacted about anything serious affecting Thanh."

"Can't they transfer her to a hospital?" I asked.

Jake looked angrily at me. "Don't be so naive, Maggie. She has leprosy. She's not entitled to humane treatment in this damned place!" He paused and lowered his voice. "I'm sorry for being so rough. But you know that no hospital will take her." He looked over at Spence. "If we can get the Commanding Officer's permission to fly tonight, will you come with me?"

Spence nodded. "You don't even have to ask. You know what the answer will be."

"Thank you," he said, before turning and walking out of the Bastille to call his CO.

I wanted to scream after him, "You can't fly in this!" But I knew Jake had already made up his mind. There was nothing I could say that would change it.

Fifteen minutes later, Jake came back. As I observed his facial expression, I was hopeful for the first time.

"The CO says that even I can't fly with this cloud cover." He looked at Spence. "We can leave at dawn. We have a chopper. Due to the limited number of medevacs we've been making, they can do without us for twenty-four hours."

"I'd like to come with you," I said. "I want to help. It's my day off."

"Ditto for me, Sir," Lance said.

Jake grabbed my hand and looked appreciatively in Lance's direction. "That's great. We'll pick you both up tomorrow at 0600 hours."

"We'll have some supplies for you, too," I said. "I guess I'd better check with Major Bradshaw before I promise too much." Suddenly, I remembered about the immunizations at Hanh Phuc.

As usual, Kate read my thoughts before I could even put them into words. "Don't worry about Hanh Phuc. I'll go with Dr. B tomorrow. You just take care of Thanh. I know what she means to you two." Our eyes touched for a brief moment. I knew Kate could read the gratefulness expressed in them without me having to say a word.

"How about one last dance before I go, Sweetheart?" Jake asked.

We danced together to "Will you Still Love me Tomorrow?" I pressed my body against Jake's, trying to reassure him that everything would be OK. But the tension never left his body and his fear frightened me.

At 0545 hours the next morning, Lance and I were waiting near the helipad, armed with IV solutions, tubing, catheters, portable oxygen tanks, nasal cannulas, face masks, aspirin suppositories and tablets. Monsoon season was definitely upon us; I could hear Silver long before it emerged from the thick, wet monsoon clouds. I waved to Jake and Spence in the front of Silver as Lance and I threw all our supplies in, before climbing on board ourselves. Yelling to be heard above the chopper, I introduced Lance to Frank Alstead, Jake's crew chief, in charge of the flight worthiness of the helicopter, and Toby Green, his medic. My eye caught some M-16 machine guns stowed in the back corner of the chopper. "I thought we were supposed to be unarmed," I yelled to Frank while pointing to the guns.

He grinned back at me. "Preventative medicine, Maggie. Just damned good preventative medicine."

I nodded and smiled back at him to show my comprehension, then, finding it too difficult to talk further, I put on my earplugs. We lifted off. *God, he's good, I thought.* I could see nothing except clouds so thick that I wanted to reach out and grab big pieces of fluff. Yet, surprisingly, I wasn't afraid. I knew he was the best. I felt completely safe with him, even flying in this weather.

I closed my eyes and concentrated, trying to recall everything I knew about influenza. Following an incubation period of twenty-four to forty-eight hours, flu symptoms begin to appear, including sudden onset of chills, temperatures of 101 to 104 degrees Fahrenheit, possibly even higher in children, headache, malaise, body aches, a nonproductive cough, laryngitis, conjunctivitis, and nasal congestion. These symptoms usually subsided in three to five days, but weakness may persist for weeks. Children were prone to croup, but pneumonia was, by far, the most common and most dangerous complication in both adults and children. I shuddered remembering Dr. B's words. This pneumonia had a fifty percent mortality rate, even with treatment, usually from cardiopulmonary collapse. "Please, be OK, Thanh," I prayed.

As we flew, Jake was in constant communication with Frank via headsets. "Jake wants to know if you're doing OK," Frank yelled across the chopper to me.

I gave him the thumbs up. He nodded, spoke words that I couldn't make out into his headset, then tilted his head back and laughed. I marveled that Jake was able to keep everyone so calm despite the poor visibility and his own anxiety about Thanh.

It took us a little under an hour to traverse the seventy-five miles between Pleiku and Qui Nhon. Jake gently set Silver down in front of the Leprosarium. We walked as a group to the Leprosarium with our arms brimming over with medical supplies.

Sister Simone greeted us. Her habit was drenched with sweat and her eyes lacked the luster seen during our previous visit. "Thank you for coming so quickly," she said with a weary voice. "There are so many sick now. I just don't know what to do anymore. Follow me to the chapel. That's where we have everyone."

Jake introduced the entire group to Sister Simone as she led us over to the chapel. As we entered the building, she looked apologetically at us and made a sign of the cross on her chest. "I pray that God will forgive us, but this is the largest room we have, so we decided to use it for our infirmary."

"I think it was the only sensible thing to do, Sister," I said softly.

Sister Simone smiled for just a moment before pointing out different areas in the chapel. "We've tried to isolate them by severity of symptoms. I'll show you what I mean in just a minute. First, why don't you put all your supplies on that table in the corner? That's where we kept our linens and medications. You'll notice that we have so little of either one left." She reached over and squeezed Jake's hand. "We're so grateful that you were able to bring so much with you." She made eye contact with each one of us in turn. "God bless you for coming to care for His children in their hour of need."

"Where would you recommend we start, Sister?" I asked after we had organized all the supplies on the table.

"I'll get Sister Jeanne for you. She's been in charge and can answer all your questions."

She returned in just a minute accompanied by a short, robust sister. After brief introductions, it only took Sister Jeanne a few seconds to let us know that she definitely would be in charge. She placed her hands firmly on Toby and Frank's shoulders. "We lost three during the night. I need your help burying them outside. Sister Cecile will help you. You'll find her in the back of the chapel on the right side." She released them and they obediently headed to the back of the room.

I couldn't wait any longer for Jake to ask. I had to know. "How is Thanh, Sister?"

Sister Jeanne looked into Jake's eyes. "'I'm sorry. I don't think she'll be with us much longer. She's in the back with two little boys who are also quite ill. Come. I'll take you to her."

Even exhausted, she walked so quickly that Jake and I almost had to run to keep up with her. We passed by so many pallets on the floor, all bearing Vietnamese adults or children of all ages. Their clothing was soaked with sweat as they tossed and turned on their makeshift beds. Coughing and soft moaning were almost constant.

"Sister, is there anyone who hasn't got the flu yet?" I asked.

Sister Jeanne stopped and turned to face us, brushing beads of perspiration off her forehead with the back of her hand. Her face was flushed. "Madame Kelleher, I can't answer that question. I'm afraid most of us sisters are working even though we feel poorly. Perhaps, everyone does have influenza. I don't know. No. I didn't say that correctly. I don't want to know. I just want to save as many as we possibly can."

She turned and started walking briskly again, not stopping this time until she reached the back of the room. I saw Toby and Frank to the right with Sister Cecile, but Sister Jeanne directed us to the left. She reached out for Jake's hand. "She's right behind these sheets. She's been asking for you today. Every time she wakes. I know she'll be so happy to see you; if she'll only wake up one last time for you."

I refused to believe her. "But Sister, we've brought IV fluids, portable oxygen, and medication. Perhaps, with some interventions, Thanh can still recover."

Sister Jeanne shook her head slowly. "Not this time, Madame. The Lord is calling her to join the rest of her family at His side. She has endured enough pain in this world. The poor child has suffered enough. I think she was simply waiting to say goodbye to Jake. She loves him so." With tears in her eyes, Sister Jeanne gently pulled the sheets apart to expose a small, completely enclosed area. She gestured towards the opening. "Please, go in now. I'll let you see her alone."

I followed behind Jake as he stepped through the opening in the sheets. Little Thanh's pallet was in the far-left corner. Her respirations sounded moist, even from a distance. We knelt beside her.

Jake gently stroked her hair. "Thanh, Thanh, it's me. It's Jake. I'm sorry it took so long for me to come. I'm sorry, Thanh. But I'm here now and I won't leave you."

She didn't open her eyes. Jake reached for her tiny left hand. It was clenched so tightly. He gently opened it, revealing the Wentletrap seashell. He carefully returned the seashell to her hand and closed her fingers around it, then clasped her small hand in his own large one. He turned his head towards me. "She remembered, Maggie. She still has the Wentletrap. But she feels so hot. What do you think? What can we do for her?"

I placed my stethoscope on her chest and listened. Her lungs were full. I heard crackles throughout all lobes and her airflow was so diminished. Her nailbeds were blue and the skin around her mouth and lips was dusky, as well. Her cheeks were so flushed. Judging from her skin temperature, she was probably over 105 degrees Fahrenheit. I wrapped my fingers around her right wrist to feel her radial pulse. It was rapid and thready. I noticed that her nostrils were flaring and was fairly certain I would also see her rib cage retracting with every inhalation beneath her nightgown. Her poor little body was fighting for every breath. I was so afraid for her life, but I didn't want to tell Jake. Not yet. I gently grabbed his hand.

He turned to look at me again. "Well, is there anything we can do to help her?"

"I'm not sure yet. If you're OK staying alone with her for a few minutes, I'll go speak to Sister Jeanne about what they've done for her recently."

He nodded understandingly at me, then turned back immediately to whisper to Thanh.

I found Sister Jeanne kneeling over a small boy. "Please, drink this for me," she said softly but firmly, holding a cup up to his lips, while simultaneously lifting his head and shoulders off his pallet.

"Sister Jeanne. I can see that you're quite busy, but I need to know the last time that Thanh had any medication to bring down her fever."

She gently removed her arm from the child's back, allowing him to lie back down on his pallet. She turned towards me, with tears forming in the corners of her eyes. "We ran out of aspirin on Wednesday night," she said hoarsely. "She hasn't had any since then. No one has."

I rubbed her back. "It's all right, Sister. I understand. We'll give her some now. We brought enough for everyone."

"Thank you. God bless you," she said before turning back to care for the child.

I quickly walked to the front of the chapel and gathered some supplies for Thanh, and returned to her bedside with portable oxygen, a face mask, IV supplies, and an aspirin suppository. Jake was still kneeling next to her, gently stroking her arm while she continued to fight so hard for every breath. I placed the supplies on the floor next to her pallet and knelt next to him. "She really needs to be on a ventilator," I whispered.

"I know that," he said in a low, tight voice. "What do you want me to do? You know as well as I do that the Vietnamese hospitals won't take her. We'll just have to make do with what we do have for her."

Together, we gently rolled her on her side so that I could insert the aspirin suppository. I set up the portable oxygen and handed the face mask to Jake to put on Thanh.

While Jake was gently placing the mask on her face, her eyelids fluttered open. "Jake. I knew you would come." She closed her eyes again.

Jake held her small hand in his and spoke softly. "I'm here, Thanh. I won't leave you."

I reached for her arm to start an IV line, but Jake grabbed it. "No, Maggie," he said, his voice on the verge of tears. "It will only hurt her. We both know it won't do any good. We just came too late. We came too damned late." Tears were beginning to trickle down his face but he wouldn't let go of Thanh's hand to wipe them away.

"I understand, Jake. You're right. But it's not your fault. You came as soon as you could." I rubbed his back before continuing. "I think there are still a few more things we can do to make her more comfortable. She's burning up and that makes her body require more oxygen. We could give her a sponge bath to cool her down a little more? It will take the aspirin a while to work."

Jake still couldn't speak, but he nodded his head in agreement. I ran to get a washbasin, face cloths, and a towel. When I returned, we began to sponge her off, doing one body part at a time so her temperature wouldn't fall too rapidly, possibly causing her to seize. As we were finishing sponging off her right leg, she began to stir. She opened her eyes and looked right into Jake's eyes. She looked like she wanted to speak, so he gently removed her face mask.

"Please, take me to the beach. I want to go there with you and Maggie. Like we did before." She closed her eyes and her breathing became even more irregular.

Jake gently placed the mask back on her face, then looked at me. "What do you think? What should we do?"

I scanned the confined space that had been hers for the past three days or more. "I know the sisters meant well, Jake, but the outside air with be fresher and moister, too. It can't hurt her and she wants to go. Let's wrap her in a blanket and go for it."

A few minutes later, we were walking down the steep, narrow path to the beach. Thanh, even wrapped in a heavy blanket, looked so tiny and delicate in Jake's arms. I carried a tank of portable oxygen behind them so she could breathe easier. Jake found a protected spot on the beach where the wind wouldn't hit us full force. He sat down with Thanh still cradled in his arms. I sat right next to them. She hadn't opened her eyes once during our walk down to the beach.

Jake stroked her head, running his fingers through her long, black hair. "We're on the beach now, Thanh. Just like you wanted. Maggie's here too. Just the three of us. Me and my girls. Just like in September. Maybe, in a few minutes, we'll go look for seashells again. What do you think, Thanh?" He gently removed her face mask so she could see the ocean clearly and talk to us if she wished.

Slowly, she opened her eyes. She looked around for a few minutes, gazing in the direction of the South China Sea, but it seemed so difficult for her. "Thank you, Jake." She looked at me. "Thank you, Maggie." She lifted her arm slowly and placed her hand on top of Jake's. "Chau yeu chu, chu Jake."

He gently leaned down and kissed her cheek. "Chu cung yeu Thanh. I love you, too."

She smiled up at him, and then her eyes closed again. Her respirations slowed until her chest stopped moving all together. Her left hand relaxed and the Wentletrap fell out into the sand.

Jake rocked her back and forth in his arms with tears streaming down his face, whispering to her, over and over again. "Thanh oi, chu yeu con. Chu yeu con rat nhieu..." I had never seen him suffer so. His strength had soothed me so many times. And now, when he needed me, I could think of no words to ease his pain. So, I simply tried to be there for him. I sat silently next to him, rubbing his back, holding back my own tears with all the strength I had.

After about fifteen minutes, Jake collected himself. He softly kissed Thanh's head and then turned towards me. "Please, go ask Sister Cecile for a shovel," he said hoarsely. "I want to bury her on that bluff, overlooking our beach."

The sisters joined us and said prayers over Thanh's lifeless body, before Jake gently lowered her into the earth. He carefully placed the Wentletrap into her left hand, and then covered her delicate body with dirt. He made a small cross of bamboo and pounded it into the soft dirt above her grave. I looked down at her small grave-site, then gazed out over the South China Sea. Some of the cloud cover had lifted, allowing rays of light to stream down through the remaining clouds. I felt as though Thanh was up there, watching over us from heaven.

We spent the rest of the day working with the sisters, tending to the sick. Around noontime, the two young boys, who had been in the back with Thanh, died within minutes of each other. Toby and Frank buried them. Sister Jeanne looked so exhausted, so flushed as she stood in prayer over their graves.

I wrapped my arm around her shoulders. "Why don't you rest for a few hours, Sister? We can take care of everyone for the rest of the afternoon. It may be the only break you get for a while."

She nodded. "Merci beaucoup, Madame Kelleher. I will rest for just a bit."

We spent the afternoon giving sponge baths, administering aspirin, pushing fluids by encouraging those that could to drink and providing IV fluids to those who were too weak to do so.

We set up portable oxygen for the more critically sick. By 1600 hours, the conditions at Ben San Leprosarium had improved somewhat. There were still ample supplies remaining for the sick. We said our goodbyes to the sisters. They assured us that some nurses from Qui Nhon would be coming in the morning to provide additional support. We hugged them tightly before boarding Silver. I waved goodbye to the sisters as Jake lifted off, then gazed past them, past the Leprosarium, to Thanh's tiny gravesite overlooking that vast turquoise sea. "Thanh hoi, co yeu chau" I whispered. "We'll never forget you."

...Maggie's voice faded into a silent reprieve. It had been so painful recalling Thanh's death that she couldn't tell Lydia anymore right now. She looked into Lydia's warm, understanding eyes. "I think this would be a good time for some tea." That's all she needed to say. Lydia got up quickly and went into the kitchen.

Maggie laid her head back against the back of the sofa and tried to bring Thanh back into focus. It wasn't difficult. She remembered her long, silky black hair, her luminous brown eyes, her delicate facial features, her tiny hand clenched so tightly around the Wentletrap, her solemn promises, her rare laughter, her graceful walk, her soft voice, her quiet dignity, even in death. Maggie knew she would be grateful forever for the deep, permanent imprint Thanh's fleeting dance of life had left on her heart.

CHAPTER EIGHTEEN
Hanh Phuc

Lydia and Maggie sipped their hot tea in contemplative silence. Maggie spoke first. "Do you remember how I called myself 'Humpty Dumpty' on the afternoon that we first met?"

Lydia nodded. "I remember your words quite clearly. Tell me. Do you still feel that hopeless about the possibility of recovering?"

"No. Not quite. I feel like you've patched me up, glued a lot of my shell back together. Piece by piece. I know it's been a long, difficult process." Maggie looked directly into her eyes. "Thank you. But, I'm just not sure that, even you, will be able to finish the job. I honestly don't know how to tell you the rest. I've never attempted to tell anyone before."

"Can you remember it all clearly?"

Lydia's words angered her. She thought Lydia knew her so well and yet she asked such a question. *"Can I remember it?" Can't she see? That's what's so disturbing to me. I remember it too clearly. I can't forget anything. I see their mutilated bodies every night... Every night.* Her hands began to tremble, forcing her to put her teacup down on the coffee table. She stared at the teacup for several minutes, steadying her nerves, before looking back at Lydia. "Tell me again. Tell me how reliving this nightmare with you, this nightmare that replays in my mind every day, will help me forget?"

Lydia put down her teacup, got up, walked over to the sofa and sat down next to Maggie. She reached out for Maggie's hand and clasped it in her own, then looked directly into her eyes. "I'm sorry. You misunderstood me. I can't promise that you'll ever be able to forget your nightmare. In fact, I know that you'll remember it always. I just want to help you put it in the right perspective. Sometimes, if we're too close to a picture, we see it out of focus. We must learn to take a few steps back to view it clearly. Only then, can we learn and grow from it to allow us to move past it. That's what I hope to help you do. After you share your memories with me, I want to help you put them behind you, back in the past where they belong, so that they will stop incapacitating you in the present."

"Do you really think that it's possible to do that?"

Lydia squeezed her hand firmly. "Yes. I promise I'll help you do just that. I'll help you forgive yourself and start living again. Perhaps, even tonight."

Maggie was doubtful, but something about Lydia's strong, confident presence reassured and encouraged her. Perhaps, it really would be all right. For the first time, she saw a resemblance of Lance in her. She felt safe sharing her story with Lydia. She leaned her head back against the back of the sofa, closed her eyes, and began speaking softly.

...While flying back to Pleiku in the back of the chopper with Lance, Toby, and Frank, fleeting images of Thanh and Jake together bounced through my head. Her death seemed so meaningless and my mind overflowed with 'ifs." If only we had known sooner. If only it hadn't been monsoon season. If only she didn't have leprosy. If, if, if. I hated that word almost as much as I hated Vietnam. After spending nine months in Nam, I had begun to question the existence of God almost daily. If He really existed, why would He allow this war to continue? Now, with Thanh's death, I found my faith in a Divine Being almost nullified. There weren't many threads of faith left to cling to. Why would God have a child live only to see her family burn to death in their own home, to develop leprosy, and to die, all before her ninth birthday? The only thing that made sense to me was that there was no all-powerful God. I knew such a Being would never have allowed such pain in little Thanh's life.

Then my thoughts focused on Jake. I knew that I would miss Thanh, but I also knew that her death wouldn't hurt me as deeply as it would him. I had seen them together, witnessed their joy, their close bond. Thanh had rescued him from the horror of Vietnam so many times. Now, her death would be his greatest horror of all. I tried to think of ways to comfort him, but I realized that nothing I said or did would change anything. How could I help him forget? Should I even try? I had never felt so alone or quite so helpless in my entire life. Answers had never seemed to be so beyond my grasp.

As we flew further inland, I noticed the cloud cover was dissipating rapidly. I looked around, trying to forget about Thanh's death for a few minutes. In the distance, I could see the Annamite Mountains. We were almost back to Pleiku.

Suddenly, Frank was shaking my shoulder. "Jake wants to talk to you. Put these on," he yelled, placing a headset on me.

I heard Jake's voice. "Sweetheart, please listen carefully to me. Don't panic. Just listen. I just radioed the 71st to tell them our estimated time of arrival. They told me that Kate and Dr. B haven't come back yet, although they were expected back two hours ago. They can't reach them over radio. It's probably nothing."

"Yeah, it's probably nothing," I answered while I felt as if all the life had been pulled from my body, leaving such a cold, sharp pain in my chest.

Jake continued in his calm, reassuring voice, "I told them that, because it's so clear now, we'll swing a little to the southwest before landing to check on them. We'll be there soon. Do you understand?"

"Yes." I was terrified, yet couldn't think of anything else to say. Frank yelled in my ear that I could keep the headset on. I nodded then prayed, "Please, God, if you really do exist, take care of them for me."

Within minutes, I saw Ia Drang Valley below us. I peered down intently, searching for the little path through the jungle that lead to that familiar formation of six Quonset huts. Finally, I found it. Almost instantaneously, I noticed the smoke, rising ominously from an overturned army cargo truck with a red cross painted on its side. "Oh my God, Jake!" I screamed into the headset. "Can you see it? Do you see the truck? That's Hanh Phuc. Please, land now! Land now!"

"I see it, Maggie, but we can't land until we determine if the area is still hot. We'll know soon enough. Tell everyone to strap in tight."

I motioned to everyone to strap in. We descended steeply at a very rapid rate. Receiving no enemy fire, Jake set Silver down about twenty feet from the overturned truck. I heard his voice again, "I want you to stay in the chopper, Maggie. Give the headset back to Frank. Some of us will get out and look around."

"No!" I screamed back at him. "I'm coming. You can't keep me in this chopper unless you tie me down." Jake said nothing in response. His silence infuriated me. "Did you hear me, Jake? I meant every word."

"All right. All right. But you'll carry an M-16 like the rest of us. Understood? Do you know how to use it?"

"Yeah. They showed us at Fort Sam. And don't worry. If those bastards did anything to Kate or Dr. B, I'll use it."

"OK. Just take a deep breath and relax. I'll be back there in a second."

Within a few minutes, with our flak jackets and helmets on securely, carrying our M-16's, Jake, Toby, Lance and I began walking towards the truck. Spence and Frank remained behind with the chopper to maintain its security.

"What do you think happened?" I asked quietly, as we walked alertly towards the truck, looking for any signs of movement around us.

"Looks like it took a direct hit from a grenade," Toby said.

"Why?" I asked. "Why would anyone do that? They must have seen we were trying to help their own people. Didn't they see the red cross?"

"Sure, they saw the red cross," Jake said angrily. "Just like they see them on our medevac choppers. The fact that we're on a mission of mercy doesn't mean a thing to these people. I don't understand them. I guess by their rules, during war, anybody or anything is fair game."

We walked in silence the rest of the distance to the truck, stopping just to the left of it. One military policeman (MP) must have been inside or standing near the vehicle when the grenade hit. His body had been blown apart. I forced myself not to feel anything and fought off the almost overwhelming urge to retch. A second MP was a short distance from the truck, lying face down on the ground that had been discolored by his blood.

Lance knelt down beside him and wrapped his fingers around the MP's wrist. "No pulse."

Jake turned towards me, squeezed my hand and looked deeply into my eyes. "Are you sure you still want to go with us?"

A part of me wanted to run back to the chopper and get away from there as fast as it would fly, but the urge to find Kate and Dr. B was so much stronger. I had to know. I nodded my head. "I was supposed to be here today, Jake. I should have been here. Not Kate."

"Please, don't say that, Maggie. I've already thanked God that today you were with me instead." He gave me a quick hug and stroked my face with his hand. "OK. You can come with us." He turned to the rest of the group. "Let's go. We'll put their bodies on Silver later, after we check the whole area."

We walked down the path and around the corner towards the first hut. Phuong emerged from the hut, limping, with a bruised face, holding her left arm against her chest with her right hand. I ran towards her. "Phuong! What happened to you?"

"Go away!" she said loudly in broken English. "We don't want your help. Leave now. They come back!"

Toby walked up to Phuong, carrying his first aid supplies. "Let me look at you, Phuong," he said firmly.

"No! You go now!" she screamed, backing away from him quickly. "They come back!"

"Who's coming back, Phuong?" I asked.

"Go. Please, go now!"

"We're not leaving without Kate and Dr. Bennett," I said. "You may not want our help, but I'm sure they do. Where are they?"

She pointed behind the second hut, then followed quietly behind us as we walked in that direction. As we rounded the corner of the hut, Dr. Bennett, like the MP earlier, was lying face down in the dirt in a puddle of his own blood. As in so many of my recurring nightmares, I found myself immobile, unable to do anything but stare at Dr. B, lying so still on the ground.

Lance knelt down beside him and felt for a pulse, looked up at us and shook his head, then gently rolled him over. A baby, who also had been shot, was beneath his body with Dr. B's arm still wrapped around her.

Phuong was still with us. I turned to face her. "Tell us what happened," I said firmly, angrily. She didn't answer. I walked over to her and shook her by her right shoulder. With my voice on the edge of hysteria, I yelled at her, "Where's Kate? Tell us now, Phuong!"

Jake walked over to us and pulled my arms off of Phuong's shoulder, releasing her. His actions angered me. "Damn you, Phuong! Tell us what happened. Please, tell us. Where's Kate? Where is she?"

"I tell you and you go?"

I nodded. "Yes, Phuong. If that's what you want. After you tell us, we'll go."

Phuong began speaking. It was difficult to hear her, but I strained, determined that I wouldn't miss any of her words. "You bring food. They come take. You bring clothes. They come take. You bring medicine. They come take."

"Who, Phuong? Who comes and takes everything from you?"

"You call them Viet Gong."

"You mean Viet Cong?" Jake asked. "Are you saying there are Viet Cong guerrillas around here?"

"Yes, yes, Viet Gong guerrillas. They everywhere. They always watch. They see you come. When you leave, they come. They take. They take everything. They say we be sorry if we get anything they cannot take. So, I say 'no' to shots for a long, long time. Then they no come. I think they gone. I say 'yes' to shots."

She stopped talking and tears began to fall, dampening her

face and clothes.

"Please continue," I said gently. "I know it's difficult for you to talk about it, but we have to know what happened."

She began speaking again. "Kate and Dr. Bennett come early today. They give shots. They ready to leave when we hear loud explosion. Kate say, 'Hide the children in the last hut. Hurry!' We listen to Kate. We hurry. Many Viet Gong walk through Hanh Phuc with big guns. We cannot hide from the guns. They find us. They bring us over there," she said, pointing with her finger. "They tell me I bad let children take medicine from America. They ask me where children are. I do not say. They punch me and push me down hard. I point to where children are. I get up and walk behind them."

For the first time, Phuong began to speak loudly. "They see Dr. Bennett running with baby. They shoot again and again until he fall to the ground. They laugh. Then, they find Kate. They ask again where children are. Kate say, 'Hurt me, not children. I gave the children medicine.'

"They laugh. They throw Kate to the ground. They take turns lying on Kate and hurting Kate. Kate screams. Kate cries. They cut Kate with swords. Kate stops crying. Kate lies still. Kate dead."

"Stop, Phuong," I said, in an almost whisper. "Please, don't say anymore. Just bring me to Kate. Where's Kate? Where is she, Phuong?"

"Come. I show you."

As I began to follow her, I felt a strong pull on my arm. I turned to face Jake, while angrily trying to release myself from his strong grip. "Let go of me!"

"Lance," Jake said, "please, bring Maggie back to the chopper. We'll bring back the bodies in a few minutes."

"No! I'm not a child, Jake. You can't protect me from life. I know we're at war. This war is a hideous, bloodthirsty monster that's ripping us all apart. But I can't go back to the chopper. Not without seeing her. Didn't you hear me? I was supposed to be here today. Not Kate."

"And what good will it serve for you to see her this way? It's over now, Maggie," Jake said softly. "You don't need to do this. You don't need to see her. Not like this. Let us help you." He pulled me close. "Please, I want to help you."

I pulled away from him with all my strength, but I couldn't free myself. Frustrated and angry, I looked right into his eyes and firmly said, "I will see her, Jake. You can't stop me. Don't you understand? I need to see her."

He released me but avoided my eyes. "Have it your way then. You've always been too stubborn for your own good. I give up. I can't help you if you won't let me, but we will go with you to find her and the children." Jake turned towards Phuong. "Where are the children? We must help them if they were hurt."

Phuong looked at Jake with eyes of steel. "No! You say you leave after you find Kate. We no want help. You help enough."

"Please, Phuong," Jake pleaded. "We must treat the children if they were hurt."

Phuong stood her ground. "No. I sorry. Your medicine costs too much. I cannot take anymore. Children not need help."

Jake started to say something else, but I interrupted, "Where's Kate, Phuong? I still don't see her."

Again, Phuong pointed. This time, I ran in that direction until I saw her. Kate's red hair caught my eye first, then worked as a magnet, pulling me towards her. I knelt down beside her. Kate's face was the only part of her body that hadn't been mutilated by their swords. Gently, I lifted her head and placed it in my lap. I stroked her hair and kissed her head, but I couldn't cry for her. Carefully, I removed her dog tags from around her neck, kissed them and then placed them in my right hand, closing my fingers tightly around them. I sat there with Kate's head in my lap, clutching her dog tags, with 'WHY' reverberating in my head until I thought it might explode. Suddenly, Jake's strong arms were around me, lifting me up.

"No!" I yelled. "I want to stay here with her. Don't you see? It should be me. It should be me lying here."

But Jake wouldn't put me down. He turned to Toby and

Lance. "Please, bring Kate's body. I'll take Maggie to Silver, then I'll be back to help with the others." He spoke softly as he carried me back. "I'm here with you, Maggie. Try not to think about it anymore. I won't leave you, Sweetheart."

"Shut up!" I tried to yell at him, but my voice was barely audible. "You're not listening to me. It was supposed to me. It shouldn't be Kate."

"OK, Maggie. I hear you. Let's not talk about it anymore while we go back to the chopper."

When we got back to the chopper, Jake gave me a towel to wipe Kate's blood off my hands. I wiped off her blood, then hugged the towel to my chest. Still, I couldn't cry for her. In silence, I watched them load the bodies. Not one of us spoke as we flew back to Pleiku. The English language was devoid of words to describe the intensity of emotions churning inside of us.

A cold Pleiku fog was descending upon us when we arrived back at the 71st. Still clutching Kate's dog tags and the bloodied towel, I went to our hooch to gather her personal belongings to send back to Doc and Mama O'Brien with her body. That's when I decided to open her journal. I had watched her write in it, faithfully, every night, but she had never allowed me to read her work. I sat down on her cot and slowly opened its cover. Once I began reading, I couldn't stop. It was as if she was still in the room, talking to me, only she was saying words she had never before spoken. I was seeing a side of Kate that I had never known, a side that cried for help, but had never received any. I knew I should place her journal with her body bag, but I just couldn't. I desperately needed to get to know this side of Kate. So, Kate's body was flown back to California, but her spirit remained with me."

"...That's my nightmare, Lydia. I clung to Kate's journal, reading from it daily while I finished my tour in Nam. Even now, it still comforts me. Sometimes, when I look in the mirror, it's her face I see staring back at me." Maggie held up her hands. "And her blood still covers my hands over twenty years after her death. How am I supposed to move past her senseless death?

How am I supposed to forget what they did to Dr. B, Kate and the Military Police? And what about Dr. B's girls? He loved them so much. What did they ever do to deserve losing such a beautiful father? Oh, Lydia! What happened to God? Why did He abandon us in Vietnam? Why did He let all that happen? He was supposed to take me. Not Kate."

Maggie put her face in her hands. She didn't see the point of saying anything else. She had told Lydia everything that she felt was pertinent about Kate's death. And somehow, she knew Lydia wouldn't be able to help her. She knew no one ever could.

CHAPTER NINETEEN
Kate's Journal

Why doesn't she say anything? I've just bared my soul to her, and she responds by sitting there, filling the room with this unbearable silence. Finally, unable to endure it any longer, Maggie removed her hands from her face and peeked over at Lydia. She was weeping. Somehow, beyond all comprehension, watching those tears trickling down her face, comforted Maggie. She reached for Lydia's hand and squeezed it tightly. They sat together in silence.

When Lydia was again composed, she spoke softly to her. "I've known you for about a year now, Maggie. I thought I was prepared for your story. I was wrong. I find myself searching for words, but none of them seem appropriate. I apologize for my inadequacies."

"Please, don't be sorry, Lydia. Believe it or not, I felt a strange sort of comfort as you cried. I don't know why."

"I'm glad. Perhaps, you don't feel so alone anymore," she said, giving her hand a squeeze. "There's somebody else who knows about the hell you've lived through."

"Perhaps," Maggie replied, giving her a grateful smile. "Or maybe it simply makes up for my inability to cry that day. You've cried for both of us."

"I didn't realize that you didn't cry. Have you ever truly grieved for them?"

"I don't know... Maybe... I know I often cry now, especially when I read from Kate's journal."

"I'm glad you were able to find some solace in Kate's work. Do you look at her journal frequently?"

"For years, I looked at it every night before I went to sleep. Then I met Adam, and, as you know, I hid from my past. I rarely opened her journal for those five years. Now that he's out of my daily life, I find myself needing to talk with Kate again. I've been reading her poems daily for some time now."

"May I see her journal? I think it will help me understand everything more clearly. But you don't have to show it to me if it will make you feel uncomfortable in any way."

"No. It's perfectly OK. I want you to see it. I think it's important for you to know everything."

Thirty minutes later, Lydia had thumbed through much of Kate's journal. Again, she looked as if she might cry. "Her work is beautiful you know. Kate was a gifted writer. I can see why you clung to this journal. She has a style of writing that makes you feel that you're standing right beside her, enduring everything with her."

Maggie nodded her head in agreement. "The sad thing is that, back in Nam, I never knew that she was suffering. She was a pillar of strength for me. Every time, and there were hundreds of them, that I needed someone, she was there for me. I don't understand why she never leaned on me in the same way."

"How do you feel about her not sharing her own pain with you?"

Maggie thought about Lydia's question for a few minutes while images of Kate danced through her mind. At first, she was always smiling, then slowly memories of her with an angry face, a sad expression, and finally, even with tears in her eyes, began to emerge. She was confused. Had Kate really expressed those emotions in Nam or was she just imagining them now? "I don't know. Maybe she did reach out to me, but I just didn't see it. It's my fault. I should have been there for her. I guess I feel guilty. And hurt. And even a little angry. What gave her the right to suffer alone and die without me being able to do a thing for her?"

"In Vietnam, when you were hurting, what did you do?"

"I generally didn't have to do anything. Jake or Kate or Lance always seemed to be there for me. They just knew what to do. I wouldn't have made it without them."

"Talking about it with good friends soothed you then?"

"Yes, I guess that pretty much sums it up. And sometimes, we didn't even need to talk. They were just there for me with warm embraces and caring eyes that bandaged my hurt."

"Now, I want you to think carefully about this before you answer. How did Kate deal with her pain?"

She closed her eyes and focused on Lydia's question, trying to remember just one-time Kate had come to her for support in Nam. The thousands of hours that they had spent together in the ER flowed together chaotically, and yet she couldn't recall a single instance when Kate had asked her for help. All she could remember were the countless times Kate had propped her up so she could go on. She opened her eyes and looked at Lydia. "Well, one thing I know for certain is that she didn't talk about it with me. In fact, I don't remember her asking for help from anyone." She nervously rubbed her hands together. "I'm sorry. I never really thought about it before. I don't know."

"Yes, you do," she said, holding up Kate's journal. "Yes, you really do know."

"You're suggesting that her writing helped her get by?"

Lydia nodded. "I know that it did. I've read her words. So much pain is interwoven with them that I can almost feel her soul bleeding. She didn't lean on you, Maggie, because she didn't have to. She was able to let go of her heartache through her writing. Her journal is one of the most beautiful pieces on Vietnam that I've ever read. I can see why you've read it daily for so many years." She paused before continuing. "But I think you know that it doesn't belong to you."

Suddenly feeling ashamed, Maggie looked away from her. "I know. You're absolutely right. But I'm just not sure I can give it up. I need her here with me."

"Perhaps, you can let go of it without having to give it up completely?"

Maggie looked inquisitively at her. "What are you implying? I don't understand."

"You've told me before that her father is still alive?"

Maggie nodded her head. "That's right. He still has a medical practice in San Jose."

Lydia looked into Maggie's eyes and softly said, "I think you know that her journal belongs to him. But I'm also fairly certain that her work is good enough to be published. I think the world has a right to know what you nurses endured in Vietnam. Perhaps, Kate's death wouldn't be so meaningless if you allowed her to be your voice."

Maggie thought about her proposal for a few minutes before responding. "It would be hard for me to see Doc again. I went to see him last August when Kate was just a few months old. I promised him that I would be back, but I never kept that promise."

Lydia patted her hand. "Well now, you have a very good reason to go back. You have to let go of the past and start living in the present. I'll help you learn to do that."

Suddenly, Maggie needed to get out of the room. She felt as if she were suffocating. "Let me get us some more tea," she said, getting up quickly. A few minutes later, she returned, feeling a little more relaxed. She handed a fresh cup of tea to Lydia then sat down in the armchair across from her.

"Thank you," Lydia said, taking a sip. "This is delicious."

They sipped in silence for a few minutes. Lydia gently broke into Maggie's thoughts. "I thought about Hanh Phuc while you were making our tea. I know that people can learn to move past their nightmares, but only if they're able to face their emotional responses to it. I don't think that you've accomplished this task. I noticed that one emotional theme seemed to repeat itself throughout your recounting of that day. Why do you feel it should have been you, not Kate that died?"

Maggie set her teacup down on the coffee table and tried to steady her nerves. *Hadn't Lydia been listening to her?* She could feel herself becoming so agitated that she feared she would scream at her. Somehow, she forced herself to answer the question civilly, but her voice was still tight with masked anger. "Don't you remember that I was supposed to be helping Dr. B with the immunizations that day? Kate went in my place."

"Yes, I remember," she said softly. "Do you remember that Thanh was critically ill? Thanh was dying, Maggie, and she and Jake needed you much more than the orphans did that day."

"I remember," she said angrily, "but-"

Lydia interrupted her. "There are no buts," she said firmly. "Jake and Thanh needed you. You made the only correct choice. You would have been acting selfishly, inhumanely not to go with Jake. You were obligated to go. You must stop feeling guilty about that decision. Maybe, God felt Kate's work in life was completed while yours was not."

"God!" Maggie exploded. "What does God have to do with this? There is no God! If He existed, I'm certain Kate and Dr. B would be here today."

Lydia waited for her to calm down before continuing in a gentle voice. "When did you stop believing in God?"

"I stopped believing in Him that day. I asked for His help. He gave me nothing. Nothing! How could there be a God when Thanh, Kate, and Dr. B died that way? There is no God, Lydia. He's just a magical fantasy for people to waste their prayers on."

"I hear what you're saying, but I still believe in God. I think it's too easy to blame Him whenever atrocities occur that are beyond our understanding. I've found that people are generally behind the horror. People start wars. Not God. And people have the power to stop them. He gave us free will. I'm glad that He did. But sometimes it comes with an expensive price tag. The Civil War, the Kennedy assassinations, Vietnam, Kate and Dr. B's deaths. You can blame free will for all of them. We humans are free to do good, but we are equally free to do great evil. I realize that I can't make you believe in Him. I just want to be certain that your disbelief in Him is based on concrete knowledge and logic, not on anger and hate."

Her words descended on Maggie like an inferno. She didn't even attempt to stop her rage this time. She allowed years of pent-up anger to spew out of her. She stood up and stormed around the room, speaking in a loud, uncontrolled voice. "Over the past year, I've come to love and respect you. Now, when I need you the most, you speak to me with the same cold, philosophical jargon that Adam throws at me." She stopped pacing and looked across the room to where Lydia was still seated on the sofa. "I'm sorry if my disbelief in God doesn't sound logical to you. But I don't give a damn! He doesn't exist, Lydia! Do you hear me? I don't know why I know that. But I do." She felt that familiar knot forming in her throat. She struggled to stifle her emotion. She walked across the room, stood directly in front of Lydia, and looked down defiantly into her eyes. "I saw their mutilated bodies. Do you really think God would have let them die like that?" She paused, then in an almost whisper continued, "I just know there is no God, Lydia. I am sorry if it offends you."

Lydia stood up and faced her. With a soft, gentle voice she said, "It doesn't offend me. I understand what you're saying, probably because I have been there, too. I, along with so many other Jews, lost everyone that I loved to the hands of cold, brutal hatred. Like you, I doubted God's existence for over two decades. It took me twenty-three years to find my way back to Him. I don't expect you to do it today." She grabbed Maggie firmly by both shoulders. "Look in my eyes, Maggie," she said urgently. "Look back at that scene at Hanh Phuc again. Who killed Kate? Who killed Dr. Bennett? You're right, Maggie. God didn't do it. They may have worn different uniforms, had different faces, but it was the same people who killed my family." She squeezed her shoulders tightly. "Who killed them, Maggie? Answer me! Now!"

Maggie began to sob without any hope of stopping. "Viet Cong guerrillas. Damned Viet Cong guerrillas."

Lydia hugged her tightly. "That's right, Maggie. It's not your fault. It's not God's fault. We were at war and people get killed in war. Sometimes brutally. And sometimes, it's the people that we love the most that suffer and die on us. I don't know why. All I know for sure is that it's not God's fault. He is never behind the evil and hatred. People are. Very confused people, consumed with hate."

"I know. I know. What you're saying is really true. I believe it, too. I just miss her so much. I want her to come back."

"I understand. I know you miss her, just like I miss my family. But you may be a little luckier than me." Lydia released her from her arms and reached for Kate's journal. She handed it to her. "She's right here, Maggie. She never really left you. I think you've known that all along. But she doesn't belong to you, alone. I know that you'll do the right thing."

Maggie nodded her head, then sat back down on the sofa, placing Kate's journal on her lap.

Lydia sat down next to her. "You know, I firmly believe what they say, that God never closes a door without opening a window. After you lost Kate and Dr. Bennett, who helped you get by?"

"Jake," she said without hesitation. "Jake took my beatings. He was my rock. I swore at him, slapped him, and ran away from him as hard as I could, but he stayed with me through it all. Lance was there too, but it was mostly Jake. After Kate died, all that I had left was Jake. I clung to him like a child clings to his blanket."

"But he's not here now. What happened between you two? I don't think you've told me the whole story yet. Have you?"

She shook her head. "No. I know I should tell you the rest now."

CHAPTER TWENTY
Ice

Because of Kate and Dr. Bennett's recent deaths, morale at the 71st was understandably low over the Christmas season. Most days, I felt as if my soul were one with the dismal monsoon clouds. As usual, Lance, Spence, Jake and I sat together during our holiday dinner. Despite their company, I felt incredibly lonely. After dinner, we went to the Bastille and sat together in a small circle listening to music, drinking, and talking. Kate and Dr. B's chairs were glaringly vacant. Our conversations were forced with too many gaps that lingered on uncomfortably long. In a much larger circle, across the room from us, were about a dozen nurses, medics and doctors. All of them were fairly new to the 71st, having arrived in intervals during the past few months. They were loud and boisterous and so full of life. For some unknown reason, as I observed them, I felt myself growing angrier and angrier until I had the urge to walk across the room and slap them. "Jake," I whispered. "Please, take me away from here. I can't stand it any longer."

He looked at me with such concern drawn across his face. We said our goodbyes, then walked to my room. We lay on the bed and I snuggled against him, trying to regain some strength from him.

"What's the matter, Sweetheart?" he said softly, brushing his lips against my hair.

"I don't know. Everything! Nothing feels right. I can't stand being here anymore. I hate that Bonnie has been assigned to Kate's room. I want Kate's name to still be on that door so badly. I want to sit on her cot and talk with her at the end of the day like we used to. It was hard enough to cope when I was able to do that. Now, without her, it's unbearable. I would give anything to just leave and forget this place. But where would I go? Even home won't feel right without Jason. Everybody that I love seems to be dying."

"Now, wait just a minute," Jake said, hugging me tightly. "I'm right here and you can't get rid of me. Maybe home doesn't feel right because you're imagining the wrong home. How does a home with me sound? Do you think you would be comfortable and happy living with me?" Jake paused and got down on one knee next to the bed, then reached for my hand and held it tightly. "Margaret Rose Taylor, will you marry me? Before you answer, I think it's only fair that you know that I come with a whole sack full of faults, but I love you so damned much. I've never loved anyone more. I never want to let this feeling go… I'm asking if you can be my forever." He reached into his pocket and pulled out a small, beautifully wrapped package. "Merry Christmas, Sweetheart," he whispered, handing his gift to me.

My hands were shaking, but I was still able to tear off that delicate, gold wrapping paper and open the small black-velvet box inside. Jake had given me a large solitaire diamond ring set with two delicate pearls on either side of it. I looked down into his deep-blue eyes with tears filling mine. "Oh, Jake, it's beautiful. Yes, I will marry you. And I want you to know that you will always be perfect in my eyes. I can't wait to be your wife. In some ways, I feel like I already am."

We made love, then talked and planned for hours. Finally, hope was blowing my way. My tour would be up on March 21st and Jake's on June 1st. We decided on a late September wedding in Monticello, Georgia to accommodate his large family. After all, I only had Mom left, but was hopeful that Doc and Mama O'Brien might also journey to Georgia to be a part of my wedding day. I still wanted them in my life. Jake's marriage proposal rescued me. Thinking of him, I would smile as I worked. I felt everything would be all right. I just had to make it through a few more months.

We all geared up towards the end of January, fearing another escalation of the war like the Tet Offensive of January '68. Tensions were high, but the war continued at its usual pace. We all breathed a hell of a lot easier as February dawned.

February 4, 1969. Like the typical day in winter monsoon season in Vietnam's central highlands, it was cold, damp and cloudy. Both sides must have been a little irritated, because the pace in the ER was unusually heavy. I continuously calmed and patiently taught the new nurses. Lance walked over to me as I was starting an IV line on a frightened eighteen-year-old who would need his right leg amputated. I smiled up at Lance as he approached, then continued to search for a suitable vein. "Sergeant Powers, perhaps, you can tell Private Castille what surgery will be like?" I looked into Private Castille's eyes and smiled gently. "He's a little anxious."

Lance touched my shoulder. "Maggie," he said in a voice barely above a whisper. "I don't know how to tell you this."

That's all he had to say. I knew immediately. "Where is he?"

"Spence said that he'd be landing with him in about ten minutes."

"How is he?"

"He's alive, Maggie," he said squeezing my arm. "He's alive, but Spence says he's been shot up pretty bad."

"Did you tell Captain Pollard?"

He nodded. "She knows. They're getting a spot in the OR cleared for him."

"I want to help him when they land."

"I don't think that's a good idea. Let me and Captain Pollard handle it. We'll take good care of him for you."

"But I need to be there. I want to help him."

"I heard you, Maggie. You can be there. Just let us do all the work. OK?"

I nodded. A knot was forming in my throat making it difficult to speak, but I had to know one more thing. "Do you know what happened to him?"

"No. I figured Spence would tell us when they arrived."

I nodded in agreement, then suddenly started crying and

couldn't stop.

Lance pulled me into his arms and held me tightly. "Jake will be all right, Maggie. Come on now. You know that no one can really hurt that big lug. He's not going to die on us."

After a few moments, my throat relaxed. I calmed down and pulled away from Lance. "Thank you. I'm OK now. They must need you outside and I have to finish up with Private Castille before I can join you there."

Captain Pollard and Lance were busy triaging patients when I walked outside ten minutes later. I wanted to help, but I couldn't do anything but stare at my diamond and think about Jake. I so wanted to look into his dark-blue eyes, run my fingers through his sandy hair and hear his gentle voice. But mostly, I just wanted to wrap my arms around him and protect him from this place. As the minutes passed, one memory after another rushed to the surface. I would see each one clearly, for just an instant, before it sank beneath the water again and was replaced with another unforgettable moment with Jake. I relived so many precious memories. I saw him removing his shirt the day we met, kissing my hands, chasing me on our beach in Qui Nhon, telling us the story of the Wentletrap, throwing me into the South China Sea, holding me in his arms on my birthday, spinning Thanh around with such joy in his face, giving me the book with its beautiful inscription, holding me, just holding me close so many times and sheltering me from this brutal world, laughing so boisterously with his head tipped back, and kneeling next to my cot and asking me to be his wife. I desperately needed Jake in my life. I wanted to pray, to ask God to take care of Jake for me, but I couldn't. I knew it would do no good. Instead, I alternated between staring at my diamond and up into those thick monsoon clouds.

I heard the sound of a chopper approaching. As it emerged from the clouds, I saw that familiar splash of silver and my heart began to pound in my chest. Silver's engine died almost immediately after landing. Spence jumped out to help Frank unload the wounded. They avoided all eye contact with me. Nothing scared me more than that. I walked over to Silver. One, two, three stretchers came out, and still, I didn't see Jake. Finally, Spence and Frank carried out a fourth one. Toby was leaning over it, holding up high a pint of blood that was still infusing. I could tell from their faces that it was Jake, even before they got close enough for me to see who was on the stretcher.

I walked over to them. I stared down at Jake, lying so still on the stretcher with his eyes closed and his face ashen. I reached out for his hand and held it tightly. "Jake. Jake. It's me. It's Maggie. I'm here. You made it to the 71st." He didn't respond. Not a muscle twitched, not an eyelid fluttered. A sharp pain tore through my chest making it difficult to breathe. I squeezed his hand, hoping by some miracle this would cause him to open his eyes and he would come back to us, but he didn't respond to my words or touch.

I heard Toby begin his status report, but I didn't look up. I couldn't stop studying Jake, hoping I might see some movement to give me just a spark of hope to cling to. "We've given him three liters of IV fluid. We just ran them wide open and this is the second pint of blood up on him. His pressure has been hovering around 80/45, pulse 120 and respirations 30. He's got a gunshot wound to his chest, another to his abdomen and another bullet grazed his head. Thank God, that one is just a surface wound. He lost consciousness ten minutes ago. His pupils are still equal and reactive. His breath sounds are absent on the left side. He needs a chest tube now." Toby stopped talking abruptly. I looked up momentarily and could see his eyes brimming over with tears. "Captain Pollard, if he doesn't go to the OR now, I don't think he'll make it."

"I hear you Sergeant Green. He's on his way there now. You did a great job with him. You may have saved his life."

I felt a hand on my shoulder. I turned and looked at Captain Pollard. "Lieutenant Taylor, take the rest of the day off."

"But Captain Pollard, have you seen the ER? I can't just walk out on you like this."

"Yes. Yes, you can. You need to. That's an order, Lieutenant."

Too worked up to speak, I just nodded my head gratefully.

She squeezed my shoulder firmly. "We're all praying for him. He's going to pull through, Maggie."

I wanted to believe her words, but I no longer shared her faith in prayer. I was terrified that her prayers would be as unanswered as all mine had been in this God-forsaken place.

A few minutes later, we watched the OR staff take Jake back to the OR. While he was in surgery, I waited with Spence, Toby, and Frank. We didn't say very much, but we were there for each other.

After the first hour, I turned to Spence. "Please, tell me how it happened." He looked at me with eyes still so red and swollen. I felt badly for making him talk about it, but I had to know. He looked away from me without saying anything. I grabbed his hand and held onto it tightly. "Please, Spence."

He slowly turned back to me. "You know I love him, too, Maggie. But he's so damned stubborn."

I nodded. "I know, Spence. That's why we love him so much. Isn't it?"

His lips almost turned up into a smile. "Yeah. I guess that's why."

"Thank you for bringing him so quickly, Spence."

For some reason, my words seemed to agitate him. He got up and nervously paced the hall for a few minutes. Finally, he returned and sat back down next to me. He looked directly into my eyes. "You have to know that I wanted to bring him in a lot sooner. But he wouldn't let me. He just loves them all too damned much for his own good. He'd rather die himself, than take a chance one of them might not make it." He stopped talking and began to clench and unclench his fists.

I reached over and gently stopped him from clenching his fists. I looked pleadingly into his eyes. "Spence, please, tell me."

"OK. I'll try to get through this. We got a call over the radio. Three men down, critically hurt, halfway up the mountain in the middle of the damned jungle. Really nothing out of the ordinary for us. They claimed the area was no longer hot, but then they always claimed that so we would come. Twenty minutes later, closing in on their coordinates, we had them on the radio again. I saw their red signal smoke. I pointed it out to Jake. We saw no safe place to land. The jungle foliage was so thick and the ground too steep. The area still seemed quiet so Jake decided to use the jungle penetrator. Do you know what that is?"

I shook my head. "Not really. I'm afraid I'm not very mechanically inclined. Jake has mentioned it a few times, but I've never completely understood it."

"That's all right. I'll try to explain what it is. A jungle penetrator is about three feet long and weighs only about twenty pounds. It's shaped like a bullet. We attach it to the end of our electric hoist cable. It has three paddle seats that are folded up as it descends down through the jungle canopy. Because of its streamlined shape, it can go through just about anything. That's the beauty of the beast. Once it reaches the wounded, those on the ground pull down the seats and strap the wounded in tightly. The tricky part is that you have to hold the chopper perfectly still through the whole process. Any movement on our part in the air is exaggerated tenfold for the penetrator and somebody on the ground could get seriously hurt. Do you understand so far, Maggie?"

I nodded. "I think so."

"The penetrator had almost reached the ground when all hell broke loose. Shots seemed to be exploding everywhere. I remember losing it. I told Jake that we had to get the hell out of there. I looked over at him. He'd been hit. Blood was splattered all over his shirt. I told him that I would take over, but he refused to let go of the controls. 'We almost have them. They need us,' he said. 'She'll swing too damned much for you. I can't let them get hurt any more than they already are.'"

Spence paused and rubbed tears from his eyes and face. I put my arms around his shoulders. "It's OK," I said softly.

After a few minutes, Spence pushed my arm away from his shoulder. "I knew Jake was right. I couldn't do it anywhere near as well as he could... If only I had practiced more. And Jake just wouldn't abandon them or risk hurting them. His voice stayed so calm. He held Silver so steady. I maintained radio contact with the ground and Frank and Toby in the back of the chopper. Eventually, our side returned fire so the bullets stopped tearing us up. Miraculously, the penetrator returned to us and Toby and Frank pulled the boys in. I turned to Jake to give him the thumbs up. Blood was pouring from him by that time. He looked half-dead. I called Frank up front. Somehow, I was able to take control of the chopper while Frank pulled Jake to the back. I radioed the 71st and flew here as fast as she would go." He looked me in the eyes. "That's the whole story. You can thank Toby and Frank for stabilizing him. I really thought he was gonna die on us. I don't know, Maggie. I've never been so afraid. He's got to make it."

I reached over and squeezed his hand for a moment then let go. "Thank you." Those were the only words I could offer to comfort him, for his fears mirrored my own. For an additional hour, we remained there without really speaking. We simply sat together, recalling our own private memories of Jake.

They wheeled Jake out of the OR at 2045 hours, alive but still comatose. We walked beside his stretcher to Post-op. Spence asked the OR nurse for an update. Still so fearful for his life, I wasn't sure if I wanted to hear it, but bits and pieces filtered over to me.

"Missed major organs. Had to remove his spleen. Still feeling the effects of the concussion from his gunshot wound to his head. Will have to keep his chest tube in for several days. Should pull through just fine. He's one lucky bastard. Someone must have been watching over him."

Jake was going to be OK. Overjoyed, over the moon, but still not quite believing this really could be true, I gave my tearful hugs and said my goodbyes to Spence, Frank, and Toby. With relief in their hearts and written across their faces, they finally were able to return to their base. But I couldn't leave him. I felt if I were to leave his side, then I may not find him here when I returned. I stayed with him all night, watching him rest and assisting the Post-op nurses with his care.

He started to stir around 0530 hours the next morning. At first, he just moaned softly, sporadically. A few minutes later, I thought I saw just the slightest movement of his fingers. When his entire arm moved a few moments later, I knew I had not just imagined his movements. Finally, his eyes fluttered open. He seemed disoriented, confused. His eyes darted around Post-op almost incoherently, but as soon as they found me, they stayed locked on me and he reached up urgently towards me. From his facial grimace, I could see the sudden movement caused him to experience acute, sharp pain. "Be careful, Tiger. You have to take it easy for a little while. Let me come to you." I smiled down at him and leaned over his stretcher to kiss him. I gently stroked his face. "I love you. Welcome back to us."

"I feel like shit."

I laughed. "You look like it, too." I smiled tenderly down at him, into those deep-blue eyes I cherished, the ones I knew I could never live without. "I take that back. You look beautiful, even with your collection of IV lines, drainage tubes, and dressings. Are you sure you have enough of them?" I leaned over and kissed him again, then stroked his hair. "Seriously, Sweetheart, are you comfortable? That little motion seemed to have caused you considerable pain. Can I get you some medication?"

"You're not going to hover over me, now? Are you?"

"You're damned right I am. I don't trust you a minute with these Post-op nurses. Haven't you heard the rumor? Army nurses are sleeping with everyone."

He grinned back at me. "I heard. They won't come near me though. Something about me already being taken. Can't understand where they got all this misinformation."

I waved my diamond in his face. "Does this refresh your memory? Or do I need to resort to harsher tactics?"

"What kind of screwed-up nurse are you? You mean to tell me that you would beat on a helpless patient."

I cupped his rugged face in my hands. "Oh Jake, you may be a patient, but I know you'll never be helpless, unless you continue to play hero. Promise me that you won't take chances anymore. I don't know what I would do without you. I love you." I gently kissed him. He responded to my kiss, but didn't say a thing.

Over the next few days, I continued to work my shifts in the ER, but I stole every moment I could to spend with Jake. He recovered more quickly than any of us expected. He really pushed himself. "Some people will do anything to go home first," I teased him. He didn't respond. "Jake, you are going home? I know your wounds bought you a ticket home."

"Maggie, can we talk? Come sit next to me."

I nervously sat down next to him on the bed. Afraid what I might see there, I avoided his eyes.

"I still want to marry you, Sweetheart. I just want to change the date."

"What are you talking about?!"

"Maggie, don't be angry," he pleaded. "Please, listen to me. I want you to understand. I thought I was dying up there. I really thought I was leaving you. I couldn't stand it. I prayed, Maggie... I prayed so hard. I promised God that if He just saved my life, then I would sign up for another tour. I'd save some more poor souls for Him if He would just save me for you. He kept his promise. Now, I have to keep mine."

Needing to put some distance between us, I got off his bed and stood next to it. I looked into his eyes. "Do you know how ridiculous you sound?" I said angrily, then paused to calm myself. With a much gentler voice, I continued. "I've never had a near-death experience, but I've heard that everyone prays when they're afraid they're dying. Everybody makes deathbed promises. But they don't usually keep them." I smiled at him and stroked his hair. "You've already served over here for almost two years. I'm sure God is pleased with you. I'm sure He thinks you've done your part and it's time for you to go home now... I need you to come home with me, Jake. I want to be your wife. I want to have your children."

"I want that too, Maggie. And you will get that. I still promise you forever. You just have to wait one more year for me. Just twelve more months. I have to honor my promise to God. That comes above all else."

"Jake, stop! Look at yourself. Do you realize how close you came to dying this time? Spence, Toby, Frank, me. We all were afraid you weren't going to make it."

"Yes," he said softly. "I do realize how close I came. That's my whole point. I didn't pull through on my own. God gave my life back to me. Now, I have to do my part for Him."

Tears began to form in the corners of my eyes and my throat tightened making it difficult to speak. "But Jake, I don't think you'll live through another tour. You take too many risks. You can only push your luck so far. Please, Jake. Please, don't do this to us."

"I'll be fine. I have to do this. I don't admit this to many people, but I know that I'm a damned good pilot. There are not many who can fly under the dire conditions that I can. Oh, there are a few. Major Patrick Brady for one. I was stationed with him at the 54th. Did you know he received the Medal of Honor last January? You talk about using up luck, but I don't believe it can happen for a minute. Pat Brady evacuated over fifty wounded in a single day. One very dismal, cloudy day. He went through three helicopters doing it, too. Think about it, Maggie. They shot him down three times and he still wouldn't abandon his mission. He lived up to our Dustoff doctrine, 'No compromise. No rationalization. No hesitation. Fly the mission. Now...' I must live up to it, too."

Seeing the sheer determination in his eyes, I realized that nothing I could say would change his mind. Jake was going to sign up for another tour. Slowly, painfully, I removed his engagement ring from my left hand. I handed it back to him.

He grabbed my wrist. "What are you doing, Maggie. I don't want the damned ring. I want you." He looked as if he might start crying. "I love you. Don't do this to us."

"I love you, too, Jake. Somehow, I know that I always will... But I can't keep your ring. I've been here almost a year now. I know how fragile our lives really are. But I also know that you don't see that. You lie here denying the reality, the finality of death while recovering from injuries that could have just as easily killed you. You're like a moth, Jake, dancing so beautifully above the flame. Perhaps, you think because you dance so well that the flame can't hurt you. Or maybe, its inherent danger tantalizes you. I don't know why. And it doesn't really matter. What is significant to me is that, each day, you fly just a little closer. And I know, without doubt, one day, if you remain here in Vietnam, that flame will consume you. Even if you refuse to admit it to yourself."

Sobbing uncontrollably, I pulled my arm away from him. "Oh, Jake, I've seen too many people that I love die. I won't watch you die, too!" I ran out of Post-Op without looking back, to the sound of him calling my name.

I know that Jake eventually recovered and went back to active duty. He reached out to me so many times, but I refused to see him. Spence was my link to Jake. He stayed in contact with me. He told me that he had tried to talk Jake out of signing up for another tour, but his efforts were as futile as mine had been. Spence said that he understood why I couldn't wait for Jake. For some reason, I felt better knowing that at least he understood.

I said goodbye to Lance less than one week later. After completing his second tour in Vietnam, he was going stateside. I had never been so completely isolated in my entire life. I worked my shifts, then walked back to my hooch alone with my memories and Kate's journal. Nothing affected me. No matter how young they seemed. No matter how gruesome their injuries were. No matter how many came through our doors. I didn't flinch. I was numb to it all. That's when they started calling me "Ice." Not to my face, of course. But I heard them. And yet, it didn't bother me. Nothing did anymore.

"...That's about it. I guess you've heard it all now, Lydia."

Lydia looked intently at her. "Thank you for having faith in me and trusting me with so much of your past, Maggie. I know it's been a difficult night for you."

Maggie nodded. "I got through it. Somehow. Actually, it feels good to have shared with you."

"Good," she said, smiling for just a moment before becoming serious again. "We still have a little unfinished work. Two questions come to mind. The first is 'Why do you think they chose to call you 'Ice?' Why not robot? Or Stone?"

Her question surprised Maggie. It seemed so irrelevant. "I don't know."

Lydia's face became quite animated and excited. "Robot. Stone. Ice. They all conjure up the same image when applied to a person. Or don't they?"

"I guess so. I picture someone walking through life without feeling a thing. Making motions, but without heart or feeling. Pretty much how I was my last weeks in Nam."

"No, Maggie! They're not the same. I think you've missed something important." She leaned a little closer to Maggie. "A robot will always be a robot and stone will always be stone. But ice, Maggie, ice melts. Just like you have over the years. You can feel again; even if you don't want to because it hurts so much. Can't you? You've come a long way in just the past few hours. You're almost there."

"I don't understand, Lydia. Where do you want me to go?"

Lydia smiled at her. "Ah. You've asked the other question for me." She touched Kate's journal in Maggie's lap. "I think you already know one journey you have to make. With time and contemplation, I'm sure you'll think of the other. In my office, months ago, you talked about crossing a bridge. It's time for you to cross it. It's the only way that you'll completely heal. You'll always mourn Jason, Kate, Thanh, Dr. Bennett and all those you lost in Vietnam, but you must stop mourning for those you may not have lost." She stood. "Maggie, I think it's time for me to go home. You have my cell phone number. Please, don't hesitate to call me any time of the day or night if you need me." She smiled down at her. "Don't get up. I'll walk myself out and leave you to your thoughts."

Maggie listened to her footsteps on the hardwood floors, the front door open and softly close, and her car fade into the night. She didn't have to think for long. She knew where Lydia wanted her to go. Perhaps, she was right, after all. Maybe, it was the only way she could recover completely.

CHAPTER TWENTY-ONE
Letting Go

Tearfully, Maggie read through Kate's journal, one last time, before turning off her bedside lamp to sleep. She felt as if she were about to give away a part of herself. While reading Kate's journal had comforted her for years, sometimes, simply touching the words, feeling the actual paper upon which Kate had written, consoled her as well. But she knew Lydia was right. She knew that it was time to let go of her. She deeply regretted that she was returning Kate's work too late for Mama O'Brien to cherish and was anxious about what response Doc would have to the very belated gift. She slept fitfully, awakening repeatedly throughout the night and finding it more difficult each time that she awoke to return to sleep.

The next morning, as she drove along the coast towards San Jose, she alternated between stealing glances at the breathtaking California coastline and gazing down at Kate's journal, lying beside her on the front seat. Less than forty-five minutes after leaving her home in Carmel Valley, she drove through the black wrought-iron gates of St. John's Cemetery. Doc had chosen to meet here. She was grateful he had. Many times, throughout the past year, she had wanted to visit her gravesite, but had felt too guilty to call Doc just to ask for directions.

Just as Doc had described to her on the phone yesterday, up ahead, on her left, she could see a much narrower road. She slowly turned on to it. Rows of gravesites were on either side of her car now, with tall pine trees in the background. Black wrought-iron benches were positioned every thirty feet or so, serenely dividing each section of gravestones. Abruptly, the line of firs to her left ended and the whole world seemed to open up before her. Far below, jagged bronze-colored cliffs jutted out into the deep-blue waters of the Pacific, almost becoming one with that ocean. The Pacific was alive, a brilliant multi-colored monster, angrily spewing out frothy, white foam. Then, just as suddenly as the fir trees had stopped, the tall, silent line of green sentinels watching over the cemetery began again.

Doc's white Continental was parked beneath the first tree of this new formation. She parked her car behind his, then slowly got out, tucking Kate's journal safely into her large, black-leather Coach handbag and slinging it across her right shoulder. Doc was kneeling on the grass in front of three small, white marble crosses. He started to rise when he heard her footsteps on the gravel walkway.

"It's all right, Doc," she called out. "Don't get up. Stay where you are. I'll join you." She knelt beside him and stared at Kate's headstone. "Doc," she said softly. "May I touch her cross?"

He nodded. "Yes. I often do myself."

Slowly she moved her fingers over each letter of her name, thinking about her the entire time. Happy childhood memories mixed with the more painful memories of her in Nam. She felt so alone, so sad. Finally, she dropped her hand to her side and stared down at the vibrant red and yellow flowers on their graves. "The flowers are beautiful, Doc."

"Um," he growled. "Mama used to plant such delicate pastel ones for Kate. I tried to imitate her the first Memorial Day after she left me. The damned things wouldn't take for me. I couldn't stand it. My girls were dead and the damned flowers were dying, too. I went to a local greenhouse. 'Give me something pretty that will grow well despite my foolish attempts at gardening,' I told him. He gave me marigolds and geraniums, telling me they were extremely hardy and would bloom all summer long. It's been marigolds and geraniums ever since." He slowly stood up. "Now, if you don't object, this old man is going to sit on that bench for a few minutes. My knees just can't take much abuse these days."

She quickly stood up beside him, interlocking her arm with his. They walked in silence to the bench. *Perhaps, he's waiting for an explanation for my prolonged absence she thought. He certainly deserves it.* They sat down on the bench in the shade and looked out over the Pacific. "It's really quite something," she said.

Doc nodded. "I remember how you and Kate loved to go to the beach. When I'm sitting here, I often think of you two racing around, kicking up the sand, and splashing in those waves. I don't know how you could even get into that cold water. The northern Pacific is pretty to look at, but she's a bear to get in."

Maggie laughed. "I agree with you now. But back then... Back then, we could do anything."

He smiled and grabbed her hand and squeezed it. "I'm glad you came back. Again. I missed you." He looked right into her eyes. "You know Mama and I loved you, Maggie. Our other daughter. That's what we called you."

She smiled. "I certainly stayed in your home enough to earn that name."

They both laughed. "Seriously, Maggie, it was much more than that. Kate loved you. It didn't take us long to see why." His eyes saddened. "You're not going to stay away for another year now?"

"No, I'm not. I promise. Really, there's no good excuse for this past year. A lot has happened in my life. Still, none of it excuses me for forgetting you like this. I'm truly sorry, Doc."

He patted her hand again. "There now. That's enough. Tell me what's wrong. I can see something is bothering you."

She gazed back out over the Pacific. So often in her life, she had felt as mixed up as that ocean. There were so many emotions churning and spinning around inside of her, at times, she felt as if she would explode. She turned back to Doc. "Adam left me this year."

"No! Why? If you don't mind my asking?"

"Because he found out that I had served in Vietnam." She held up her hand. "Wait. Before you say anything, let me explain. It wasn't all his fault. I never told him about Nam. I kept so much from him. I was afraid to tell him who I really was."

"You're not making any sense, Maggie. There's nothing wrong with whom you really are. He must have been a fool to leave you."

"There's more to it than I want to get into now. I guess what I'm trying to say, quite badly I'm afraid, is that it's OK that he's left me. It just took me a few nervous breakdowns to realize it. I've been seeing a terrific psychologist, Dr. Lydia Rothschild. Have you heard of her?"

Doc shook his head. "Can't say that I have, but I'd be happy to check her out for you."

"No, Doc," she said, smiling at him. "That's not necessary. I already know that she's one of the best, especially for Post-traumatic stress disorder. It's because of her that I'm sitting with you now."

"Maybe, I should look this lady up, after all," Doc laughed. "I like her already."

She sighed and looked back over the Pacific. She opened her handbag and pulled Kate's journal out. She hugged it to her chest, one last time, before turning back to Doc and handing it to him. "Doc," she said quietly, "This belongs to you. It's Kate's. She wrote it in Vietnam. I'm so sorry. I know that I should have given it to you years ago. But I couldn't." Tears were forming in the corners of her eyes. She brushed them away before continuing. "It may hurt you to read her words, but they're real. She describes what most of us went through. I think you have a right to know." She stood up. "Why don't you look at it alone, for a while? Maybe then you'll understand why I couldn't let go of it. Take your time. Don't worry about me. I'll take a walk."

Twenty minutes later, walking back towards his bench, she watched him. Head bent over Kate's journal, he wiped at his eyes every few seconds. *I'm sorry, Doc, she thought. But you had to know.* She sat back down next to him on the bench and put her arm around his shoulders.

"Oh, Maggie," he said hoarsely. "Did Kate really go through this?"

"Yes. We all did. She speaks for us all. I wasn't sure if I should give her journal to you. I didn't want to hurt you."

He looked at her with tears in his eyes. "I'm so grateful that you did. I want to know everything that she went through. I want to know it all."

She patted her journal. "It's all here, Doc. Right here."

He seemed quite agitated and his eyes told her that he wanted to ask her something else. She squeezed his hand. "I'm right here. What is it?"

He looked directly at her with his red, swollen eyes and tears trickling down his cheeks. "Were you there? Were you there when they killed my baby?"

She looked away from him. Her throat tightened. "No. I'm sorry. I wasn't with her." She looked back at him, with tears forming in her own eyes now. "But I was the one who found her body. I held her and rocked her in my arms until they took her away from me. I wish I had been there. But I wasn't. I wasn't with her when she needed me the most."

She felt Doc's arms around her. They hugged each other tightly, both trying to rid themselves of so much pain. Finally, they separated, allowing their arms to fall uselessly to their sides.

Doc read for a few more minutes, then closed her journal. "I think that's enough for today." He looked down at Kate's journal then back at Maggie. "I'm glad you weren't with her when she died because, if you were, you may not be sitting with me today. I am grateful to still have you."

She nodded her head. "You may be right. It took me so long to admit it, but I am grateful I didn't die with her, too. I want to apologize again. I know that this must all have been quite a shock for you today." She looked back over the ocean, gathering her thoughts for a few moments before continuing. "I've made reservations for Washington D.C. I'm flying out to say goodbye to Kate, among other things. Would you like to come with me?"

Doc shook his head. "No. I went there the year they put up that damned wall. I hated it. So many names... Too many names. I don't like to think of her there. I don't want to remember her as just one among thousands. She was too special. She's here, Maggie. Right here with Mama and me. And the ocean she loved so much."

"I understand." And she really did. She kissed him softly on the cheek and gave him a warm, loving hug. "Bye Doc. I'll call you when I get back home from Washington."

Doc waved his hand after her. "Go on then. You'll call me when you remember this old man again."

She smiled sincerely at him. "I mean it this time. You can expect a call from me soon after I step back off that plane. I want you to be in my life again. I missed you."

Maggie called Lydia soon after she got back home from her visit with Doc. It was important that she knew Kate's journal was finally where it belonged. She also wanted Lydia to know about her early morning flight to Washington D.C. But mostly, she just wanted to hear Lydia's voice. Lydia was her anchor. Lydia had kept her safe in the harbor for over a year now. They had weathered more storms than she cared to remember. But she knew it was time to pull up the anchor and sail out of the harbor alone.

She dialed Lydia's cell number and smiled when she heard Lydia's voice on the line. "Hello."

"Hello, Lydia. It's Maggie." ...

"Yes, I gave her journal to him." ...

"I don't know. I guess I feel sad and lonely, but mostly relieved. Like it was something I should have done years ago." ...

"I guess he took it OK. He cried but then thanked me. I'm going to keep in touch with him to make sure he's all right." ...

"Before you hang up, I want to tell you something important. I'm leaving for Washington D.C. in less than twelve hours. I thought perhaps that was the other destination you had in mind for me." ...

"I want to say goodbye to Kate, Dr. Bennett, Chris, DJ and so many others. I'm going to look for Jake's name, too. I know it's there. I guess it's time that I faced the truth." ...

"No, you don't have to come with me. Thank you for the offer, but I think I should do this myself." ...

"That's right. Katie will be fine. Adam's coming for her and Camille in just a few hours. I guess I have no excuses not to go. It's time." ...

"Let me see now. My flight lands back in San Jose at noon on Thursday." ...

"Are you sure? You know you don't have to pick me up." ...

"OK. That would be great. See you at noon on Thursday." ...

Maggie placed the phone back on its cradle, then stretched across the bed and closed her eyes. She sighed. She knew it would be difficult to make this journey alone, but, thanks to Lydia, she also knew she was strong enough to do it. She owed so much to that remarkable woman.

CHAPTER TWENTY-TWO
The Wall

Maggie gazed into the still waters of the Reflecting Pool, marveling at the perfect image of that slender column of white visible on its surface. Just one amongst hundreds of tourists, she moved considerably slower than most, for she was in no hurry to reach her destination. She knew the waters would take her there... eventually. A few ducks floated gracefully by. A group of children, standing a few feet from her, began to throw bread crumbs to them. They laughed and their voices rose excitedly as the ducks squawked and raced towards the bread crumbs. She smiled, recalling Jason and herself so long ago. She sighed, then turned around, crossed the street, and walked up the clean, white steps of the Lincoln Memorial.

Its whiteness struck her. That color seemed to symbolize Washington, itself. All its monuments were white and clean and beautiful. She touched one of the columns, leaving her hand there for a few seconds, enjoying its coolness. Finally, she walked over and stood directly beneath the statue of President Lincoln. She stared up at him. His compassion was embedded so deeply into that marble that she felt he could help her even now. *Speak to me, she thought. You lived with such pain and suffering, yet were able to see us through to the end. How? Despite the hate, pain, and death threatening to tear us apart, you, somehow, held us together. How did you do it?*

She waited patiently. She hoped, but silence was her only answer. As she turned to walk back down the stairs, his words, engraved into the sidewalls of the memorial caught her eye. She stood still and read them slowly. Certain phrases reached out and grabbed her. "For those that gave their lives that the nation might live…It is for us the living rather to be dedicated here to the unfinished work…That from these honored dead we take increased devotion to that cause for which they gave the last full measure of devotion…That we here highly resolve that these dead shall not have died in vain." She realized that she was mistaken. There was no silence here.

"Thank you," she whispered, peering up at him again, before turning and walking back down the steps of his monument. She crossed the street again, walked past the Reflecting Pool, and headed left in the direction of the Vietnam Memorial. Suddenly, surrounded by people, she felt so alone. She stopped, opened up her purse, and removed Kate's dog tags. She ran her finger over her name. "Help me, Kate," she whispered. She closed her fingers around her dog tag and squeezed tightly. With renewed strength, she began walking towards her final destination.

She rounded the corner, then stopped again. She could see it now. *Black. It was so black. Everything in Washington was white except this monument. Why? And it was so immense, so much bigger than she had imagined it would be. Both ends of the wall were an identical height, growing symmetrically taller as they approached the center, where the wall achieved its greatest height. The perfect symmetry of the wall unnerved her. She wanted to scream, "No! You're wrong! There is no such perfection, no such balance in death."*

Slowly, she walked forward a few more steps until she could see the names etched into that black granite. So many names. Her throat tightened. For each name on that wall, she pictured a soldier's body on a stretcher, so many broken boys in pain, lying across the floor of their ER. She began to cry, but for once, she didn't try to stop herself. Finally, she could cry freely for them and for herself. They had given everything, but she, too, had lost so much. Suddenly, she understood the black. Black was the only color this monument could be.

Still choked up, she walked even closer and began to move along the walkway in front of the wall. Every few steps, she would reach out and touch a Jacob or William. Kevin or Samuel.

Having known only a few of them, she mourned for them all, not just for their loss of life, but for her country's loss of so many young souls. After traversing the entire length of the wall, she walked away from it and stood still to observe from a distance. She squeezed Kate's dog tags tightly and remembered Vietnam. Fleeting images of Jake, Kate, Dr. B, Thanh, Chris, DJ and hundreds of others that she had watched die in that ER in Pleiku, thousands of miles from home, raced chaotically through her mind until she couldn't bear it any longer. She turned her back to that wall and walked back to her hotel, without accomplishing anything that she had intended to do.

Early the next morning, she returned to the Vietnam Memorial. Yesterday, it had affected her so deeply that she had only been able to see the wall, itself. Today, seeing how many others had journeyed to this wall overwhelmed her. She stood back and watched them. Many slowly walked its entire length, in silent respect for the dead, and then chose a spot to stand and quietly reflect, just as she had done yesterday. Then she noticed that some didn't understand the memorial at all. They talked in loud, excited voices and their cameras clicked until they, too, began to feel the enormous power of this black wall. Soon their voices faded and their cameras ceased. Finally, for the first time, she noticed them. They reacted much differently to the simplistic beauty of this wall. They reached out with tears in their eyes and longingly fingered each letter of the names of their sons or brothers, husbands or fathers, friends or lovers. They tenderly placed roses beneath their loved ones' names or slid letters of love and anguish beneath the crevices of the wall. She knew that they realized that their letters would never be answered, but perhaps, through the process of writing them, they had begun to heal from the wounds that had penetrated so deeply into the fabric of their souls. She prayed that a blanket of peace would begin to wrap around their souls as she watched their tears fall for their beloved who had given up their lives for our country in that tiny, misunderstood land so far from here.

Somehow, through watching them, her feelings of isolation

began to recede. At last, she knew that she was not alone. Through them, she found the courage to do some of what she had come here to accomplish. She slowly, tentatively walked towards the National Park volunteer. "Excuse me. I know some names." She pointed to the wall. "Some names. Somewhere on this wall..." Her voice drifted off. Unable to continue, she turned to walk away.

Suddenly, she felt a hand on her shoulder. "It's all right," he said softly. "Just tell me their names, one at a time. I'll help you find them all. I promise."

She turned and looked gratefully into his warm, brown eyes. "Thank you," she said hoarsely. "Katelyn. Katelyn Marie O'Brien."

As she watched him look through that massive book of names so quickly, she realized that he had worked here for some time. He smiled and looked up at her. "I know where your Katelyn is now. Come. Follow me. I'll show you." He stopped in front of a panel, then reached up and touched her name. Seeing Kate's name on that black granite hurt... It hurt so much. She began to cry uncontrollably. He put one of his arms around her shoulders and she leaned her head on him for just a few minutes, until she had the strength to pull herself away from him.

He looked directly into her moist eyes and softly said, "Can I help you with a rubbing of her name? You can take it home with you."

She nodded. "Thank you. I'd like that very much."

He returned a few minutes later with a small, rectangular piece of white paper and a large, black crayon. He placed the paper over Kate's name and began to rub the black crayon back and forth, back and forth.

Suddenly, she had to do the rubbing herself. "Please," she said urgently. "May I take over?"

He nodded and placed the crayon firmly in her hand. "I'll wait while you finish, then we'll find the others." Thirty minutes later, she had completed rubbings of Kate, Dr. Bennett, Chris and DJ's names. "Do you have any more names for me to find?"

She began to sweat and could feel her heart pounding. She looked into his eyes again, hoping that some of his warmth and strength would help her cross that final bridge. "Yes. There's one more. John." She stopped talking and looked back towards that enormous black wall.

"I'm sorry, Ma'am," he said gently. "But I need John's full name or I won't be able to find him for you. There's so many you know, over fifty-eight thousand in all. Do you remember John's last name?"

She nodded her head but still couldn't speak. He allowed her time to regain control of her emotions. "Never mind. I can't do anymore today."

"Are you sure, Ma'am? I'd be happy to help you find your John."

"No. I'm sure." She stretched out her hand to him. They shook hands firmly. "Thank you. I'll always remember what you did for me today." She walked away from him, back towards her hotel, hugging her rubbings tightly against her chest, fighting off tears.

She returned to the Vietnam Memorial just before dusk. It would be her last opportunity to learn if Jake had survived the war, for her flight back home took off early the next morning. The crowds around the wall had thinned considerably. Again, she watched from a distance. She noticed a man with sandy colored hair, sitting in a wheelchair with his back to her. His build was similar to Jake's and his hair the exact color and style. He just sat there, staring at the wall. Could it be him? She began to walk towards the wheelchair. The closer she got to him, the more he seemed to resemble Jake, until she was certain that it was him. Her heart raced and her hands began to shake. She stopped directly behind his wheelchair. "Jake," she said softly. He didn't move. "Jake," she called out to him a little louder.

He turned his wheelchair around and faced her. "Excuse me, Ma'am. Can I help you?"

It wasn't Jake. She started to cry.

He reached out his hand to her and she clung to it. "You were there, too?"

She nodded, still unable to speak.

"I was there from April '69 until May '70. Sometimes, I swear I'm still there. Or maybe, I just wish that I were still there so that I could do it again. Only right this time. Maybe then, I would be staring at them instead of their names on this damned wall."

She felt his pain. She knew it well. "No!" she said loudly. Then she softened her voice. "Please, stop thinking that way. Someone once told me that we're not gods. We're only humans and we can't make perfect decisions." She touched his shoulder. "I'm certain that you did your best. That's all we could do. Remember them, but don't hate yourself. It's been so long now. You... Me... We have to start living again."

She thought she saw a few tears in the corners of his eyes. "Thank you," he said with a rasp in his voice. He turned his chair back around and they stared at the wall together, in silence for a few minutes.

"Where were you stationed?" he asked.

"I was at the 71st Evacuation Hospital in Pleiku."

"You were a nurse then?"

"Yes. And you?"

He smiled. "I was a Dustoff pilot. But never up north like you. Mostly down south in the Mekong Delta region."

"Did you know Major Kelleher?"

"Sure! Hell, didn't everyone know the Lone Ranger? I'm not sure all the tales about him were true. It doesn't really matter now. I think we just needed a few real heroes to hang on to, to help us get by."

She nodded. "He really was a hero, wasn't he? ... You wouldn't know what happened to him? Sounds like you were in the same area around the same time."

"No. Last I heard his chopper went down in Cambodia."

"Cambodia?"

"That's right. Cambodia. You know, where our troops never were supposed to be. Strange how many we had to medevac out of there."

She hesitated for a few moments before asking, "Did you hear if he survived that crash?"

"I honestly don't really know. There were so many stories circulating. Some say he and his whole crew died. They swore his chopper was engulfed in flames within seconds."

"No! That can't be true."

"I don't know if I believe it myself. Probably because there's just as many that claimed that story was bullshit. They said that Lone Ranger and his crew had gotten medevacced out of Cambodia. But then again, there's some who are just as positive that he and his crew are missing in action, taken as P.O.W.'s."

"What do you believe?" she said, almost inaudibly, so afraid to hear his answer.

"To be honest, I don't know what to believe. But it would be easy to find out something about him. We can ask the Park Ranger if Major Kelleher's name is on this wall." He started to wheel his chair in that direction.

"No!" she said vehemently, grabbing his wheelchair with both hands and pulling back to impede all its forward motion.

He turned his chair back towards her, his countenance changing from surprise to sadness when he saw the tears in her eyes. "I understand," he said, reaching up and taking hold of her hand. He squeezed gently before letting it go. "There's a few names I haven't been able to look up myself."

An awkward silence lengthened between the two of them. Finally, she said, "It's been good talking with you, but it's getting late. I really should be going now." They shook hands.

"Good luck to you," he said.

"You too," she said smiling at him. "By the way, did you know that from the back you look just like Major Kelleher?"

"No. Now ain't that something." He smiled for just a moment before a familiar sadness returned to his face.

As he turned his wheelchair around to face the wall again, she walked slowly away from him, back to her hotel for the last time. She would fly back to California in the morning with her most important question still unanswered. She knew that

Lydia would chastise her in her own quiet way, but she didn't care. She knew that she had made the right decision. His name was the only rubbing that she would never be able to do.

CHAPTER TWENTY-THREE
Crossing the Golden Gate Bridge

As Maggie walked down the jetway pulling her small suitcase behind her with the rest of the passengers deplaning from flight 1207, she scanned the crowd up ahead searching for Lydia. It only took a few moments to locate her, her island of safety, in the middle of that noisy, bustling crowd. Lydia smiled at her as she approached. Maggie was reassured when she saw her endearing, wrinkled outfit and her loose, dangling wisps of gray, but it was Lydia's face that warmed her spirits the most. Upon seeing it, she knew she was home at last.

Lydia stretched up to give Maggie a quick kiss on the cheek, then wrapped her arms around her in a warm embrace. Finally, she let go of her. "Welcome home, Maggie," she said, handing her a half-dozen long-stemmed yellow roses. "I hope you had a good trip."

"Thank you, Lydia. I did," she said, simultaneously embarrassed and pleased by her gesture of friendship. "They're beautiful, but you didn't have to give me these. Just being here for me was more than enough."

"Ah, but I did have to give them to you. You've returned from, what I believe to be, the most difficult journey of your life." She smiled up at her. "I wanted you to know that you have arrived home safely and that a friend is here for you. And nothing speaks the words of friendship more fluently than the yellow rose."

"Thank you, again. I don't know how you do it, but you always seem to know what to say, what to do. I'm grateful for your special gift."

"That's enough flattery for one day," she said brusquely, with just the hint of a blush on her face. "It will get you nowhere. Shall we go find my car now?"

Maggie was touched by Lydia's embarrassment, feeling just a little closer to her upon realizing that she, too, was only human after all. They walked out of the terminal together and headed for the short-term parking garage. It didn't surprise her that Lydia hadn't yet asked her about her trip. She never failed to keep her promise of not asking grueling, personal questions.

Lydia found a spot for Maggie's suitcase in the cluttered trunk of her '69 black Mustang. *A classic just like her, Maggie thought.* As they headed towards Salinas, they filled her Mustang with idle conversation. Maggie told her about Washington's suffocating humidity, the crowds around the monuments, and the irritating, little boy who sat behind her on the plane, kicking her seat all the way across the country. She laughed at all the right places as Maggie shared her trivial stories and still didn't press Maggie for any significant details. About halfway home, Maggie turned towards her. 'Thank you, Lydia," she said softly, "for not asking."

Lydia glanced at her for a brief moment before looking back at that traffic. "You're very welcome. Where can I take you now?"

"I don't know. I guess home."

"Are you sure?"

Maggie thought about her question for a minute. Suddenly, she knew where she wanted to go. "Can we go to your office instead?"

Maggie walked around Lydia's waiting room, studying those Civil War faces. "You know, I saw them in D.C.," she said quietly. "For some reason, I missed them the first day, but I saw them everywhere the second time I visited the wall." She stopped just below a soldier's face that appeared to be in more intense pain than the others. "They looked just like him."

"Why do you think you missed them the first day?"

"I don't know. Wait! That's not true. I do know. I didn't see them because I couldn't concentrate on anything but that wall. That immense black wall. Have you ever seen it, Lydia?"

She nodded. "A few times. Each time, initially, it overwhelms me. Just as it did you. But after a few minutes, I begin to feel a strange kind of peace or comfort. Something I've never felt anywhere but there."

"I know what you're talking about. I felt it, too. But it wasn't until I focused upon the actual people at the wall that I received an even more tangible comfort, along with the courage to do some of what I went there to do."

They stopped talking. Lydia didn't probe further. She allowed Maggie a few more minutes to study the Civil War soldiers' faces in silence. "Would you like to go to my office now?" she asked softly.

Maggie nodded and followed her through the door. She walked over to the display case and peered down through the glass. "So many of them died here," she said quietly.

Lydia nodded, but didn't say anything in response.

"Do you think they were able to identify all the bodies?"

"Unfortunately, I know that they weren't able to identify many of them. Some bodies were injured beyond recognition. Our military didn't start using dog tags until forty years after the end of the Civil War. Some soldiers sewed their names into their shirts because they were so fearful of dying anonymously; but many did not take this extra step. So, they were buried without anyone knowing who they were... Some just never came home."

"Do you think that the families of those that never returned searched for them?"

"I don't know. Maybe. Or perhaps, they just knew. After a certain passage of time, they just knew that they weren't coming home. Not ever."

"Like you knew about your family?" Maggie asked softly.

Lydia looked away from her.

"I'm sorry, Lydia. I didn't mean to hurt you. I'm just trying to understand why I couldn't do everything that I had intended to do in Washington."

"So, you didn't look for his name?"

Maggie walked away from the display case towards the window without answering her question. As usual, Lydia allowed her to have some space. After a time, Maggie walked back across the room and sat down in an easy chair. Lydia joined her.

"I visited the wall three different times, and each time I had every intention of looking for his name." Maggie looked directly into Lydia's eyes. "No. I just couldn't look for his name. I'm sorry if I've disappointed you. I guess some bridges are just not meant to be crossed in our lifetimes."

"You didn't disappoint me, but do you know why you couldn't look for it?"

She nodded her head. "I realized that I wouldn't ever to able to look for his name the last time I visited the wall. There was a man sitting in a wheelchair that day with his back to me. He looked just like Jake. Each step that I took closer to him, he looked more like Jake. I was so excited, Lydia. It didn't matter to me that he was in a wheelchair. I was just so excited, so happy, so completely overjoyed that he was alive. Jake was alive!" Her throat began to tighten. She looked away from Lydia.

"It wasn't Jake?" she asked, after a few minutes had passed.

She shook her head. "And I knew at that moment, that I would never find him. Not in a wheelchair or anyplace else. I knew that he had died."

"But you're not sure of that?"

"Yes! Yes, I am," she said with conviction. "I'm as sure of it as I am that the sun will set tonight and rise again tomorrow morning. I know he's dead. I just can't face reading his name on that black wall. I promised myself that I would never do a rubbing of his name. Never Jake's name." She paused and looked into Lydia's eyes, desperately wanting her to understand. "Even though I never crossed the bridge the way you had hoped I would, I feel that I have crossed it. In my own way. I have navigated to the other side and I feel a sense of peace that I've never felt before. Perhaps, I've finally healed."

Lydia said nothing for a few moments. "Perhaps, Maggie. Perhaps. I guess only time will tell." She glanced at her watch then back at Maggie. "Would you like to go for a drive with me? Call me an old Fuddy-dud if you like, but I've always enjoyed symbolism. Since you've crossed your final bridge and feel fully recovered, I'd like to take you somewhere to commemorate this momentous occasion, but it will take a few hours to get there. Do you want to go? Is that too much time?"

Maggie smiled at her. "Adam is keeping Katie tonight. I do have the time. Truth be told, I'd love it."

Two hours later, Lydia parked her Mustang in the Golden Gate Bridge Visitor Plaza. She turned towards Maggie. "I remember a happy memory that you once shared with me about this bridge. I've brought you back here today to remember those happy times in your life, but mostly to celebrate your healing. You've come so far. I'm proud of you."

She smiled shyly at Lydia. "Thank you. I know that I wouldn't be here today without you. I owe you so much." She opened her door and stepped out of the car, but Lydia remained seated behind the wheel. She leaned back in. "You're not coming?"

She shook her head. "No, Maggie. I may have helped you, but you made the journey on mostly your own steam. Go now. Walk across that bridge. Remember. Celebrate. I'll be right here when you're ready to go home."

"OK. Thank you for bringing me back. This means so much to me."

"My pleasure. Take your time now. I have nothing else planned for the day."

As Maggie began to walk across the bridge, she stared up at it, smiling to herself when she noticed that the top was, again, buried in puffy, white clouds. *It's so beautiful she thought, taking in its massive dimension and its brilliant color.* Soon however, the beauty and serenity of the scene around her blurred as her mind focused on so many faces, so many memories. At first, she remembered Kate, for it was with her that she had originally crossed this bridge. Then she thought of her mom, Jason, Thanh, Dr. B, DJ, Chris, and so many others. Finally, she remembered

Jake. Once his image entered her mind, she couldn't think of anything else.

She stopped midway across the Golden Gate Bridge and stared into the turbulent, dark-blue water below her. For years, she had felt as mixed up and agitated as that water appeared to be, swirling so angrily around the bridge. But not anymore. While she still felt remorseful and sad, remembering everyone she had lost, she no longer felt guilty or responsible for their deaths. For some unknown reason, she was standing here today and they were not. Perhaps, some day she would learn the reason why. Then, again, maybe she would never know. It just didn't matter to her anymore. She was grateful to be alive and to have Katie, Lydia, Camille and Doc to share her life with. That's all that really mattered to her.

"Are you always this serious?"

His question shot through her like an electric current. She turned quickly and looked into his face. She reached up and touched his cheek, with a tight knot forming in her throat. "It can't be. It can't be."

He gently pulled her hand away from his face and kissed it softly. "Yes, it can be," Jake said, his voice, too, on the edge of tears.

And then they were hugging tightly and crying together unashamedly. After more than twenty years, the arms she had ached for were finally around her. After a time, they were finally able to pull away from each other.

"How did you know I would be here today?" she asked, looking into his deep-blue eyes, still doubting that this was really Jake standing next to her.

He laughed. "I'm sure you can guess. An unusual woman contacted me a few weeks back."

And suddenly she knew. "So, you've met Lydia?"

"Yes. I've had the privilege. She's quite a woman."

"Believe me. No one knows that better than me. How did she find you?"

"You must have told her that my family was from Monticello,

Georgia? She found me through them."

She nodded her head. "That's right. I did. Isn't she something?"

"She is." Jake suddenly looked uncharacteristically serious. "Would you consider spending the rest of the day with me? There's so much I want to tell you... So much you need to know."

Without hesitation, she said, "Yes. Just let me tell Lydia first. She's waiting for me at the Visitor Plaza." She turned to walk back across the bridge.

He laughed, grabbing her arm. "Hold your horses, Woman. You don't have to. I told her that I would text her." He pulled out his Motorola cell phone and sent a text to Lydia. She texted him back immediately and he smiled as he read her message. "She says not to worry about your luggage. You can pick your roses and suitcase up anytime you'd like. She wants you to enjoy your time with me."

"I should be angry you know. You two had this all planned. Why wasn't I part of it?"

He laughed. "There's that sweet pout I remember so well. Seriously, now, I wanted to surprise you. Lydia told me that you needed a little more time."

"And what else did she tell you about me?"

For an answer, he cupped her face in his hands and tenderly kissed her, then pulled her into his arms again. He released her and looked deeply into her eyes. "I'm so sorry for all your pain. I tried to find you for so many years. I guess it was my mistake not to try immediately when I got back to the States. I might have found you then. But I had my reasons. By the time I started looking, your mother had already passed away and no one in your neighborhood knew where you were. At one point, I even hired a detective. Every time he got close, you had moved again and we had to start over from scratch. Finally, about six years back, I moved to San Francisco. I just knew you were out here, somewhere," he said gesturing with his hand.

He stopped talking and looked out across San Francisco bay

for a few moments, then back at her. "I saw your wedding photo in the paper two months after I moved out here. I moved back to Georgia one week later, but couldn't stop thinking about you. Was he good to you?" he said softly.

"Yes, in his own way." She reached up and gently stroked Jake's face. "But he never knew me. Not like you do. No one ever has. Did Lydia tell you that Adam and I are getting a divorce? We've been separated for over nine months now."

Jake nodded. "She did. I wouldn't have come without knowing that. I could never do anything to hurt you. Not again."

She could see tears forming in his eyes. "Jake, please stop. Don't you know that you never did anything to hurt me?"

"No, Maggie. That's not true. You were right. I shouldn't have signed up for another tour. I paid too much. I lost you for so long."

"I missed you, too, Jake. That's why you couldn't find me. I just kept moving and looking for something. But I never could find it. I know, now, that I was looking for you, but I thought you were dead. I've always known in my heart that you died over there."

"You've always been wrong then," he said with a huge grin, but it faded quickly and he became serious. "I have to tell you something important. The reason that I didn't look for you when I first got back is because I'm not whole anymore."

"What are you talking about?"

"This." He pulled up his right trouser leg to reveal a prosthesis in place of his right leg which had been amputated just above the knee. "I lost my leg in Cambodia in January of '70."

"Jake," she said angrily. "Are you forgetting that I was a nurse in Nam? What's a damn leg? You're whole to me. I'll take you any way that I can get you, even in a wheelchair with no legs at all." Her voice softened. "Someday, remind me to tell you a story about how devastated I was not to find you in a wheelchair." She saw the confusion in his face. "Don't worry about it now. There're too many other things we have to catch up on. Like when you were in Cambodia, did Silver go up in flames?

Were you medevacced out? Or were you taken as a P.O.W.?"

"So many questions," he interrupted her by pulling her back into his arms and kissing her fully on her lips. He smiled down at her. "Don't worry, Sweetheart. I'll tell you everything in time and I have millions of questions for you, too. First things first, though." He reached into his shirt pocket and removed a tiny, wrapped package. He looked deeply into her eyes. "I've been saving this for you for years, Maggie." He handed it to her with tremulous hands.

Her hands were shaking as well but she successfully unwrapped the package. Inside the small box was a Precious Wentletrap. It was incredibly beautiful, just as she had remembered it to be. This one had a small crack along its base, but that tiny flaw didn't detract from its intrinsic beauty. She gently removed the delicate shell from the box and placed it in the palm of her left hand. She slowly turned it over, studying it from all angles. She looked up into Jake's eyes. "Thank you. It's so beautiful."

"You'll notice that it's not perfect. Just like me." He reached for her hand. "Do you remember what the Precious Wentletrap signifies?"

She nodded with tears cascading down her face. She couldn't speak.

He gently pulled her into his arms again. "I'm sorry, Darling. For so much. I love you. I always have. Now that you have this Wentletrap, I know that you'll always know that."

Still too choked up to speak, she hugged Jake tighter so that he would know that she did understand. She understood the true meaning of the Precious Wentletrap.

EPILOGUE

Maggie patted the dirt around the last Geranium, enjoying the feel of the cold, damp soil against her hands. Then, with another Memorial Day planting successfully completed, she paused to admire her work. She gazed at the red geraniums and gold marigolds which now brightened their headstones. Although he had been buried for almost seven months now, the outline of Doc's grave was still visible in the ground. She reached out and lovingly fingered the engraved letters of his name and the dates of his birth and death- September 12, 1925- November 23, 1999. She missed him dearly. During the last six years of his life, he had been more than a grandfather to her children, but his years of waiting were finally over. She smiled, thinking of him reunited with his girls. She looked away from their headstones, out over the Pacific. Feeling sufficiently rejuvenated by its splendor, she knelt before their three white crosses and said her goodbyes. "I miss you. Take care of them for me, Doc. I know we'll all be together again... Some day." She slowly rose to her feet, walked to her car, and drove back home.

Arriving home, she found Jake and Katie playing chess in the Great Room. It still amazed her, that at eight years of age, Katie knew how each chess piece moved and could play competitively. She kissed Jake softly on the lips and lightly stroked Katie's hair.

Katie pushed her hand away. "Stop it, Mom! I need to concentrate." Irritably, she looked up at her, then back down at the chessboard. She began twirling her hair loosely around her finger.

Maggie smiled at Jake before looking back at her. "I'm sorry, Katie."

"How did it go today? Did you have any problems?" Jake

asked.

"No problems. I guess it went all right. It's always a little difficult for me to go there. But this time I think it might actually have been just a little easier.... And it was a gorgeous day for a drive along the coast. You know I enjoyed the time to myself, too. Are the boys napping now?"

"Yes. Camille surprised us with a visit for a few hours. They played so hard with her. You know how she is."

She smiled and nodded. "I wish I'd been home to see her. I miss her."

"I know you do, Honey. I think she misses you, too. She stayed for a long time. I think she was hoping that you'd come home early. At any rate, the boys have been sleeping for about ninety minutes now. If you play your cards right, you may have a few more minutes to relax before they stir."

"Dad! Mom! Please! I need to think."

They looked at each other, fighting the urge to laugh. She was always such a serious little thing. Maggie grabbed the newspaper off the coffee table, plopped down on the sofa, and began flipping through the pages. The close-up photo on page twenty-five caught her eye. It pictured a female major in the Air Force. Something about her was so familiar. It was those eyes. She still couldn't place her so she read the caption. "It can't be!" she said excitedly, under her breath. "Jake!" she said, jumping up and running across the room towards him. "Look at this photo. Do you recognize her?"

He took the newspaper from her. "Let me see. No. I don't think so. Why?"

"Look at it again, after you read the caption." She gave him a minute.

"Major Jennifer Bennett...first female to be given command of a combat wing." He looked up at her. "You think this is Dr. Bennett's Jenny?"

She nodded. "I know it is. Look at those eyes. They're his. He'd be so proud. She's flying like the wind now, just like she always wanted to do."

Katie looked up at them. She didn't have to say anything this time. They knew she was upset by their talking. "I'm sorry, Katie. We'll try to contain our excitement until you finish your move," Maggie said.

After visiting St. John's Cemetery and seeing Jenny's picture in the paper, Maggie was overwhelmed with the desire to stimulate a few more memories from Nam. They were usually buried deeply in the back of her mind now. Thanks to Lydia. She was such a free spirit these days, out exploring the world since her retirement in December. They never knew when she would knock on their door next and entertain them for a few hours with tales of her latest escapades. Maggie knew, too, that sharing her adventures with them was just an excuse for the visit. Lydia really just wanted to make sure that she was still doing OK.

As Maggie walked across the room, she gazed at Kate's portrait that hung above their fireplace. Kate belonged here with them. She was happy that Doc had chosen to give her portrait to them before he died. She stopped in front of their built-in bookcases and picked up her Precious Wentletrap from its protective home on the top shelf. She studied all its delicate surfaces, tracing its thin, decorative lines of beige with her finger, before closing her fingers around it and squeezing gently. It was real! She looked across the room towards Jake. He was sitting with his back to her, but somehow sensed he was being watched. Suddenly, he turned around. She smiled at him and mouthed, "I love you."

He smiled back at her with that endearing boyish grin of his, then waved his right hand in her direction. "Leave me alone, Woman. Can't you see I'm concentrating?"

She laughed, then gently placed the Wentletrap back on the top shelf before picking up Kate's book. It had been a long time since she had read it. They had bought a hard cover edition when it first came out in the fall of '94. Appropriately enough, there was a picture of the Women's Vietnam Memorial on its cover. The anguish on their faces brought her back for just a few moments. *The Voice of Nam* was the title Doc and Maggie had chosen for her work. Within three months of its publication, it had become a bestseller. She hugged it to her chest, kissed the cover, and then returned it to the bookcase. She didn't need to open it for she had memorized every word years ago. Sometimes, she just needed to touch Kate again, for just a minute.

She heard a muffled, "Mommy, I'm thorsty!"

Smiling, she quickly walked upstairs to the boys' bedroom. After two years of infertility treatment, they had been blessed with healthy twin boys. Joseph was still asleep, but Jason was sitting up in his bed. "Did you have a good nap, Sweetie?" she asked, stroking his blond curls.

"I thorsty."

She picked him up in her arms. "Come on. We'll get you a drink." When they returned, Joseph was awake as well. "Would you boys like Mommy to read you a story?"

"Yes! Yes!" they screamed excitedly, jumping up and down.

She smiled down at them. "You two are the wildest two-year-old's that I know. Come here." She hugged them tightly. "Which story would you like Mommy to read today?"

"Muver Goose. Muver Goose," they yelled in unison.

"Now, why doesn't that surprise me, boys?" she laughed, while grabbing their "Mother Goose Book" from their bookshelf. "Which rhyme do you want to hear first?"

"Humfy Dumfy!" Jason screeched, jumping up and down again.

"Yeah, Humfy Dumfy," Joseph chimed in.

"OK. Calm down and come sit on Mommy's lap." She sat down on the floor and pulled them to her, then began reading.

Humpty Dumpty sat on the wall;
Humpty Dumpty had a great fall;
All the king's horses and all the king's men
Couldn't put Humpty together again.

"Humfy Dumfy broke Mommy?" Joseph asked solemnly when

she had finished reading the poem.

"Yes, Honey. Humpty Dumpty is broken."

"They no can fix Humfy Dumfy?" Jason asked in a husky, sad, little voice.

"That's right. They can't fix poor Humpty Dumpty."

"Why?" Jason asked.

"Yeah, why come?" Joseph asked very loudly.

"I'm sorry boys. I don't know why. I guess he was just too broken. Do you remember the battle you had with your ceramic dinosaur piggy banks? They broke into so many pieces. Daddy tried so hard, but he just couldn't glue them back together."

They nodded their heads.

"Well, it's the same with poor Humpty Dumpty. Look at this picture," she said, pointing at his shattered shell. "See how broken he is. Into hundreds of pieces. No one could glue him back together either." Her explanation didn't help. They seemed so sad. "Stand up boys. Let's hug again."

They wrapped their chubby arms around her and squeezed as hard as they could. As she hugged them back, a lump formed in her throat and tears began to trickle down her face. When they stopped hugging, they saw her tears.

"Mommy broke too?" Joseph asked.

"No baby," she said through her tears. 'Mommy's not broken." She smiled at them. "Mommy's fine. She's just happy. Very, very happy. Now, which rhyme shall we read next?"

<<<<>>>>

Made in the USA
Middletown, DE
21 January 2021